WITH DEATH

A gripping small town crime mystery full of twists

P.F. FORD

A Prequel to The West Wales Murder Mysteries

Previously published as
I Hope You're Happy Now

JOFFE BOOKS

Revised edition, 2023
Joffe Books, London
www.joffebooks.com

First published in Great Britain
as *I Hope You're Happy Now* in 2017

Cover art by Dee Dee Book Covers

ISBN: 978-1-83526-090-6

To my amazing wife, Mary — sometimes we need someone else to believe in us before we really believe in ourselves. None of this would have happened without your unfailing belief and support.

CHAPTER ONE

'Oh no! She's been sick all down your back,' said Freddie Albright, as he watched a trail of sick trickle down his daughter's jacket.

'Oh God, no, not now,' gasped thirty-seven-year-old Sarah Southall. 'It's my first day back, and I'm already running late.'

'I know it's your first day back,' said her father, wearily, 'that's why I'm here to help with the baby, remember? Now give her to me, change that jacket, and get going!'

He took the baby gently from Sarah's shoulder. 'There now,' he said to the baby, 'let's wipe that face of yours while your mum gets off to work. We can manage just fine, can't we?'

'You are sure about this, aren't you?' asked Sarah, as she struggled out of her jacket. 'You know where the child minder is, and don't forget she has to be there by nine and—'

'Will you just get off to work,' said Freddie, testily. 'I have looked after babies before. Your mother trusted me with you and your sister.'

'I do trust you, but you were younger then—'

'I'm sixty-eight, not ninety-eight. I can manage just fine, if only you would let me.'

'Alright, alright, I'll just grab another jacket and I'll be gone.'

As he rocked the baby gently in his arms, Freddie listened as Sarah stomped up the stairs to her bedroom. A few seconds later she came stomping back down again, then rushed into the kitchen.

'Right,' she said, doing a quick inventory, 'jacket, bag, phone, car keys. So, that's it then, I suppose I'd better go.'

She looked fondly at her dad, and then longingly at the small bundle in his arms.

'Don't do that,' said Freddie, 'the more you think about it, the harder it is to leave her. She'll be fine, trust me.'

Sarah tried hard to swallow the lump in her throat, but it was no good, she just couldn't speak with it there. She took a couple of steps over to her dad, kissed the top of his bald head, stroked the baby's cheek with a finger, then turned and walked from the kitchen.

Freddie didn't make a sound until he heard the front door close, then he let out a long, weary sigh. A few seconds later he heard Sarah's car start, and then she was gone.

'I thought she was never going to leave, didn't you?' he asked the baby. She grimaced up at him. He knew it was probably wind, but preferred to think of it as a smile. Next she seemed to frown in concentration, and then shortly afterwards let out a little grunt.

'Ah, that'll be a full nappy then, will it?' said Freddie, getting up from his chair. 'Come on, let's get you changed, then we'll be ready to take a slow walk round to Wendy's.' He plodded slowly from the kitchen and up the stairs, careful to make the journey as smooth as possible for little Laura, his first grandchild.

'I don't really know why she needs to go back to work,' he told the baby. 'It seems pointless to be working and paying for a child minder. When Sarah was born, her mum stayed at home.'

Freddie had been quite taken aback when Sarah and her husband, Kenny, had announced Sarah was pregnant. He had been delighted, of course, but he'd always thought he was never going to be a grandfather, what with Sarah being well into her thirties, and her sister being even older and single.

CHAPTER TWO

Detective Sergeant Sarah Southall thought the worst thing about the first day back at work was all the catching up that needed to be done. It was bad enough when she had a week off, but this time she had had six months maternity leave, and that meant a serious backlog. She had been asked to take over a case involving a handbag snatcher who had been operating in the local market, and a series of burglaries. A new young DC had been working on the cases, but Sarah's boss DI Henderson had asked her to use her experience to assist and guide him.

By three o'clock that afternoon, she should have had plenty of time to read and digest the reports, but with so much other stuff to catch up on she had only just got to the bag-snatch reports. Now her head was beginning to ache and she needed some fresh air. She decided perhaps a walk around the market would be a good idea.

She hadn't met DC Parrott yet as he had been in court that morning, and obviously things had dragged on into the afternoon. This was a pity as she had really wanted to speak to him in person before starting on the cases, but she thought it wouldn't hurt to take a look around the scene of the crimes.

She was just getting ready to leave her desk when her phone began to ring.

'DS Southall.'

'Oh, right, this is DC Parrott. I was told to report to you when I got out of court.'

'That's excellent timing,' she said. 'I've just crossed the boredom threshold as far as catching up on crime reports is concerned. I was just going down to the market to take a look around. Why don't you meet me there, inside the main entrance?'

'That sounds like a plan,' said Parrott. 'I'll make my way down there now. I'm on foot so you'll probably get there before me.'

* * *

As she walked across the car park towards her car Sarah heard someone calling her name. She turned to see who it was, and her heart sank.

'Hello, Grinder,' she said, as the man puffed to a halt in front of her.

DS Graham 'Grinder' Boulting was a rather nondescript, unhealthy-looking individual, with the sort of badly thinning hair that would benefit from its owner accepting the inevitable and admitting he was going bald. Sarah thought a short haircut would have looked so much better than the rather pathetic comb-over he insisted upon. He was one of the shorter detectives, being only an inch or two taller than Sarah, which made him one of the few she could literally look in the eye.

The fifty-year-old Grinder had been a DS for as long as anyone could remember, and would best be described as a steady detective rather than a spectacular one. His dogged pursuit of suspects, and a questioning technique that relied on monotonously wearing people down rather than using clever questioning to outwit them, had spawned his nickname.

He was the last person Sarah wanted to see at the end of a boring day, but he was a colleague and she couldn't ignore him.

'Sarah,' he gasped. 'It's good to see you back.'

'I just couldn't keep myself away any longer,' she said, with a heavy dose of irony that was completely wasted on him.

'So how are you?'

'I'm fine,' she said. 'I'd be happier with a nice juicy murder to get my teeth into, but I'll have to make do with the small stuff for now. Anyway, I haven't really got time to stop and chat. I've got to go and look at a crime scene, and then get home to rescue my dad from the baby.'

'Oh, right. I actually wanted to ask you about the baby.'

'Oh, the baby is fine,' said Sarah, looking pointedly at her watch. 'Look, we'll catch up another time. I really must go.'

She turned and headed off towards her car.

'Right,' said Grinder, disappointed, his voice fading as she walked away from him. 'I haven't seen you for months, and when I do you're too busy to talk to me. Of course you are . . .'

Sarah climbed into her car, started the engine, buckled her seatbelt and put the car into gear. It was only as she began to move away that she realised Grinder was still watching her. Glad to escape him, she gave him a cheery little wave as she drove off.

Hesitantly, he raised a hand to wave back and watched until the car turned left out of the car park and was gone from view, then he walked slowly through the doors into the building and made his way to the canteen where he ordered his usual cup of tea and two digestive biscuits. Customers were few and far between at this time of the day, and as he surveyed the room, those few who were present studiously avoided making eye contact with him.

He sighed heavily as he walked over to a corner table, pulled out a chair and sat down. As usual, he was on his own, with no-one to talk to. Normally he would sit and dwell on his loneliness, but today was different. Today Sarah was back, and at last he had something to look forward to.

* * *

The market was housed under a huge, ornate, arched Victorian roof, built of cast iron and glass. Sarah could never walk in here without looking up to admire the roof, which had been painstakingly restored and repainted in a vibrant shade of green. Three rows of huge brick and cast iron pillars supported the centre of the roof, and ten-feet-high red-brick walls bordered the perimeter. The main, open-plan, floor was reached by a grand staircase which led down from a platform just inside the main entrance, allowing a view across the entire area of the market. There were additional entrances in each corner, and as Sarah stood to take it all in from her vantage point she realised it would be quite easy to evade capture with so many paths between various stalls, and so many exits. She could see exactly why someone would be able to target this place and how they could do so again and again without being caught.

Parrott had said he would be coming on foot, which meant he would come in from the far end, but there was no sign of him yet, so she stood for several minutes just watching and observing, until someone tapped her on the shoulder. She spun round to find a man in uniform with the word 'Security' emblazoned across the front of his hat.

'Can I help you, miss?' asked the man. He must have been seventy, if he was a day, and Sarah wondered just how secure he could possibly be.

Discreetly she showed him her warrant card. 'DS Sarah Southall,' she said. 'I'm here to try and put a stop to your mini crime wave.'

'Well, good luck with that, luv,' said the man, 'you're going to need it. That young detective you sent down here doesn't seem to be getting anywhere.'

'Well, there's two of us on it now,' she said, 'so perhaps we'll be able to make some progress. What's your name, then?'

'Len, Len Newman.'

'And you're the security, are you?' asked Sarah, dubiously.

Newman smiled. 'Well, that's what they call me,' he said. 'I doubt if I could stop a stroppy toddler at my age, but I suppose I'm better than nothing.'

‘I’m not being funny, Len,’ said Sarah, concern in her voice, ‘but you could get hurt. Doesn’t that worry you?’

‘Yes, but I need the money. Being a pensioner is all very well, but you want to have a life, don’t you? Without this job all I can afford to do is sit at home watching crappy repeats on the telly. If that’s how it’s going to be, I might as well be dead. At least this way I can afford to take my missus out for a meal now and then, and we get to go on holiday sometimes. It’s worth a bit of risk to have a life. Besides, I never get to hear about these thefts until they’ve already happened, so I’m not really in much danger.’

Sarah turned so she was standing alongside Len and they were both looking across the market. ‘So tell me,’ she asked, ‘which is the hotspot?’

‘If you mean, “where do the crooks operate”,’ he said, raising an arm to point, ‘it’s mostly down that far end, where the jewellery and mobile phone stalls are situated.’

‘And what’s the most common crime?’

Len looked at her suspiciously. ‘You should know all this, it’s been reported to your young lad.’

‘I’ve just spent several hours reading his crime reports, so I do know it all, but you’re here on the ground, so you might be able to offer a different view about what’s happening. You’re the security man, so you should have your finger on the pulse.’ She thought it highly unlikely he would know anything worthwhile, but it wouldn’t do any harm to appeal to his ego.

Len chuckled quietly. ‘Ha! That’s what you call it, is it? Having your finger on the pulse? The only pulse I’ve got my finger on is my own occasionally, just to make sure I’m still alive.’

‘Go on, you don’t look that bad,’ said Sarah, warming to him.

‘Oh, hang about, here you go,’ said Len, suddenly serious and pointing to the corner again. ‘Look! There’s something going on now.’

Sarah looked across at the corner. Len was right, something was definitely going on.

‘That little shit’s nicked someone’s handbag,’ he said, as a young man suddenly bolted along the pathway between the stalls, a bag clearly visible under his arm. ‘Someone’s chasing him. It’s that young detective of yours.’

Now Sarah could see the pursuer. He was a good way behind, and the crowds of shoppers in that area weren’t helping. It was clear to her that Parrott would be very lucky not to lose the thief in the crowd.

‘I’m going to try and head him off,’ she said. ‘You stay up here and keep an eye on him, and then if I miss him at least we’ll know which way he went. Here, hold this for me.’ She slipped off her handbag and passed it to him as she took off down the steps and began to sprint towards the corner where the runaway was headed.

‘Police, excuse me!’ she called as she dodged her way through the shoppers meandering between the stalls.

Meanwhile, heading towards the same corner exit as Sarah, but from a path at a right angle to hers, and unaware of her presence, the teenage bag thief looked over his shoulder and, convinced he had made good his escape, began to slow down. This was a pity because, having lost DC Parrott, if he had continued at his original pace he would have been long gone before Sarah even got near. However, his overconfidence proved to be his undoing, and by slowing down he only ensured they arrived at the corner at the same time.

Sarah saw the boy coming from her left as she approached the corner. Totally unaware of her impending arrival he had slowed right down to walking pace, trying to blend in and look innocent, just occasionally glancing back over his shoulder to make sure he was not being pursued. Then, suddenly and quite unexpectedly, he found himself being swept up in a rugby tackle that sent both him and his assailant flying from the path and crashing into a painstakingly built display of wicker laundry baskets. The stall-holder howled in dismay as the assorted baskets creaked and sighed under the weight of the two bodies wrestling amongst them.

The breath had been knocked from the boy, but the baskets had provided a soft enough landing to ensure he was otherwise unhurt, and although he had been caught unawares by his attacker, he was determined he was not going to be detained. He swung the handbag he was carrying at Sarah's head, failing to make contact and losing his grip on the handle, but doing enough to make her dodge to one side. As she shifted her weight, he took a swift kick at her standing leg, dumping her on her backside before she disappeared under an avalanche of falling baskets. The boy scrabbled for the bag he had dropped, taking just long enough for Sarah to recover and lunge at him again.

'Come here, you little bugger,' she yelled, as she dived and grabbed his legs. He managed to pull one leg from her grip but, despite delivering several kicks to her ribs, her tenacity got the better of him, and she finally brought him to the ground. She had put on a little weight since she was last on duty, but she knew how to use it to her advantage against the skinny youth, and an 'accidental' elbow to his groin finally allowed her to gain the upper hand as he forgot about fighting and clutched at his bruised wedding tackle.

'Ah, you cow! You kicked me in the balls. That's assault, that is!' he screamed.

'It was an elbow actually,' she hissed, quietly, into his ear, 'but I think you'll find I'm allowed to use reasonable force to resist your attempt to assault me, and these accidents sometimes happen in such situations.' Sarah was breathing heavily as she finally manoeuvred herself into a sitting position on top of the boy, who was face down, still clutching his battered equipment.

A tidy crowd had gathered to watch the impromptu wrestling match, and there was a smattering of applause as it became clear Sarah had overcome the bag-snatcher. As she looked up in surprise at the crowd, a familiar voice spoke to her.

'I've brought your bag, luv,' said Len the security man. 'I guessed you might have your handcuffs in it.'

'You're a diamond, Len,' she said, 'can you just bring it over here while I get his hands behind his back.'

Fifteen minutes later the boy was led away by two uniformed police officers. Sarah had finally been joined by Parrott, and they spent another ten minutes trying to pacify the holder of the wicker stall. Sarah even offered to pay for the damage herself, but it was no good; he made it clear he was determined to make a complaint.

'Miserable git,' said Parrott as they walked away. 'It makes it difficult to feel protective towards people when all they do is complain.'

'Yes, I know what you mean,' agreed Sarah, 'but, on the bright side, I've probably made him a very happy man. Just think how important he's going to feel when he makes that complaint!'

'Thanks for catching the boy,' said Parrott. 'If I had been just half a minute earlier I would have caught him red-handed, but he had just enough of a head start.'

'I could see he was making good use of the crowd,' said Sarah, 'but he was so focused on avoiding you he had no idea I was coming from the other direction. But it was you that flushed him out, all I did was bring him down.'

'I suppose it's your collar, then,' said Parrott, gloomily.

'Now that would hardly be fair, would it?' she said. 'You've done all the donkey work, and you spotted him making his escape. I think we should put it down to good teamwork. I think you can have the credit for this one.'

'Oh, wow! Really?' said Parrott, immensely pleased.

'Yes, really,' said Sarah. 'Of course, it means you have to do all that paperwork, but like I said, you did all the work, I didn't really do much at all.'

'Don't forget the wicker basket avalanche,' said Parrott, with a grin.

'Don't remind me. I'm sure I'll be hearing all about it tomorrow when that complaint comes in.'

'I'll try to resist the temptation,' he said.

'I hope you'll do more than try,' said Sarah. 'In the meantime, you can buy me a coffee and tell me about these burglaries.'

* * *

'So, all the victims are single women in their thirties?' asked Sarah.

'Well, one's separated from her husband, and another's divorced,' said Parrott, 'but I think that's just splitting hairs. I think the relevant thing is they all live alone.'

'And no-one's been hurt?'

'No. Somehow he always seems to know when they're going to be out of the house.'

'D'you think he's watching them?'

'I suppose it's got to be a possibility,' said Parrott. 'I just wish I had somewhere to start. He never leaves a trace of evidence, and there's not even anything distinguishable about any of the stuff he takes. There's nothing big, and it's all easy to dispose of.'

'Well, if we can't work backwards from the crime scene, or the proceeds of the crime, maybe we need to start from the other end, and work out how he selects them,' suggested Sarah.

'The only thing they seem to have in common is what I told you: they're all single, in their thirties, and living on their own. Oh, and he's stolen a pair of panties from each one.'

'A trophy hunter?'

'That's what DI Henderson thinks,' said Parrott. 'He thinks we'll find a drawer full of them when we eventually catch the guy.'

'There must be something linking them,' said Sarah. 'He seems to know their movements. He can't be relying on luck each time.'

'Well, I'm sorry, but I haven't found it,' said Parrott.

Sarah looked at her watch. 'I tell you what,' she said. 'Why don't you get back to the station and get your bag-snatcher sorted out. I'll take all the burglary reports home and go through them. Maybe a fresh pair of eyes can spot something.'

'And if you can't?'

'Then perhaps we need to interview them all again.'

CHAPTER THREE

It was 8.15 a.m. Sarah became aware of the silence that seemed to engulf her as soon as she entered the small flat. It was as if she had passed into another world, where evil had triumphed over good, at least for the time being. She paused to absorb the atmosphere. After a few seconds she became aware of the low murmur of voices in a room off to the right. A ghostlike figure dressed in a white forensic oversuit quietly went about his business in a room off to the left, but it was the room on the right that she was drawn to. This room contained the victim.

'Morning, sorry I'm a bit late,' she said as she entered the room.

A body was lying on the floor, a forensically booted and suited figure knelt either side of it. They both looked up as she spoke.

'Morning, Sarah,' said her boss, Detective Inspector Don Henderson.

'Didn't you choose the best week to come back to work?' added Dr Christine Morgan, the forensic pathologist. 'I wouldn't worry about being late, though, we're all far too late to help this poor girl.'

'Don't fret, you haven't missed much,' said Henderson. 'We've barely started.'

Sarah picked her way carefully across the room and stopped by her two colleagues, looking down at the body.

'What do we know so far?'

'There was a fight, which we think started out in the hall, and ended in here,' said Henderson.

'You don't need to be an expert to see she's been strangled,' said the pathologist, 'but apart from that, I can't really tell you much until I do the PM.'

'Has she been—?'

'Sexually assaulted? I can't say for sure, but there's nothing obvious to suggest it, so initially I would say no. She did fight whoever did this. She has three broken nails, and there's some sort of material under her fingernails.'

'Skin?' asked Sarah.

'Could be, but we'll have to wait and see.'

'I suppose that's something to hang on to,' said Sarah.

Henderson sighed heavily as he got to his feet. 'Well, if the pathologist isn't going to solve the crime for us, I suppose we'll just have to get on and do some detective work.'

Dr Morgan looked up at him with a sad little smile. 'But that is what they pay you for, isn't it?'

'Only when we're not pushing paper,' said Henderson, offering a weary smile in return. 'Never forget our prime purpose is to fill in forms, write reports, and try not to offend any minority groups.'

'Oh dear, did someone get out of the wrong side of the bed this morning?' She looked up at Sarah. 'I'm so glad you're back, he's been so miserable without you to do all the work for him.'

'I've missed him too,' said Sarah, with a wry smile. 'Mind you, I have spent the last six months looking after a baby, so it's not much different, really.'

Henderson pretended to look hurt. 'Hello, I am here, you know. Let's just remember who the senior officer is, shall we?'

Morgan and Sarah grinned at him.

'Anyway, joking aside, I think you can remove the body now, Chris,' he suggested, before turning to Sarah, 'and perhaps we can give Chris some space and make a start in the bedroom.'

* * *

'The bed's been used,' said Sarah, as soon as they entered the room.

'I wonder if she was alone,' said Henderson. 'We'd better get the guys to bag up these bedclothes and take them away for testing.'

'Is it just the two of us?' asked Sarah, as they began searching through drawers, looking for anything that might help.

'These flats are pretty small,' said Henderson, 'so I thought it best to keep the numbers down until forensics have finished. I've got Grinder speaking to all the neighbours, but I'm not holding out much hope. Chris reckons she's probably been dead for hours, so I'm assuming nobody heard anything or we would have been notified earlier.'

'Who found her?'

'A neighbour from one of the flats upstairs comes down every morning at six o'clock to take her dog out. She saw the front door was open and could see there had been some sort of a fight, so she called 999. Fortunately she didn't go inside and find the body. It would have been a bit of a shock.'

Sarah pulled a face. 'Is Grinder speaking to her?'

'I thought she'd had enough shocks for one day, so I said we would speak to her,' said Henderson.

'He's got no better then?' asked Sarah.

'Still as dull and boring as ever, I'm afraid,' said Henderson. 'But he's also still as persistent as ever when questioning witnesses, so he's not all bad news.'

He slid open a drawer in the bedside cabinet and peered inside. 'Aha! I spy a passport. Come to me, my little beauty.'

He rummaged around in the drawer to make sure there was nothing else of interest, before turning his attention to the passport. 'Oh well, this is a start. At least now we know who she is, and what her face looked like before she was strangled,' he said. 'Her name is Miriam Daniels, and she's thirty-seven years old.'

'Same age as me,' said Sarah.

Henderson looked at the photo in the passport, and then across at Sarah. 'Not just the same age,' he said. 'She's a ringer. You could be sisters!'

'I already have one sister and she's more than enough to cope with,' said Sarah. 'I certainly don't need any more.'

Henderson placed the passport carefully into an evidence bag. 'He's been missing you, you know, Grinder.'

'Oh please, don't start that. All I did was offer the bloke some support when his wife died. Someone had to.'

'Yes, and as a result he thinks you're some sort of angel. Still, I suppose he's harmless enough,' said Henderson. 'And I don't suppose I would manage something like that any better myself.'

'None of us know how we would deal with something like that until it actually happens,' said Sarah. 'I'm not sure I would be able to cope — Hello! What have we here?'

She produced a large box of condoms from the drawer and held them up for Henderson to see.

'There's no law against buying in bulk,' said Henderson. 'I've not seen anything to suggest she's a—'

'No, but it does suggest she has an appetite,' said Sarah.

'You think she invited someone round?' asked Henderson.

'Well there's no sign of a break-in, is there?'

'Not that anyone's found,' agreed Henderson, 'but that's not really a surprise.'

'Look, I've been away for six months,' said Sarah, 'so I'm a bit out of touch with what's been going on. I have read the burglary reports, but until I can get up to speed, you're going to have to bear with me for a few days.'

'Sorry, my fault, I'll try to remember that,' said Henderson. 'If you've read the reports you will know there have been a few burglaries. They have all involved women living on their own, just like this one, and each time there's been no sign of forced entry.'

'But no-one has been hurt in these other cases.'

'No, but that's because in all the other cases the owner has been out.'

'Maybe Miriam wasn't supposed to be here,' said Sarah. 'Perhaps she was asleep when the guy let himself in. She wakes up, hears a noise, goes to investigate, and he attacks her. She fights back, so he strangles her, and then flees the scene, leaving the front door wide open. Do we have a time of death?'

'Chris reckons seven or eight hours ago, give or take,' said Henderson, 'so that would make it around one a.m.'

'Bearing in mind it was Sunday night, and assuming none of the neighbours was out partying, they were probably all in bed by midnight at the latest. That would explain why no-one would have seen the front door was open until the neighbour came down at six,' suggested Sarah.

'And if they were all asleep, it's quite possible they wouldn't have heard anything,' added Henderson. 'Check her underwear drawer, can you?'

'Pardon?'

'The victims always report he takes a pair of panties. I suppose it's some sort of trophy,' said Henderson. 'I suspect when we finally catch him he's going to have dozens stashed away.'

'Yes, Parrott told me about your "trophy" theory,' said Sarah, 'but without an inventory, how am I going to know?'

Henderson looked briefly crest-fallen. 'Bugger! You're right. We're not going to know, are we?'

They continued searching, working their way from room to room, finally finishing back in the small lounge where the body had been found.

'So, no handbag, no purse, no laptop, no tablet, no mobile phone, no diary, and a calendar on the kitchen wall with sod all written on it,' said Henderson.

'No helpful information, but it looks like a robbery gone wrong,' said Sarah.

'We'll go with that for now,' agreed Henderson, 'subject to what Christine and the forensic team come up with.

There's not much more we can do in here, so we'd best go and have a chat with the neighbour who found her.'

'Look at those flowers. They look quite fresh,' said Sarah, walking over to a small vase of flowers perched on a small table. 'I bet they haven't been here long.'

'Boyfriend?' asked Henderson.

'Maybe, or perhaps she's someone who just likes having flowers around the house,' said Sarah. 'I do.'

'Yes, but what if she had invited someone round? She loves flowers, he arrives carrying them, so she lets him in. It explains why there's no sign of a break-in.'

'That works,' agreed Sarah, 'but it also suggests her killer arrived during Sunday evening, and I reckon those flowers are a couple of days old; one or two of them are starting to look a bit iffy.'

'There's a florist in town—'

'I think that would be a waste of time,' said Sarah. 'If some guy bought these for her, he was a cheapskate. You can get stuff like this in any petrol station for less than a fiver.'

Henderson muttered a curse as he stalked off to the kitchen where one of the forensic technicians was just opening a pedal bin.

'There's a bunch of flowers in the other room,' he said to the man. 'We think her attacker might have brought them with him, so I want you to keep an eye out for some sort of wrapping paper. You might even get really lucky and find a card with a name, but I wouldn't hold your breath on that one. If this is our usual guy, he never leaves so much as a fingerprint.'

'I'll see what I can do,' said the technician.

Henderson had barely made the short walk back to join Sarah when the technician called out.

'Sir? You might want to see this.'

Henderson and Sarah rushed through to the kitchen. The technician was holding a card wrapped in a small polythene bag. Henderson took the card and studied it. 'That's bloody weird,' he said.

'What is it?' asked Sarah.

Henderson passed her the card without comment.

'I thought you said her name was Miriam?' said Sarah.

'That's what the passport says,' said Henderson, 'you saw it for yourself.'

'So who's Sarah?'

'Search me,' said Henderson. 'Maybe you're right about the condoms. Perhaps she is a sex worker and that's her alias.'

'There again, maybe the flowers weren't for her but were for someone else,' said Sarah. 'Perhaps that's what she argued with her boyfriend about.'

CHAPTER FOUR

The neighbour who had reported what she thought was a break-in was Mrs Manson. A sprightly, bright-eyed eighty-two-year-old, she lived by a strict routine which included rising at 6 a.m. every day to take her dog Toby down the three flights of stairs that would allow him to relieve himself in the small communal garden outside. As Sarah knocked on the door, Toby made his owner aware of their presence with a series of deep, baying barks.

'That sounds like the hound of the Baskervilles,' muttered Henderson. 'She's supposed to be a little old lady, how can she handle a bloody great dog like that?'

As the door opened, Henderson took an involuntary step back, half expecting a huge hound to launch itself at him. He needn't have worried, as Toby proved to be nothing like the monster he sounded. A good-natured five-year-old Basset hound, he greeted them with a slowly wagging tail and an amiable expression framed by his large, floppy ears.

'Mrs Manson?' asked Sarah, showing her ID. 'My name's Detective Sergeant Southall, and this is Detective Inspector Henderson. We'd like to ask you a few questions if we may.'

'Come in, dear, come in,' said Mrs Manson, stepping back to let them in. 'Don't mind Toby, he's all bark. He has very little brain, I'm afraid, but at least he lets me know when I have visitors.'

Her flat was identical in layout to that of the unfortunate Miriam Daniels, and she showed them through to the small lounge where they sat down and waited as she rushed off to the kitchen, soon returning carrying a tray.

'I thought you might like a cup of tea,' she suggested cheerily. She removed a woolly tea cosy from the tea pot and set two cups ready. 'It's still quite warm,' she assured them, as she began to pour.

'Er, not for me, thank you,' said Sarah, correctly guessing the tea had been made hours ago and would be well stewed by now.

'Oh,' said Mrs Manson, clearly disappointed. She directed a smile at Henderson. 'How about you, Inspector?'

Silently cursing Sarah for being so quick off the mark, and not wishing to disappoint their witness further, he reluctantly accepted the cup of tea she passed across to him. Sarah could see from its colour that she had made the right choice, and returned Henderson's frown with a knowing smile. Just to add to Henderson's discomfort, the dog ambled past him, depositing a layer of hairs across the front of his trousers. He looked down at his trousers and then turned his dismayed face to Mrs Manson.

'He always moults at this time of year,' she confided, 'gets hair everywhere.'

'You don't say,' said Henderson through gritted teeth.

'I understand you called the police earlier, Mrs Manson,' said Sarah. 'Can you tell us exactly what you saw?'

'Well, I always get up at six o'clock every morning,' she began. 'It's for Toby really. He needs to pee, you see, and if I don't take him out . . .'

Sarah caught Henderson rolling his eyes, but ignored him.

'Right,' she said, 'so you took Toby downstairs, and what did you see?'

'Well, I didn't see anything on the way down. Toby's always in a hurry, you see, but when we came back up the stairs I could see Miriam's front door was open,' said Mrs Manson. 'I called out, but there was no answer, so I went to the door. I was going to go inside, but as soon as I saw the mess in the hall I thought there must be something wrong, so I came up here and called the police.'

'Could the door have been closed when you came down?' asked Henderson.

Mrs Manson thought about this. 'It could have been, I suppose. And now you ask me, I couldn't say for sure one way or the other.'

'So someone could have come out of Miriam's flat and left the door open after you had gone down with Toby?'

'I would have seen them,' she assured them. 'There's only one way out, and no-one passed me.'

'Is there anywhere they could have hidden until you came back to your flat?' asked Sarah.

'Oh no, dear, this is the top floor. The only way out apart from the front door is the fire escape to the roof, and that was firmly closed.'

'And you're quite sure you didn't hear anything?' asked Henderson.

'It was as quiet as a grave. It was so quiet it was rather unnerving. I'm afraid that's why I didn't venture into the flat.'

'Please don't feel guilty about that,' Henderson assured her. 'You did the right thing.'

'Is Miriam alright?'

Sarah looked at Henderson. She had assumed Mrs Manson had known.

'Er, no, I'm afraid not,' said Henderson. 'I'm afraid she's dead.'

'Dead?' The dog had decided to sit next to his owner, but now he suddenly found himself hoisted into the air and clutched to her chest. 'But I could have—'

'Trust me, you couldn't have done anything for her, Mrs Manson,' said Sarah. 'She was dead long before you got there.'

Visibly shaken, Mrs Manson clutched the dog tighter still. 'Oh my goodness . . .'

It was a good ten minutes and a pot of fresh tea, made by Henderson, before Mrs Manson was able to continue.

'Did you know Miriam very well?' asked Henderson.

'Not really. We always spoke if we met, and exchanged a bit of small talk. She seemed to keep herself to herself, and I'm not one to pry.'

'Had she lived here long?'

'Four or five months, I think.'

'Do you know where she worked?'

'She said something about an animal shelter, you know, where they take in mistreated animals.'

'Did she have a boyfriend?'

'Oh yes, she'd been seeing someone. I never actually got to meet him, but I saw her with him, and sometimes he would be leaving in the mornings just as I was taking Toby out. Off to work I expect.'

'He didn't live with her?'

'Oh, no, he wasn't a regular visitor. He only stayed now and then.'

'Could you describe him?' asked Henderson.

'I'm afraid my eyesight's not that good,' she said. 'I can tell you he was about your height, but he didn't look as old as you. I'd say he was about mid-forties.'

Sarah caught Henderson's expression and suppressed a smirk. He was forty-four.

Ten minutes later Henderson decided they had all they were likely to get from Mrs Manson at this stage. They had a very vague description of Miriam's boyfriend, although he wasn't convinced it would be much help. Maybe Grinder had managed to come up with something from the other neighbours.

CHAPTER FIVE

'Okay, let's get this show on the road.' Henderson looked at the faces turned his way. There were eight in all, a mixture of his small team, and two or three others drafted in to make up the numbers.

'This is a preliminary briefing to ensure you all know as much as we know. It's not a great deal, but it's a start. We haven't got any handouts yet, so you will need to take notes.' He paused, and took a sip of his tea, to allow everyone to prepare.

'This morning, shortly after six a.m., we received a call from a concerned resident of a small block of flats in Cardinal Street. She reported finding a neighbour's front door open, and damage in the hall that suggested all was not well. Officers were sent to the scene and on investigation they found a body inside the lounge of flat number 6.'

He pointed to a photograph on a board next to him.

'It's a bit fuzzy, because it's a copy of a passport photo, but this is the victim, Miriam Daniels. Miriam was thirty-seven years old and lived on her own. She had been strangled. There was no sign of a break-in, which suggests either: a) she let her attacker in, or b) her attacker had a key.'

He paused again, to allow everyone to finish their note-taking.

'Are we linking this to the PKN burglaries?' asked a voice.

'We found no handbag, purse, laptop, tablet or mobile phone at the scene,' said Henderson, 'so we have to consider it's a possibility.'

'Surely it's a cert, isn't it?' asked another voice.

'I understand why you think that, but let's not jump to conclusions,' said Henderson. 'Yes, it looks like a robbery, but, in the other cases the burglaries took place between nine and ten, and all the victims were out of their homes. The pathologist has suggested this murder happened after midnight, when you would expect most people to be at home. If we're suggesting the other burglaries all happened at a time when the victims were likely to be out of the house, why would he suddenly decide to strike when someone almost certainly would be at home?' He let this sink in before continuing, but another voice cut in.

'Maybe she was supposed to be away.' It was Grinder. 'Surely you can't rule him out just like that.'

'I'm not ruling anyone out,' said Henderson, patiently. 'I'm just saying we shouldn't close our minds to any other possibilities, because, like I just said, there are differences. One I didn't mention is that every one of the previous victims was unattached. We understand from one of her neighbours that Miriam had a boyfriend.'

'She did?' asked Grinder, in surprise. 'No-one I spoke to mentioned a boyfriend.'

'Maybe you just haven't spoken to the right people,' said Sarah. 'Don't forget, half the owners had already gone to work and haven't been interviewed yet.'

'Anyway,' said Henderson, 'at this stage it's important we find this boyfriend and speak to him.'

'So he's number one suspect?'

Henderson nodded. 'He's all we've got at the moment.'

'Do we have a name?'

'I'm afraid not,' said Henderson. 'All we have is a card with "Just for you" written on it. We think the card may have been attached to the flowers she had in her lounge, and we're assuming the boyfriend brought them with him.'

'Any forensics?' asked another voice.

'It's very early yet, but they have found a single footprint, right foot, size nine.'

The faces said it all.

'Yes, I know,' said Henderson, 'we've got sod all to go on really, but in the meantime I want someone to check the locality for CCTV. You never know, we might get lucky. Grinder, I want you to find and visit the animal shelter where she worked, see what you can find out about her. Two of you can take the photo of Miriam and try all the local shops, pubs etc., see if anyone recognises her. They might have seen her with this boyfriend. We need a better description of him if we can get one. Parrott, I want you to get online. See if Miriam had any sort of social media going. Start with Facebook.'

Parrott was a fresh-faced, naively innocent-looking twenty-five-year-old, who was neither as naive, nor as innocent, as he appeared. 'Yes, sir.'

'That's it then,' finished Henderson. 'I want to know the minute anyone finds anything that might be even vaguely relevant. We'll meet up again at seven tomorrow morning.'

As everyone made their way off to start work, Sarah sidled up to Henderson. 'Is it me,' she asked, 'or is Grinder getting argumentative?'

Henderson pulled a face. 'He's definitely got more tetchy recently, but I expect this morning he's got the hump because you're back at work and you've barely spoken to him. I told you he was missing you.'

She rolled her eyes. 'Oh, ha, ha, very droll. I'm sure he's got better things to do than worry about me.'

Henderson made a point of looking doubtful, but she wasn't going to take the bait.

'About this burglary thing,' she said. 'I'm still catching up with that, but it sounds as though it might be important.'

'I can help you catch up,' he agreed, 'and I'd like you to go back to that flat and have another look around.'

'Did we miss something?' she asked.

'We didn't find any photographs,' said Henderson. 'Don't you think that's odd? You'd think she might have one or two of her family or boyfriend. I just think it's a bit odd for a woman to have no photos. Mrs Manson said she'd lived there for four or five months, so it's not as if she'd just moved in.'

'Yes, now you come to mention it, it does seem a bit weird.'

Henderson looked past her at Parrott. 'Parrott!'

The young detective looked up. 'Sir?'

'Can I borrow you for a minute?'

The young DC made his way over.

'I know you spoke to DS Southall about the burglaries yesterday, but you've spent more time on them than anyone else, so I want you to let her pick your brains.'

'Sure, no problem,' said Parrott, with a shy smile at Sarah.

'In that case you can accompany her back to the crime scene. You can talk about the burglaries in the car,' said Henderson. 'Don't worry, you won't be out long. I know you're itching to get on Facebook, but your fan club can wait for a while.'

* * *

'I've just realised you must be the new arrival they sneaked in while I was away. Am I right?' suggested Sarah, as she pulled away.

'I wouldn't exactly say I was sneaked in,' said Parrott. 'I had applied to join CID months before, but they told me there wasn't an opening.'

'And then I went on maternity leave and made the space for you.'

'I'm not a replacement,' said Parrott, hastily. 'I'm sure I'll soon be back in a uniform now you're here.'

'Don't worry, I'm only teasing,' said Sarah. 'And I wouldn't worry about being pushed out. It's not going to happen; we need all the help we can get. You must have noticed that by now.'

'Yeah, I suppose that's why I got stuck with these burglaries.'

'We all have to start somewhere. You've had help, though, haven't you?'

'Like you just said, we're short on numbers. The boss has been great, looking over my shoulder and advising me, but I worry that I'm not making enough progress. It makes me wonder if perhaps I'm just not cut out for this sort of work.'

'Rubbish!' said Sarah. 'You just need a bit of help, that's all. What does the boss say?'

'Oh, he seems happy enough, but I know he'd like to see some progress.'

'If he says he's happy then he's happy,' Sarah assured him. 'He'll soon let you know if he thinks you're a problem. As for wanting to see some progress, you have to remember he's got someone above him demanding results, and then there's someone above that person demanding results . . . and let's be honest, we'd all like to solve every case within a few days, but that only happens on TV. Sometimes there's just nothing to go on, and when it's like that you just have to keep chipping away until you find something.'

She looked across at him, but he didn't look convinced. 'Trust me, I'm a detective,' she said, 'and God knows I've had my fair share of cases that drag on and on.'

Now Parrott smiled. 'Knowing that makes me feel a bit better. From what I've heard you've got a pretty good reputation.'

Sarah smiled to herself. 'Well, I can assure you that's not because I solve cases in five minutes. It's because I'm a bit like a dog with a bone. I don't give up, even if it takes months. Anyway, tell me about these burglaries.'

'But we did that yesterday, and you've read the reports.'

'And now we're going to do it again. You do want my help, don't you?'

'Well, yeah, of course.'

'Right. So?'

'There have been five so far, spread over a period of about eight weeks, and there are similarities that make us think they're all by the same guy.'

He used the fingers of his right hand to make his points.

'One: in every case it's been a woman who lives alone. Two: it happens during the evening every time, and the women are always out. They come home and discover they've had a visit. Three: he only takes small valuables, like cash, jewellery and small electronics; nothing bigger than a laptop has even been taken. Four: there's never any sign of a break-in. Five: he always steals a nice, clean pair of panties. The boss thinks they're a souvenir.'

'So, how do you think he gets in?'

'I'm guessing he has a key,' suggested Parrott. 'But how would he do that for every one? I've tried to find a locksmith connection, or someone who cuts keys, but it's got me nowhere.'

'They don't leave keys outside?'

'No, they all have more sense. I figure he only pinches small stuff because it's easier to carry and easier to get rid of, but I've not managed to trace any of it yet.'

'What about forensics?'

'Now that would be nice,' said Parrott, 'but it seems our guy is ultra careful.'

'What, nothing?'

'Not even so much as a hair off his head, or a fibre of any sort, and definitely no fingerprints. Forensics reckon he might even be one of them.'

'Wow, that is careful,' said Sarah, 'but it explains why you're not getting anywhere. There's nothing to go on, is there?'

'Yeah, but what if he's the guy who killed this woman and I could have stopped him?'

They had just turned into Cardinal Street, and Sarah brought the car to a halt, switched off the engine and turned to Parrott.

'Now look,' she said, 'you can't think like that. For a start, we don't know that it is the same guy, and even if it is, you're not responsible for his behaviour. You can't do this job if you take it all personally.'

'Yeah, I know, but—'

'You have to remember, you're DC Parrott, not Superman,' said Sarah.

'I suppose you're right.'

'Of course I am,' she said. 'Anyway, what do I call you?'

'Sorry?'

'I can't keep calling you DC Parrott, can I? I assume you have a name?'

'Oh, right, yeah, everyone calls me Polly.'

Sarah rolled her eyes and smiled. 'Of course, I should have known. Well, come on then, Polly,' she said, opening the car door, 'let's go and have another look inside this flat.

'What's this about a Facebook fan club?' she asked as they headed slowly towards the small block of flats.

'Oh, it's nothing really,' he said, bashfully.

'Now come on, if you're going to work with me it's no good being shy. If you don't tell me I'll find out some other way.'

'I do a bit of singing, just for fun, you know? It started off as karaoke, that sort of thing. Someone put a video up online, and it got a few views, so I did a couple more. Now I've got a bit of a following.'

'Wow, so you're a singer with a real fan club. Should I be asking for an autograph?'

'I suppose you could call it a fan club, but it's just a bit of fun, a hobby. It keeps me out of trouble.'

Sarah liked the young detective and the fact that he was humble enough to be embarrassed to be talking about his singing, and his fan club. 'I'll have to take a look,' she said. He blushed at this, so she decided to drop it for now.

'So, are we looking for anything in particular?' he asked, as the PC guarding the flat stepped aside to let them through.

'We didn't find any photographs,' said Sarah. 'DI Henderson thinks that's a bit odd. It's only a small flat so it won't take long. I'm sure we didn't miss them, but we just want to make sure.'

It was barely five minutes before Polly called out to Sarah, 'I think I've found something.'

Sarah rushed into the bedroom to find Polly sitting on the bed, now stripped of its bedclothes. He had pulled open a drawer in the bedside cabinet. She walked around the bed and peered into it. As she did, he turned back a folded silk scarf to reveal a framed photograph underneath.

'Is that how you found it?' she asked.

'Yes, it was just sitting there under the scarf.'

'I'm sure we wouldn't have missed that,' said Sarah.

'Maybe you didn't look under the scarf,' suggested Parrott.

'Perhaps,' she said. Sarah remembered watching Henderson rifling through this drawer, and she was quite sure there was no way he would have missed the photograph, but she kept her suspicions to herself as she lifted the photo from the drawer.

'Well, that's a gold star for you, Polly. This is definitely Miriam,' she said, 'and perhaps this is the elusive boyfriend.'

'Is there anything written on the back?' he suggested.

Sarah quickly flipped to the back of the framed photo, but there was nothing written there. 'No such luck,' she said, 'that would have been far too easy.'

They continued searching through the rest of the flat, but there were no more photos to be found.

'Let's just pop upstairs to see Mrs Manson,' suggested Sarah as they left the flat. 'Maybe she will recognise this man.'

* * *

'So Mrs Manson thinks the man in the photograph could be the boyfriend?' asked Henderson, later. They were on the way over to the mortuary to watch Dr Morgan perform the post-mortem examination.

'Could be,' confirmed Sarah. 'But you know how vague she is, so that's not one hundred per cent definite.'

'Let's assume she's right until we know otherwise,' said Henderson. 'Where did you find that photo?'

'Top drawer bedside cabinet.'

'But that's the drawer where I found the passport, isn't it?' he asked. 'I'm sure I checked it before I opened the passport.'

'And I'm sure I watched you do it,' said Sarah.

'Maybe I'm thinking about the second drawer. Perhaps I'm losing my touch.'

'You don't believe that any more than I do.'

'Ah, but you can't argue with the evidence, can you? Parrott saw it, and I missed it.'

Although Sarah could hear him saying the words, she could see in his face that he wasn't convinced.

CHAPTER SIX

They were standing around the mortuary table, the body in position, ready to be dissected. Dr Morgan studied the face, then turned to look at Sarah. She was obviously sizing them both up.

'There's an uncanny resemblance, you know. She's just like you.'

'Maybe there is, but I bet she hasn't got my stretch marks,' remarked Sarah, making them all smile.

'You won't be surprised to hear me confirm she was strangled,' said Dr Morgan, getting down to business. 'I'm not sure what with yet, but we've managed to tease a few fibres from the wounds around her neck. My guess is they're silk, perhaps from a silk scarf—'

'We found a couple of those in her bedroom,' said Sarah.

'So she might have been strangled with one of her own scarves; that would be unfortunate.'

'What about sex?' asked Henderson.

She flashed a wink at Sarah and gave him a wicked grin. 'Really, Don, that was supposed to be our little secret, and now you've let the cat out of the bag in front of Sarah!'

Henderson looked suitably unimpressed. 'If we could just get this over with . . .'

'Oh, my goodness, you really did get out of bed on the wrong side this morning, didn't you?' she said. 'It's a good job Sarah can manage a smile.'

'If you must know, our new DCI is giving me gip about this case already. He seems to think we can solve it today.'

'Good grief, what's the matter with the man, the body's hardly cold!'

'Yes, well, you can tell him that if you like, but I'm afraid he expects a bit more from me,' said Henderson, huffily.

Christine Morgan studied Henderson for a moment. 'You've been like this ever since he arrived, haven't you?'

He said nothing; he didn't need to.

'Okay, then,' she said, 'let's see what I can tell you so far.'

'Please tell me you've got some DNA from under her fingernails.'

She picked up a clipboard with her notes. 'Sorry, the material under her fingernails was not human flesh. It appears our man was wearing leather gloves when he strangled her.'

'What?'

'Under her nails, it's leather.'

'Jesus,' said Sarah, 'she managed to claw through the back of his gloves?'

'Oh yes, she put up a fight alright. She's covered in bruises, too, but the evidence suggests she wasn't raped.'

'Is that supposed to be some sort of consolation?' asked Sarah bitterly.

'Don't take it out on me, luv,' said Morgan. 'It wasn't me who attacked her.'

'Sorry, it's just—'

'I'm on your side, you know. If I sound flippant, I don't mean to be, I just have to keep a distance or I can't stay objective.'

Henderson patted Sarah on the shoulder. He had worked with her long enough to know how she felt.

'It's alright, Chris, you carry on,' he said.

Morgan nodded her head.

'As I was saying, I don't believe she was raped,' she continued, 'but she had been sexually active earlier that day.'

'So maybe she knew her killer,' suggested Henderson, thinking out loud.

'I just find out what the bodies can tell me,' she said. 'It's up to you to decide where it all fits in to the grand scheme of things.'

She set her clipboard down well away from the body and snapped on a pair of latex gloves, followed by a pair of gauntlets that came up to her elbows. 'Now then,' she said, flexing her fingers, 'let's find out what she had for dinner.'

Henderson took in Sarah's face. He looked at his watch.

'There's no point all of us working ourselves into the ground. Why don't you go and get everything together for tomorrow's briefing and then go home,' he said. 'I can finish up here.'

'No, it's okay, I don't mind staying.'

'You're not going to miss much,' said Morgan. 'And he's right; you need to take it in turns on missing your beauty sleep. This could be a long investigation.'

Sarah looked from one to the other. 'Well, if you're sure. I would like to get home in time to feed the baby.'

'I don't want to be here all night either,' said Henderson. 'This way we can both get a decent night's sleep.'

'Okay, thank you.'

She made her way across the mortuary and out through the door. Henderson and Morgan watched her go.

'I think this is probably a bit close to home,' said Henderson, nodding his head towards Sarah. 'Our victim was the same age as Sarah.'

'She's not just the same age,' said Morgan. 'They're—'

'Dead ringers, yeah, that's already been mentioned.'

CHAPTER SEVEN

'So, to summarise, we know our victim had sex with someone on the day she died, but the forensic evidence suggests she was a willing participant. That gives us two possibilities: either the same man she had sex with was still in the flat, or sometime after midnight someone gained access to the flat. There's no sign of a break-in, so if this wasn't the same man who had been there earlier, we have to assume this person had a key.

'We believe Miriam then disturbed the intruder around one a.m. Maybe she heard a noise that woke her. Whatever, we believe she went to investigate, there was some sort of fight, and she was strangled with what appears to have been a silk scarf. We believe the killer then fled the scene, leaving the front door wide open.

'We have absolutely no forensic evidence apart from a single size nine footprint, probably from some sort of work boot with flat leather soles. The only other thing we have is a card, recovered from the waste bin, that says "for Sarah", but we have no idea who Sarah might be.'

Henderson looked around the bleary-eyed team assembled before him. Some of these people definitely did not look their best this early in the morning! 'Does anyone have anything to add to this?'

No-one said a word.

'There has to be something, somewhere,' said Henderson.

'Surely if someone had sex with her, there must be some forensic evidence, maybe in the bed,' suggested Grinder.

'We were hopeful that would be the case, but forensics say the sheets on the bed were pretty clean, and there was a freshly laundered set in the washing machine,' said Sarah.

'So it's possible someone destroyed the evidence,' suggested Grinder.

'That looks likely,' agreed Henderson.

There were some gloomy mumblings at this news.

'I also went back and spoke to the rest of the neighbours,' continued Grinder, wearily, 'but no-one saw or heard anything, and no-one else can help us with a description of the boyfriend. It seems the batty old dear you spoke to is the only one who's seen him.'

'So, basically, if forensics can't come up with anything else, we have nothing to go on,' said Henderson.

'I still think you can't rule out the PKN,' said Grinder.

'We haven't ruled out the bloody PKN,' snapped Henderson, 'but as we've got nothing on him yet, and the MO is quite different, we can't afford to ignore other possibilities.'

'Okay, you're the boss, I'm sure you know best,' said Grinder, sulkily.

'Yes, I am the boss,' said Henderson, testily, 'and, frankly, I'm disappointed with what we've got so far. This is a murder inquiry, and so far we know sod all. It's not good enough. I want to know about this woman: who did she have sex with that night? Was it the boyfriend? We've got a photograph of him, now I want a name. Where does he live? Where was he the night she died? And, Grinder, you still need to visit the animal shelter where she worked. Come on, guys, you know what needs to be done, let's get on and do it, can we?'

'Can I just butt in a moment here?' asked Sarah. She had been as disappointed as Henderson with what they had discovered so far, but there was something here she didn't get. 'Can someone explain this PKN thing to me? I'm assuming this is a reference to the spate of burglaries on single women, right?'

She looked around the team. One or two of the faces looked embarrassed.

'It's just a nickname for the guy,' said Grinder, with a broad grin. 'He always takes a pair with him, so he's the Phantom Knicker Nicker.'

There was an awkward silence.

'And you think this is funny, do you?' she asked. 'I suppose, as I'm the only woman here, I'm also the only one who thinks it must be pretty terrifying to be a single woman living in this town at the moment. Am I right?' She looked challengingly around the room, but no-one was willing to contradict her. 'As DI Henderson says, we haven't ruled this guy out. He could well be our killer. If anyone here thinks that's something we should find amusing, perhaps you should ask yourself what you're doing here.'

Henderson jumped in quickly before things could get too heavy. He knew Sarah had strong views about this sort of thing, and he knew she was definitely right in this case; he felt guilty he'd not stopped it before.

'Sarah's right,' he said. 'This is no laughing matter. If I hear anyone mention that name again, there's going to be trouble. Right, you all know what needs to be done, so let's get on with it. We need to start making some headway with this case, and we need to do it soon!'

As the meeting broke up, Sarah decided she needed some fresh air, and stomped angrily out through the back of the building to the car park. She liked most of her colleagues and had a lot of respect for their abilities, but sometimes they were just a bit too quick to make a joke of things that just weren't funny. When that happened, it was usually best if she walked away, but she'd felt she needed to say something this time . . .

* * *

Sarah stood at the barrier overlooking the car park and took a couple of deep breaths. It was a breezy morning, and the cold air blowing into her face soon made her feel better. She took a quick look at her watch and decided she could have another five minutes before she got back to work.

She heard a door bang closed behind her, but didn't look round, even though she could hear someone shuffling awkwardly. She guessed who it was. No doubt he'd come to apologise.

'Err, I just wanted to say sorry,' said the dull voice behind her.

She turned to face him. 'You just need to think sometimes, Grinder,' she said. 'And grow up. For a man in his early fifties you can be remarkably childish when you want to be.'

He looked suitably chastened by her remarks.

'I know, I know, I really am sorry.' He had one hand behind his neck and scratched at it as he spoke.

'There's no need to grovel,' she said. 'It doesn't suit you, especially when I know how surly you like to be.'

'You're looking well,' he said. 'I've missed having you around.'

Sarah groaned inwardly. She hoped this wasn't going to be a long speech about his dead wife again. She hadn't minded listening when it had first happened because she had felt genuinely sorry for him, but she had heard it nearly every day for, what was it now, three years? No matter how sympathetic you are, there comes a time when you just want it to stop.

'Yes, well, I'm sorry about that, Grinder, but I'm afraid the baby takes priority over everything.'

'Well, yes, of course,' he agreed. 'How is the little mite?'

'She's doing well, or at least that's what they tell me at the clinic.'

'Good,' he said, 'only I wanted to talk to you about her.'

'How do you mean?'

'Well, we never had any children, me and Evie, and I thought the chance had passed me by at my age . . .' He was studying her face as if he expected her to know where he was going with this train of thought.

'I'm sorry, I'm not with you,' she said.

He looked slightly crest-fallen that he needed to explain himself, but he continued anyway.

'Well, it's just that I was doing some working out on my calendar. Remember just before Christmas, when we solved that big case, and we all went out and got rat-arsed, and you and me—'

A look of alarm raced across her face, and she looked around hurriedly to make sure no-one could hear what he was saying.

'Graham, we both agreed that we would forget about that night. It didn't happen, remember?'

He gave her a sympathetic smile.

'No,' he said, 'you agreed it never happened, I didn't. And I can promise you that night isn't something I'm ever likely to forget.'

'Nothing happened,' she said. 'We were both so drunk we crashed out.'

A smirk spread across his face. 'If you say so,' he said.

'It's what bloody happened,' she said, testily. 'We were all so pissed we ended up booking rooms because we were too drunk to drive home, remember? You were so pissed I had to help you up the stairs. I felt sorry for you, that's all.'

He gave her that sympathetic look again, and had another scratch at the back of his neck.

'What's the matter with your neck?'

'It's just an itchy insect bite,' he said. 'Anyway, as I was saying, if you work the dates out—'

Sarah's face darkened and she stepped right up to him.

'I don't know what exactly you are trying to suggest,' she snarled, furiously, 'but I can assure you, you're way off the mark if you think anything happened between us!'

'Do the maths,' he said. 'If you recall, you told me your husband was away and you were gagging for it . . .'

'That's not how I remember it,' she snapped, 'and, even if I had been "gagging for it", I would have had to have been seriously desperate to turn to you.'

'I get that,' said Grinder. 'I'm not asking you to marry me, at least not yet, but we're good together, you and me, I'd do absolutely anything to make you happy. And if that baby's mine, I have a right—'

'She isn't yours!' she snapped. 'And if you really want to do something to make me happy, just get out of my bloody way.'

'Well, you think about it, and I think you'll see I'm right,' he said, as he stepped aside and she stormed back through the doors and into the building.

* * *

'Oh, there you are,' said Henderson, when Sarah joined him in his office. 'I thought we'd really pissed you off with that PKN thing and you'd cleared off home or something.'

She didn't say anything, but stood looking out of the window, breathing hard.

'You're still angry, then?' he asked, taking in her expression.

'What?' she said, absently. 'Oh, no, you're alright. It's just that sometimes you blokes trivialise things, and—'

'I know what you mean, and I'm sorry. It's my fault. I should have nipped it in the bud when it first came up, but I don't think anyone will dare to mention it again.'

He aimed a smile at her, but she seemed distracted.

'Are you alright?' he asked.

'Yeah, I'm fine. I just didn't get much sleep last night. Baby crying, you know.'

He gave her a sympathetic smile. 'Ah, yes. Welcome to my world. It doesn't change as they get older, you know. When they stop crying all the time, you lie awake wondering why they're not crying, and then you'll spend the next eighteen or twenty years lying awake wondering if they're alright. Even when they grow up and leave home you still worry about them.'

'That's something to look forward to, then,' she said. 'At least I won't get bored.'

'No chance of that now,' he said.

'So, where do you want me to start?' she asked.

'Well, we've actually made a little progress overnight,' he said. 'No-one thought to check before the briefing, but Parrott set up a social media search for Miriam Daniels yesterday afternoon.'

'Did he find her?'

'Not exactly,' said Henderson, 'but he did find a Miriam Fletcher who appears to be the same woman.'

'How does that work?'

'What he's found is a dormant profile. It hasn't been used in months, but it looks as though this was her profile when she was married. Parrott's just checking now, but looking at the last few posts he thinks maybe she stopped using it before they got divorced. He thinks maybe her husband was stalking her or something like that.'

'Do we know anything about him yet?'

'We're working on that, too. Now we've got her old address, I'm hoping we can track him down easily enough. He's got to be right up there as a suspect. If we can just get a lead on the boyfriend too, maybe we can start to make some progress.'

'Are you still getting pressure from above?'

'Just a tad,' admitted Henderson, quietly. 'Our new boss likes to think we can come up with instant results, and the bigger the case, the more instant he wants them.'

'I hope you told him we haven't got much to go on from forensics.'

'He tells me he's going to be kicking some forensic arses this morning. He doesn't seem to think they're doing their job properly, unless they come up with a full set of fingerprints and a solid DNA sample for each case.'

'He sounds like a reasonable sort of bloke. I can't wait to meet him,' said Sarah, sarcastically.

'You'll be spared that pleasure for a couple of days. He's at some conference, so it's evening telephone bollockings only at the moment.'

'That must have been a nice way to end your day.'

He gave her a rueful smile. 'Yes, discover a murder in the morning, watch a PM in the afternoon, and then get a bollocking in the evening. It was the perfect day in so many ways.'

There was a knock on the door.

'Come in,' he called.

A puzzled-looking DC Parrott pushed his way through the door. He was holding a couple of printed sheets of paper.

'Ah, Parrott, what have you got?'

'I'm not quite sure,' said the young detective.

'What's the problem?' asked Sarah.

'Let's have a look,' said Henderson.

'Well, I've managed to track down the husband,' said Parrott, laying the printout on Henderson's desk. 'His name's David Fletcher. It turns out he's got a record: six months for assault, just over a year ago.'

Henderson looked down at the headshot on the page. 'Hang on, don't I know that face?'

'That's what's confusing me,' said Parrott. 'He's the boyfriend, isn't he?'

'It is, unless he's got a twin brother,' said Sarah. 'That's a bit weird, isn't it? She divorces him, and then starts going out with him again?'

'Do we know why she divorced him?' asked Henderson.

'Unreasonable behaviour,' said Parrott.

'That's not much help, is it?' said Henderson. 'That could mean just about anything.'

'I'm trying to track down the solicitor she used so I can find out more,' said Parrott.

'Well, we now know he's got a conviction for assault,' said Sarah. 'Maybe he was violent towards her. What if he used to beat her up?'

'Then why would she start going out with him again?' asked Parrott.

'That's just one of the questions I want an answer to,' said Henderson, 'but unfortunately we're only going to get his side of the story.'

'Maybe she wasn't going out with him,' said Sarah. 'Perhaps what Mrs Manson saw was David Fletcher harassing his ex-wife.'

'Don't forget, Sarah, she said she saw him coming out of her flat some mornings,' said Henderson. 'That doesn't sound like harassment to me. It sounds like something much more cosy.'

He turned to Parrott. 'This is excellent work, Parrott, well done. I'd like you to keep searching online, see what else you can find.'

Parrott beamed with pleasure at the compliment. 'Thank you, sir,' he said, as he headed back to his desk.

'Come on, Sarah,' said Henderson, 'let's go and find Mr Fletcher and see if he can tell us what's been going on.'

CHAPTER EIGHT

They had been ringing the doorbell for a good five minutes, before an upstairs window finally opened and a wild-haired, bleary-eyed face peered down at them.

'I work nights, you know. That's why there's a sign on the door that says please don't disturb. If you're bloody Jehovah's witnesses—'

'David Fletcher?' asked Sarah, looking up at the face.

'Who wants to know?' croaked Fletcher.

'Police,' she replied, holding up her warrant card. 'I'm DS Southall, and this is DI Henderson.'

'Can't it wait?'

'I'm afraid not, Mr Fletcher,' said Henderson. 'We wouldn't be here if it could.'

'What's it about?'

'I think it would be better if we spoke about this inside your house, rather than shouting at each other like this,' said Henderson.

Fletcher thought for a moment, and then seemed to come to a decision. 'Give me a minute,' he said. 'I'm barely awake.' Then he slammed the window shut.

They waited what seemed another age, but was really only a minute or two, and then the front door opened.

'This had better be bloody good,' said Fletcher, belligerently, as he walked back inside the house, leaving them to make their own way after him.

Henderson and Sarah exchanged a look, and then followed him inside, Sarah pulling the door of the small house closed behind her.

Still not quite fully awake, Henderson flopped down on a chair at a small dining table, facing them as they came into the room.

'You are David Fletcher?' asked Henderson.

'Yes, I thought we'd already established that,' said Fletcher, testily. 'I would have told you to bugger off if I wasn't him. Now, why don't you just tell me why you feel it's necessary to ruin my sleep?'

'I understand you know a Miriam Daniels,' began Sarah.

Fletcher looked confused. 'Of course I know her, I'm married to her,' he said.

'We understood you were divorced.'

'Well, yeah, strictly speaking we are,' admitted Fletcher, 'but we're getting back together again.'

'Can I ask you when you last saw Miriam?' asked Henderson.

'Sunday afternoon.'

'Can you tell me what time you last saw her on Sunday?'

'I didn't actually take much notice of the time, but I had to clock in for work at eight, and I had to come home and change into my work clothes first. I always allow a couple of hours just in case of traffic, so I must have left her around six.'

The concern was clear on his face now. As he became fully awake, he was beginning to realise something must be seriously wrong for the police to be here. 'Why are you asking me about this? What's going on?'

'I'm sorry to have to inform you, Mr Fletcher,' began Henderson, 'but Miriam was attacked on Sunday night. I'm afraid she's dead.'

There was a sudden stillness in the room, as if all the air had suddenly been sucked out. Incomprehension filled

Fletcher's face as he looked from Henderson to Sarah, his mouth working wordlessly as he tried to make sense of what Henderson had just said.

'No, no, no,' he repeated, finally. 'No, you must've got that wrong. She can't be dead. I was going to move in with her. We were looking forward to making a new start.'

And then he did something neither Henderson nor Sarah was expecting. He began to howl, a high-pitched keening that made Sarah's hair stand on end. She looked at Henderson, but he looked equally unnerved. She made a quizzical face at him, but if he knew what they should do, he didn't seem able to tell her.

'I'll make some tea,' she said, hastily, and headed for the small kitchen. As she pottered in the kitchen, opening cupboards looking for mugs and tea, she wondered why she had suggested it. She decided it was because it was ingrained into the British psyche. It was the right thing to do: got a crisis? Then put the kettle on! Of course, it didn't actually solve anything, but it did give them all a few minutes to compose themselves. Maybe that's really what it was about, and the actual tea-drinking was irrelevant.

When she came back to the table with three mugs of tea, Fletcher seemed to have settled down somewhat. His cheeks were wet with tears, but he was no longer howling. She placed a mug in front of him and sat down opposite him, next to Henderson.

'I know this must have come as an awful shock,' said Henderson, gently, 'but we need to ask you some questions.'

'Can I see her?' he asked.

'Actually, we do need someone to come in and formally identify her,' said Henderson, adding, 'not that we have any doubts it's Miriam, it's just a formality, you understand.'

'Of course,' said Fletcher. 'I'll do it. She's my wife, so it's my job, right?'

'Perhaps we can arrange that for tomorrow morning,' said Henderson. 'Now, about these questions.'

'What? Oh, yeah, sure, go ahead,' said Fletcher.

'You say you were at work on Sunday night. Can anyone confirm that?'

'I have to clock in and out,' said Fletcher, 'and there were five other lads on the same shift, eight p.m. until six a.m. They'll tell you I was there.'

'You work that shift every night?'

'Only four nights,' he said. 'Sunday through to Wednesday, then we have the rest of the week off.'

'You say you were getting back together with Miriam,' said Henderson. 'Exactly how close were you?'

Fletcher looked puzzled.

'I understand you have been seen leaving Miriam's flat early in the morning.'

'Oh, I see, you mean were we sleeping together? Yes, we were.'

'Did you sleep together over the weekend?'

'I was there from about six on Friday evening through until six on Sunday. There's only the one bed, so what do you think?' asked Fletcher.

'Right, okay, that's fair enough,' said Henderson, hastily. 'Can you tell me why you divorced in the first place?'

'It was my fault. I got done for assault and sent to prison for three months. I lost my job, and of course, everyone thought I was some sort of violent head case after that. Miriam couldn't handle the fall-out, and wanted out. I didn't want to lose her, but I agreed to a divorce so she could start again.'

'And are you a "violent head case"?' asked Henderson.

'No, of course not,' said Fletcher.

'According to your case file, you broke a chair over someone's head,' said Sarah, 'that seems pretty violent to me.'

'Yeah,' said Fletcher, 'it's funny how no-one mentioned the bloke was coming at me with a broken beer glass, trying to cut my face to ribbons. What was I supposed to do? I couldn't run, Miriam was in the ladies, and this bloke fancied his chances with her.'

'So, it was self defence?' asked Sarah.

'I was more concerned for Miriam than I was for me, but yeah, I suppose you could call it that. The problem was this guy had all his mates with him, and they all said I attacked him. Unprovoked, they said! My word against six of them, what chance did I have?'

'Were you ever violent towards Miriam?' asked Henderson.

Fletcher looked appalled. 'No! Aren't you listening? I loved Miriam, I would never hurt her. I wouldn't have hurt that bloke if he hadn't been threatening to hurt her. I'd do it again, you know, in the same situation. I'd do anything to keep her safe . . .' His voice seemed to fade to nothing as the realisation of what he'd lost took over again.

'So how come you got back together?' asked Sarah, trying to change the subject.

'At first she didn't want to know, but then I got a job, got myself back together, and proved to her that I really wanted her back. It turns out she was as lost on her own as I was, and we just sort of started again. It was just a date here and there to start, and then we . . .' The tears were rolling down his cheeks again.

Fletcher seemed to be in bits now, and Sarah thought they were probably pushing their luck asking any more questions. She looked at Henderson, and it was clear he seemed to be thinking the same thing.

'Is there anyone we can call to come and be with you?' asked Henderson.

'No, don't worry, I'll be alright. It's just the shock, you know?' said Fletcher. 'That's what I meant about getting a conviction for assault; all my friends deserted me. There is no-one left, only Miriam, and now she's gone, too.'

'I'm sorry, but I'm afraid we're going to have to make sure you really were at work on Sunday night, I hope you understand.'

Fletcher nodded.

'Can you write down the address for us? We're here now, so we might as well go there this afternoon.'

He pushed a notebook across the table to Fletcher and he scribbled the address down for them. Henderson nodded to Sarah.

'Here's my card,' she told him. 'Give me a call later and we can make arrangements for you to come in tomorrow, and if there's anything else I can do, don't hesitate to call me, okay?'

Fletcher seemed to have lost his tongue, and he simply nodded again.

'When we get to your workplace we're going to have to explain why we're asking questions about Sunday night,' said Henderson.

'That's alright,' said Fletcher. 'I don't think I can tell them, and as for going in to work . . .'

'I don't think you need to worry about that,' said Sarah, 'I'm sure no-one will expect you to be at work tonight.'

'One more thing,' said Henderson. 'We found no laptop. Did Miriam have one?'

'She didn't have one; she wasn't a big fan of the internet. She thought people spent too much time online,' said Fletcher. 'In her world it would have been shut down so people would start talking to each other again.'

'What about a mobile phone?'

'She had one, but it was ancient, she wouldn't have a smart phone. All you could do with it was make calls and send texts. She said that was all anyone should do with a phone.'

'One more thing,' said Henderson, as he was leaving. 'There was a bunch of flowers in a vase.'

'I bought them for her on my way there on Friday,' said Fletcher. 'They weren't anything special, cost me a fiver in the petrol station down the road, but she didn't care. I could have picked a handful of daisies from the lawn and she would have been over the moon.' He smiled fondly at the memory. 'She said it wasn't the cost, it was the thought, you know?'

'Was there a card?' asked Henderson.

'For a fiver, from the petrol station?'

'No, right, of course not,' said Henderson.

* * *

'Wow!' said Sarah as she drove away from Fletcher's house. 'So he really was the ex-husband, and the boyfriend.'

'Yeah,' agreed Henderson. 'And if his alibi checks out, that's both my main suspects in the clear in one stroke.'

'D'you think he was acting?'

'He deserves a bloody Oscar if he was,' said Henderson, gloomily. 'Pull in at that petrol station, can you?'

Sarah did as he requested and parked the car to one side, out of the way. There was a stand with some cheap and cheerful bunches of flowers outside the entrance to the shop.

'Definitely no cards with them,' said Sarah, as she quickly looked through them.

'Let's see if they'll let us have a look at the CCTV,' said Henderson. 'While we're here, we might as well check he's telling us the truth.'

CHAPTER NINE

'Those are the clock cards. You can see quite clearly David clocked in just before eight on Sunday, and left right on six a.m. on Monday morning.'

Henderson and Sarah looked at the six cards laid out on the desk before them by Mr Hector. He was a small, neat man who gave off an air of tidy efficiency.

'Could anyone have clocked him in when he wasn't here?' asked Henderson.

'Inspector Henderson,' said Hector, 'it's not beyond my imagination to think that's a possibility, but we employ adults here, and we treat them like adults. No-one has to be clocked in by anyone else because we don't penalise anyone for being late once in a while. In my experience, if I play fair with my employees, they'll play fair with me.'

'But it could happen,' Sarah persisted.

'Yes, in theory, it could, but if you're suggesting someone could be away from their machine for hours on end, then you're barking up the wrong tree. Each machine has its own minder. Without a minder continually checking and adjusting, the machine stops. And if one stops, the whole production line comes to a standstill. That couldn't happen without me knowing about it, and I can assure you it didn't happen on Sunday night!'

Sarah could see she was going to get nowhere with that line of questioning so she changed tack. 'What can you tell us about David Fletcher?'

'He was a nice lad,' said Hector, as if he was talking about a ten-year-old. 'He had some bad luck, you know. He'd never been in trouble before that.'

'You knew about his conviction?'

'Of course I did. He never tried to hide the fact. It was the first thing he told me when he came for an interview. I think he thought I was going to send him packing, but as far as I was concerned he'd done his time, and he deserved a second chance. I think that's what young Miriam thought, too.'

'You knew Miriam?'

'Well, no, I'd not exactly met her. David told me all about her when he came for the interview. He showed me a photograph. That's why I employed him, he was determined he was going to prove himself. He was so excited about her being prepared to give him a second chance, you know. I was trying to find a way of paying him a bit more to cover the extra travel costs when he moved in with her. He's a bloody good employee; if I could find a way to keep him without pissing off all the other lads, then I was happy to do it. But I don't need to worry about him moving now, do I? This is such a shame, you know, it really is.'

'Do you know if he's got any family or close friends we could call?' asked Henderson. 'We had to leave him on his own. He said he would be alright, but I'd be happier if there was someone with him.'

'I'll go and see him myself,' said Hector. 'I need to make sure he understands he doesn't need to worry about coming in to work until he's good and ready, and that we're here for him if he needs us.'

'I think that would be very good of you, Mr Hector,' said Henderson.

'It's the least I can do,' said Hector. 'If we're finished here, I'll go now.'

CHAPTER TEN

'Er, sir,' called Parrott, as Henderson and Sarah headed through the main office, 'I've got something here that might interest you.'

He made his way across the office to Henderson, and handed him a sheet of paper he'd just printed out.

'I was trawling about on the internet, to see if I could find any trace of Miriam Daniels, and I came across this.'

'What's this?' Henderson was still thinking about the interview with David Fletcher, and was at a loss to take in what Parrott was showing him.

'It's her profile from an online dating agency,' explained Parrott.

Henderson passed the printout to Sarah and looked at Parrott.

'This must be out of date,' he said. 'We were talking to David Fletcher earlier, and he told us that he and Miriam had been seeing each other for weeks and were on the verge of getting back together.'

'That might be what he told you, and it might be what Miriam told him,' said Parrott, 'but look at the "became a member" date on that profile.'

'He's right,' said Sarah, pointing at the date. 'Look, she only joined this agency a couple of weeks ago!'

'Christ!' muttered Henderson, 'I really am losing my touch. It looks as if Fletcher's just spun us a whole pack of lies, and I was inclined to believe him!'

'If it's any consolation, he took me in, too,' said Sarah. 'What do you want me to do, go and arrest him?'

'No,' said Henderson. 'Let him think we believe everything he told us for now. We don't need to go and get him, he's coming in tomorrow to identify the body. We can talk to him after that.'

'Do you want me to do anything about this profile, sir?' asked Parrott.

'It's another excellent bit of work, Parrott, but I need to think about what this all means before we do anything.'

Parrott looked disappointed.

'Don't worry,' said Henderson. 'You're not being excluded. Once I decide what to do with this information you will be amongst the first to know.'

Now Parrott looked much happier.

'But I do have a job for you tonight.'

'Sir?'

'I want you to go with DS Boulting.'

'Grinder?' Parrott's lack of enthusiasm was clear.

Henderson sighed. 'Yes, Grinder,' he said. 'It's not going to be permanent. Everyone has to take their turn. You're going to speak to David Fletcher's workmates. I want to know if any of his colleagues disagree with his version of events. The thing is, there's only six of them, so you should be done in half an hour and then you can come back home. As a bonus, you get to start work later in the morning. Grinder will explain how that works. Go and get something to eat now, and I'll tell him to pick you up at six-thirty.'

'Right, I'll be ready,' said Parrott, and headed off to the canteen.

Henderson watched him go, then turned to Sarah. 'Doesn't anyone here like Grinder?'

'It's not that they don't like him, it's just that they don't like being with him. He bores everyone to tears. It's like the same record has been playing over and over for the last three years, or whatever it is.'

'Can't you have a word with him?' asked Henderson. 'He worships you. Surely he'll listen if you te—'

'He does not worship me,' she hissed. 'If anyone ever says that again there's going to be a bloody murder, right here, in this police station!'

'Ooh, dear, steady on, girl. Did I light the blue touch paper or what?' asked Henderson in surprise.

'I'm just fed up with people assuming there's something going on between me and Grinder when there isn't, never has been, and never will be.'

'Alright, cool down. That's not what I meant at all, and you know it. Who's been suggesting that?'

'It doesn't matter,' she said, now regretting losing her cool so easily.

'It sounds as if it matters,' he said. 'Do you want to talk about it, because you've been distracted all day? Something is clearly bothering you.'

'I'm fine, Don, honestly. It's just getting things settled at home, what with my dad being there helping out with the baby.'

'Finding it all a bit stressful, is he?'

'Poor old sod's worn out already,' she said, 'and it's only been a couple of days.'

'Why don't you get off early?' he suggested. 'I can manage here.'

'I can't keep doing that,' she said. 'It's not fair on everyone else.'

'Take some work home with you. I bet you haven't read all today's reports yet, have you? It's probably all routine anyway, and you can always call me if there's something urgent.'

'I feel bad about this,' she said.

'Yeah, I know, but it's not going to happen every night, is it?'

'No,' she said. 'Definitely not.'

CHAPTER ELEVEN

'Thank goodness you're home,' said Sarah's dad, Freddie, when she finally arrived just after six p.m. She didn't like to tell him she was only here now because Don Henderson had sent her home early.

'I'm sorry, Dad, but I can't just leave at five, it's not that sort of job, you know that.'

'But I'm not a young man anymore,' he said. 'We're only two days into this and I'm exhausted already!'

'Yes, I know you are, and I'm sorry. Maybe I can ask the child minder to take her for longer,' said Sarah.

Her father frowned his displeasure at this idea.

'I'm sorry,' she said, 'but I don't know what else to suggest.'

'Well, you know my views on this subject,' he said. 'In my day a wife would stay at home and look after the children, at least until they were old enough to go to school. It seems to me you're just working to pay the child minder. I can't see the sense in that.'

'Oh, please, not this again,' she said, wearily. 'We've been over this time and time again. I'm not working just to pay the child minder. I love my job; it's part of who I am, and I don't want to give it up.'

'Well, then, maybe you shouldn't have had a baby,' he snapped.

There was an icy silence. Sarah had lost count of the number of times she'd had this discussion with her father. Why couldn't he understand? Hers wasn't just a job, it was so much more.

'I don't see why you can't understand,' she said, more patiently than she felt. 'Kenny does. He doesn't expect me to give up my job!'

Kenny was Sarah's husband.

'Talking of Kenny,' continued her father, more reasonably now, 'it wouldn't be so bad if he was here to help out. He's called again this afternoon to say he's working late; that's every day for the past two weeks. And he cleared off fishing at the weekend. I don't mind helping you out, but when exactly is he going to do his share?'

'He's just taking time to adjust,' she said, hoping her explanation didn't sound too desperate.

'Adjust? Do you think me and your mum had time to adjust? Of course we didn't. Even with nine months' notice no-one ever has time to adjust, you just have to get on with it and figure it out as you go along. Does Kenny want a training course in how to cope with a baby?'

'Look, Dad, I'm sorry, but I've had a pretty crappy day, and the last thing I want is to come home to an argument with you, so can we just drop it? I'll take over now, and you can go and put your feet up. I'll do dinner after I've got her off to sleep.'

'I've already eaten,' he said. 'I never know when anyone else is coming home, and I can't wait all night.'

'Oh, right, well you go and put your feet up.'

'I think I'd rather have an early night,' said Freddie.

'But it's only half past six.'

'Which means I've got less than twelve hours before I need to get up again,' he said, heading for the stairs.

'But Dad—'

'But Dad, nothing,' he said. 'I'm tired and I want my sleep.'

* * *

It was getting on for nine by the time Sarah had found the makings of a stir fry and started to cook. She was still smarting after the argument with her dad, and at the same time she felt guilty. He had a point. He shouldn't be looking after a baby at his age, and Kenny could certainly help out a bit more. They weren't so pushed for cash that he needed to work late almost every night. Maybe she should have a word with him and get him to help out a bit more, because it was his daughter too, and quite frankly her dad was right, he was never here! Then she heard a key turning in the front door. That must be him now. Perhaps they could have that conversation over dinner.

'You're just in time, I'm in the kitchen cooking dinner,' she called.

'I've timed that just right, then,' said a familiar female voice.

For a moment Sarah was nonplussed, but then her sister popped her head around the door.

'Mandy!' she said in surprise.

'Oh, don't look so disappointed,' said Mandy, walking into the kitchen. 'Have I come at a bad time?'

'What? Oh, no, it's not that. I thought you were Kenny.'

'Ah! I can always go away again if you were hoping for a nice romantic evening.'

'Huh! Chance would be a fine thing,' said Sarah. 'He's always working. Just lately we're a bit like ships that pass in the night.'

'Well, are you sure?'

'Of course I'm sure. You're my sister, and you're just in time for dinner.'

'Oh good,' said Mandy, brandishing a bottle of wine. 'Look, I thought you could probably do with a drink!'

‘Reading my mind, now, are you?’

‘Just looking out for my little sister, that’s all. I always have your welfare in mind, you should know that. Now, where are the glasses?’

At forty-two years of age, Amanda Albright was five years older than Sarah, but unlike Sarah, who didn’t worry too much about how she looked as long as she was clean, Mandy took a lot of pride in her appearance. She was blessed with the complexion of a woman twenty years younger, and was a regular at the gym. Her skin-tight jeans and tight tee shirt were testament to the fact she was fit, in every sense of the word.

‘So how is my little sister?’ asked Mandy as she began to pour the wine.

‘Just a small one for me,’ said Sarah. ‘I can’t afford to get plastered, in case the baby wakes.’

‘And how is my little angel?’ asked Mandy.

‘Sleeping,’ said Sarah, stirring away at the wok, ‘and I’d like her to stay that way.’

Mandy pouted, ‘But I haven’t seen her for weeks.’

‘Tough,’ said Sarah. ‘You can come here anytime you want, you know that, but I only got her off to sleep half an hour ago, and I would like to eat my dinner in peace.’

‘Where’s Dad?’ asked Mandy.

‘He’s gone to bed,’ said Sarah, spooning the food into two bowls, ‘and I don’t want him woken up either. The poor old fella’s exhausted. He’s finding looking after Laura is harder work than he remembered.’

‘I bet,’ said Mandy. ‘I can imagine he forgets Mum looked after us two. All he had to do was read us a story now and then. This must be quite a challenge for him.’

‘It’s funny you should say that. He seems to think I should be here looking after Laura, not working.’

‘That sounds like my dad, still harking back to the good old days when men ruled the world.’

‘It wouldn’t be so bad if Kenny was here to help out but he seems to be working all the time these days.’

Mandy went to pass comment, then thought better of it.

'What about your work?' she asked instead. 'How's that going?'

'We've got a horrible case at the moment,' said Sarah, as she carried the two bowls over and set them on the table.

'Right,' said Mandy. 'You come and sit down, and you can tell your big sister all about it over dinner.'

'You know I can't discuss work with you.'

'I promise I won't print a word.'

'It's not that, and you know it.'

Mandy ran the local newspaper. In fact, she was the local newspaper, being editor, chief reporter and the person who maintained the website. Without her there would be no local newspaper. Because of this, Sarah was always wary of telling her sister anything that would make a good story.

'Alright,' said Mandy, 'we won't discuss work, but you've obviously got something on your chest, so tell me about it. You know I'll help if I can.'

And so Sarah explained the reasons for the current tensions in the Southall household . . .

* * *

Mandy looked at the clock. It was past 10 p.m. and Kenny Southall still wasn't home. 'So, basically, Dad's upset because he thinks you shouldn't have gone back to work, and because Kenny never seems to be here.'

'That's about the size of it,' said Sarah.

'But you knew Dad was going to be like this before he came to stay, didn't you?'

Sarah sighed. 'Yes, I suppose so.'

'So what's Kenny's problem? Have you asked him why he doesn't help out more?'

'It's a bit of a touchy subject. He says we need to have more money coming in now, and the only way we can do that is if he works as much overtime as he can.'

'So you haven't actually sat him down and had it out?'

'Erm, no, not yet,' admitted Sarah.

'That's not like you. What happened to the feisty sister who takes no shit from anyone?'

'It's difficult,' said Sarah. 'I don't think he really wanted me to have the baby.'

'What? Good grief, Sarah, what makes you think that?'

'When we were younger Kenny was keen to have kids, but it didn't seem to matter what we did, and trust me we tried all sorts, it just never happened. He always seemed pretty philosophical about it. He used to say it wasn't anyone's fault, it was just one of those things, you know? I think he resigned himself to the fact it was never going to happen. When he was forty he told me he was probably too old and set in his ways anyway. And then, right out of the blue, just after his forty-third birthday, I told him I was pregnant!'

'Bloody hell, I had no idea, you've never mentioned any of this before. It must have come as a bit of a shock to him. I expect it was difficult to come to terms with.'

'That's an understatement; even now, with the baby over six months old, he still hasn't come to terms with it.'

'Oh, God babe, is that why he stays away all the time?'

'I think so,' admitted Sarah, with a sob. 'He told me he couldn't understand why I had allowed it to happen. He said we were happy as we were. We had our own lives, for God's sake, why did I want to go and mess it all up.'

'I didn't realise he was such a selfish bastard,' said Mandy. 'Didn't he think he might have some responsibility for it happening?'

'He's never actually mentioned that,' said Sarah.

There was something about the way Sarah said it that made Mandy curious. She leaned back and studied her younger sister's face. 'Is there some doubt, then?'

'Of course not,' said Sarah.

'I don't believe this. Your eyes and your mouth aren't singing from the same hymn sheet,' said Mandy, shocked. 'Don't tell me my sweet little sister has been playing away from home? And Dad thinks I'm the wild one!'

'You swear to me you won't tell anyone about this?' begged Sarah.

'Oh, my god, you're serious, aren't you? Who was it?'

'I don't know, at least I'm not sure. No, I am sure, she's Kenny's.'

'You really don't know, do you?'

'I'm sure she's Kenny's baby, but there's a guy at work . . .'

'Well, go on,' urged Mandy.

'There was a bit of a do, before Christmas. We'd just solved a big case, and we all went out. It was a sort of victory celebration and Christmas do, all rolled into one. Anyway, we all got totally bladdered and booked rooms in the hotel rather than driving. When I woke up next morning I was sharing a bed with one of the guys.'

Mandy couldn't quite believe she was hearing this from Sarah, whom she had always considered to be something of a prude. 'Oh, wow! You are a dark horse, aren't you? Who is this guy?' she urged.

'We call him Grinder—'

'Grinder? You're kidding me. Is he really that good?'

'Trust me, that's not why he got the nickname,' said Sarah.

'So he was a bit of a disappointment, then?'

'I wouldn't know.'

'Well, either you did or you didn't.'

'I'm sure I didn't,' said Sarah.

'You're sure you didn't? That really doesn't sound too convincing, sis. Don't you remember?'

'I'd know, wouldn't I?'

'I've woken some mornings and had absolutely no recollection of what happened the night before,' said Mandy, 'but then I've always been happy to take risks in the name of pleasure. Plus, of course, I have no husband to cheat on, so I have no reason to worry too much about what I might have done. I suppose that probably makes me the wrong person to ask.'

'You should be careful, one of these days you're going to—'

'Get into trouble? Yes, so you've told me a million times before,' said Mandy. 'Anyway, enough about me, what are you going to do?'

'I'm not going to do anything,' said Sarah. 'I'm sure Kenny is the father of my baby, and Grinder is just guilty of wishful thinking.'

'Does he fancy you then, this Grinder?'

'He's over fifty, he's too old for me.'

'That's not what I asked you. Does he fancy you?'

'No, of course he doesn't. Why would he? I looked out for him when his wife died, but that was ages ago now. She's all he ever talks about. It gets on your nerves after a while.'

'But he obviously feels he can talk to you, doesn't he?'

'Well, yeah, but he's just a colleague, that's all.'

'So, what are you going to do about him?'

'I've already told him he's mistaken and my daughter is not his baby.'

'And you think that's it? End of story? And you're sure Kenny doesn't know?'

'I'm hardly going to ask him, now am I?' asked Sarah. 'Exactly how would I start that conversation? Oh, by the way, Ken, Grinder slept with me just before Christmas and he thinks he's Laura's dad, what do you think? That would go down well, wouldn't it?'

'But if the guy thinks he is Laura's father . . .'

'I didn't mince my words. I'm sure he got the message,' said Sarah.

'Let's hope you're right,' said Mandy. 'Anyway, look at the time, I have to get home.'

Sarah looked at the clock as her sister collected her things. It was just coming up to 11 p.m., and Kenny still wasn't home.

CHAPTER TWELVE

'What are you doing here, Parrott?' asked Henderson next morning at the briefing. 'Didn't I tell you to come in later?'

'Er, yes, sir,' said Parrott, visibly embarrassed, 'but DS Boulting thought you should know what we found out last night.'

'Let me guess,' said Henderson. 'Did DS Boulting also suggest you should draw straws to decide who should come in early?'

'Yes, sir, he did.'

'And did DS Boulting also just happen to have two straws in his pocket?'

'Er, yes, how did you know?' asked Parrott, then realisation dawned on him. 'Oh, right. I get it.'

'The lesson,' said Sarah, 'is that you never let Grinder choose how you're going to decide anything. He's got a double-headed coin, too. Don't worry, we've all been there.'

'Lesson learned, I hope,' said Henderson.

'Yes, sir.'

'Well, now you're here, you might as well tell us what you have to report.'

'Nothing exciting, I'm afraid,' said Parrott. 'Fletcher's colleagues all vouched for him. According to them he was there just before eight, did a whole shift, and clocked out at six with the rest of them.'

'And he was there every minute?' asked Sarah.

'None of them are there every minute,' said Parrott. 'They've worked out a sort of rota system where they take it in turns to run two machines at once, but they can only keep it up for about twenty minutes at a time. It means they can each get extra breaks during the shift, but that wouldn't even allow him enough time to drive halfway here. We tried it last night. It took us an hour: he couldn't possibly have driven all the way here, killed her, and then driven back.'

'Do you think these people are for real?' asked Henderson.

'If you mean, was it rehearsed, I don't think so,' said Parrott. 'None of the stories were identical, but they all amounted to the same thing. They seemed genuine to me.'

'What about Grinder?' asked Sarah. 'For all his faults, he can usually spot a lie when he hears one.'

'No, he thought the same as me. He was a bit disappointed about it, actually. I think he was hoping to come back with the case wrapped up for you.'

Henderson thought for a moment. 'What was the general opinion of Fletcher amongst his workmates?'

'He was pretty popular. I didn't hear a single bad word about him.'

'Did they know about his conviction?'

'The general consensus seemed to be that they would all have done the same thing. I got the feeling they regarded him as a bit of a hero for doing his time, and then trying to put his life back together and rekindle his marriage.'

'Hmm. Well, unless they're all in it together that rather takes him out of the frame, doesn't it?' said Henderson.

'So where does this dating site come into it?' asked Parrott.

'Right now, I have no idea,' said Henderson. 'Perhaps it's not even relevant.'

'Maybe we were wrong and Fletcher really doesn't know anything about it,' suggested Sarah. 'Perhaps Miriam was just stringing him along.'

‘I can’t see it,’ said Henderson. ‘Why would she do that? What would be the point? They were divorced. She didn’t have to take him back. Why do it if she was going to dump him again?’

Henderson looked at Parrott. ‘Go and have some breakfast. Then I want you to concentrate on finding the solicitor who handled the divorce. We need to know why they divorced, and don’t let them fob you off with something vague like “unreasonable behaviour”. We want the real reason.’

‘DS Boulting also told me to tell you he went to the animal shelter where Miriam worked,’ said Parrott. ‘There are only three full-time staff and a bunch of volunteers. She seems to have been well-liked, but at the same time she seems to have kept herself to herself. No-one really knew much about her, apart from the receptionist, Sonia Manning. She seemed to think Miriam was making a mistake going back to David Fletcher. When he asked her why she thought that, he got the impression she believed he was a thug.’

‘Because of the assault conviction? Or because she knew something else?’

‘He thought it was just the conviction. He says he got the impression she’s a busybody who thinks she knows a lot more than she actually does.’

‘Right, thank you, Parrott. Did DS Boulting say when he would be gracing us with his presence?’

‘Er, no, sir.’

Henderson raised his eyebrows. ‘What a surprise,’ he said.

* * *

‘Revenge?’ suggested Sarah, after Parrott had gone.

‘Sorry?’

‘Maybe Miriam was going to dump Fletcher for revenge.’

‘Revenge for what?’ asked Henderson.

Sarah pulled a face. She was out of ideas. ‘I don’t have an answer for that,’ she conceded.

Henderson let out a long sigh. ‘The problem is, we don’t have any answers for any of it, do we?’

'Did you get another phone call last night?' she asked.

'Oh, yes, a full-blown rant. If you could rate these things I'd put it at level eight.'

'He sounds a complete arse,' said Sarah.

'To be fair, it's unfortunate timing that we should have a murder occur while he's on a conference with every officer who ranks higher than him in this region. He's getting asked what progress we're making, and he's got nothing to tell them. I don't envy him trying to pacify the chief constable when we've got nothing to offer.'

'That's the price of high office, isn't it?'

'Well, yes,' agreed Henderson, 'but it must be difficult. At least if he was here, he could avoid a phone call until he had something to say.'

'You almost sound sorry for him!'

'I can't feel sorry for someone who gives me earache every night,' said Henderson, 'but I can empathise with someone who's getting earache worse than I am.'

'I suppose,' said Sarah, unconvinced.

'Enough of my woes,' said Henderson. 'We need to visit this dating agency.'

He suddenly became aware of someone standing at his shoulder.

'Are you still here, Parrott?'

'Yes, sir.' He handed a printout to Henderson.

'What's this?'

'Miriam Daniels' phone records,' said Parrott. 'It looks like she hardly ever used it.'

Henderson thumbed through the pages. 'You're right there,' he said. 'It's nearly all incoming calls, and they all seem to come from David Fletcher.'

'Anything on Sunday?' asked Sarah.

'Nuh,' said Henderson. 'The last one was just before four p.m. on Friday, and I would guess that was to tell her he was on the way to join her for the weekend.'

'That certainly doesn't contradict his story, does it?'

CHAPTER THIRTEEN

'Is this it?' asked Henderson.

Two's Company, the name of the dating agency, was emblazoned in a large fancy font across the plate glass window.

'With such powers of observation, it's no wonder you're the DI and I'm just your assistant,' said Sarah, ironically.

'At least you know all those years of training weren't in vain,' said Henderson, tongue firmly in cheek, as he pushed the door open.

The interior was tastefully decorated in shades of grey, which created a remarkably warm, inviting interior. Soft music played in the background. Sarah had been expecting something rather sleazy and was surprised to find a much more pleasant atmosphere than she had anticipated. A bell had softly jingled when they entered, and now they were joined by a forty-something man dressed in jeans, a white tee shirt and expensive shoes. At first he looked confused to see them, but soon a businesslike smile appeared on his face.

'Good morning,' he said. 'How can I help you?'

'DS Sarah Southall and DI Henderson,' said Sarah. 'We'd like to speak to the owner, please.'

'You're speaking to him. Tarquin Hemingway at your service,' said the man. 'I'm sorry if I looked confused. It's just that we don't get many couples coming in here. I'm sure you understand.'

'Do you actually get many people coming in?' asked Henderson.

'To be honest, it's nearly all done online,' said Hemingway. 'I could just as easily run this from my spare room at home. This place is just for appearances really.'

'We'd like to know about this woman,' said Sarah, producing a photograph of Miriam.

Hemingway looked at the photograph, and then looked up at Sarah. 'Should I know her?'

'She's one of your clients,' said Sarah.

'That doesn't mean I know her. If she registered online, it's quite possible I've never set eyes on her. Why, what has she done?'

'She's been murdered,' said Sarah.

'Oh my God, poor thing,' said Hemingway.

He looked shaken by the news, so Henderson pointed to some easy chairs and suggested they all sat down.

'I don't understand how I can help you,' said Hemingway. 'Like I said, most people join online, they don't come in here, so the only time I might actually see anyone is if they attend one of our speed dating nights.'

'Speed dating nights?' asked Sarah.

'Yes, it's when—'

'I know what speed dating is,' said Sarah, 'I just didn't know you organised these things. Where does that happen?'

'The Seabrook Hotel, every other Thursday night.'

'So let me get this right,' said Henderson, 'you're telling us people can join your agency and there's a good chance you might never set eyes on them?'

'That's exactly what I'm saying,' said Hemingway. 'Welcome to the world of internet business.'

'Can you access their profiles?' asked Sarah.

'No I can't,' said Hemingway. 'The whole system has been set up so that I cannot access anyone's profile even if I wanted to. It's all about data protection.'

‘Look,’ said Henderson, ‘this is a murder investigation. We need access to this woman’s profile. We need to know if anyone contacted her.’

‘Are you suggesting one of my members murdered her?’ asked Hemingway.

‘I’m afraid it has to be a possibility, Mr Hemingway,’ said Henderson. ‘Much as you may not wish to admit it, you cannot deny it’s a possibility.’

‘This is a reputable agency—’

‘But it seems anyone can join, and there’s no form of vetting,’ said Henderson. ‘Am I right?’

‘Well, yes, I suppose that’s true.’

‘So one of your male members could be stalking one of your female members, and you would have no idea?’ asked Sarah.

‘I can’t believe one of our members—’

‘I’m sure you can’t believe it,’ interrupted Sarah, ‘but unfortunately it is obviously a possibility.’

‘So this place is an open opportunity for stalkers?’ asked Henderson.

‘Of course it isn’t. Do you think I would allow such behaviour?’

‘So how do you stop it?’ asked Sarah.

‘If someone notifies me they have a problem with another member, I can have that member’s profile deleted.’

‘Surely you must have some sort of monitoring system?’ asked Sarah.

‘Er, well, not exactly.’

‘Either you have or you haven’t,’ insisted Sarah.

‘We decided monitoring would be sailing dangerously close to spying on people,’ said Hemingway.

‘In other words, you have no monitoring system,’ said Henderson.

Hemingway’s face was a picture of guilt, but he said nothing.

‘Great!’ said Henderson. ‘A stalker’s paradise!’

Again Hemingway said nothing.

'Don't you feel you have a duty to protect your clients?' asked Henderson. 'Don't you care about their welfare?'

'No-one has to join,' said Hemingway.

'That's a "no" then,' said Sarah. 'You don't give a damn.'

'I'm not sure how many laws you're breaking here,' said Henderson. 'But I intend to find out.'

'Are you going to shut me down?'

'What do you think?'

'But we bring people together. We are a service people need. We've had hundreds of success stories where people have found real love.'

'And maybe one of them found his victim,' suggested Sarah.

'You have no proof of that,' said Hemingway.

'Not yet,' said Sarah. 'And you'd better hope we don't find any.'

'I can't give you access. You'll need a warrant,' said Hemingway.

'Don't worry, that won't be a problem,' said Henderson. 'We'll get onto it right away. Come on, Sarah.'

He stood up, ready to leave.

'Are you going?' asked Hemingway, surprised.

'Don't worry, we will be back,' warned Henderson, 'and next time we will have a warrant and a search team. Just make sure you don't do anything stupid in the meantime. I expect this woman's profile to be left alone. We will know if you've been tampering.'

* * *

'Get onto that warrant straight away,' said Henderson, as soon as they were outside. 'I want a tech team crawling all over their servers as fast as we can.'

'Just as soon as we get back,' said Sarah.

'What is it with all this online dating anyway?' asked Henderson. 'I didn't need a dating agency to meet my wife.'

‘I suppose it’s called progress,’ said Sarah. ‘You can get anything online now.’

‘I’m not really sure making everything accessible to everyone is necessarily progress,’ said Henderson.

Sarah didn’t have an answer for that.

CHAPTER FOURTEEN

'So this ex-husband has to be the chief suspect, doesn't he?'

Superintendent Troy Whaffham was not a happy man. On Sunday evening he had settled into his hotel room confident he was going to make a good impression amongst the assorted senior officers gathered for the Best Use of Resources conference. He had rehearsed a speech that had been weeks in the planning, and he was certain it would add something new to the pool of ideas, if only he got the chance to present it. And with the crime figures coming from his station at the moment it was surely just a formality. They would have noticed. They would want to know how he had achieved such a startling turnaround, and when they asked, he was ready to tell them!

Then, on Monday morning he had been notified of the murder. Of course, with a crime of such magnitude, the chief constable had also been made aware. It had been a hot topic of conversation around the breakfast table, and before he knew it those precious performance figures had become nothing more than a distant memory, a situation which was soon exacerbated by the failure of his detectives to make an arrest, or even have a decent lead!

For Whaffham, it was a classic case of defeat snatched from the jaws of certain victory, and now he was back, he wanted to know why Henderson was getting nowhere fast.

'I'm afraid he has a cast iron alibi,' said Henderson. 'Five witnesses will testify he was over forty miles away at the time of the murder.'

'Is that woman certain about the time of death?' Whaffham didn't get on with Christine Morgan.

'Dr Morgan is quite certain the victim died around one a.m.'

'And she's quite sure this isn't rape?'

'There's nothing to suggest that, sir, and David Fletcher confirmed he was having a sexual relationship with his ex-wife.'

'Is it this burglar escalating?'

'We can't rule it out, but there are differences in the MO that give me cause to doubt it's the same person.'

'Like?'

'The time of entry, the fact Miriam was at home, and if we assume our guy watches his victims first, he must have known Miriam had a boyfriend and that he might have been in the flat. All the other victims were single, with no boyfriend to cause a possible problem.'

'So, really you're telling me you've got nothing, Don?'

'We're getting plenty—' began Henderson.

'But nothing that's going to get us anywhere,' finished Whaffham.

'It's only been three days,' said Henderson, 'and there are some confusing aspects to this case, what with the victim supposedly getting back with her husband and then, at the same time, joining a dating agency.'

'So, it must be someone who's met her from the agency,' suggested Whaffham.

'I think that's unlikely, sir,' said Sarah. 'According to the agency, her profile had only just gone live, and as yet she had not made contact with anyone on the site.'

'But someone could still have seen her without making contact,' said Whaffham.

'But they don't list any personal information like addresses or telephone numbers. They even have site-specific email addresses to protect privacy.'

Whaffham looked at Sarah. 'What was your name again?'

'DS Southall, sir.'

'Why haven't we met before?'

'I've been on maternity leave, sir. Started back on Sunday.'

'Ah, yes, of course. How is the baby?'

'She's doing well, thank you, sir.'

'Good, good,' said Whaffham. He seemed to have been momentarily distracted from their lack of progress so far, but it was short lived. 'Well, come on, Don, what are you going to do next? I think you should get the husband back in and find out if he knew about that dating agency. If he found out she was looking elsewhere he would have a bloody good motive.'

'When we spoke to him yesterday, we didn't ask about it because we didn't know about it,' said Henderson, 'but he's coming in to identify the body today. I'll ask him about it after that, but even if he did know, his alibi still says he couldn't have killed her.'

Whaffham heaved a frustrated sigh. 'Well somebody did it, and we need to bloody well find them soon!' he snapped. 'Tear that dating agency apart if you have to.'

There was an uncomfortable silence.

'Err, can I make a suggestion?' asked Sarah.

'Yes, please do,' said Whaffham. 'I think we're open to any ideas right now.'

'It's looking as if David Fletcher's in the clear, whether he knew Miriam was looking elsewhere or not, so it's probably a good idea to spread the net a bit and look further afield. You said yourself that someone could have seen Miriam's profile on the agency website. Maybe someone did, and recognised her. We could get a warrant to search their servers. I'm sure they probably have records of who's viewed whose profile.'

'It's a long shot,' said Whaffham.

'There is something else,' said Sarah. 'If there is some sort of predator using that site, maybe we could tempt him out into the open with a profile of our own. They also do speed dating nights. Maybe he hangs out there.'

'I'm not so sure about that,' said Whaffham. 'That means putting one of our officers at risk. I'm not sure I like that idea. We'd need to find a volunteer, someone willing to—'

'I'll do it,' she said.

'I don't think I can allow that,' said Whaffham. 'You've just had a baby, for God's sake.'

'With respect, sir, that's neither here nor there. And there aren't that many women in this station who would fit the right profile. Don't forget all our burglary victims are between thirty-five and forty, and Miriam was thirty-seven. If that's his type, it won't be any good sending in a twenty-something who looks fresh out of school.'

'I don't know,' said Whaffham.

'Sarah has a point, sir,' said Henderson. 'She is the only one who fits the bill, and has the experience to carry it off. I can post a watch on her house, and I can always send a couple of undercover guys to the speed dating nights.'

'I'm really not happy about this,' said Whaffham.

'You said yourself we need a result,' said Henderson. 'What if I'm wrong and it is the burglar escalating? Maybe he's clever enough to change his MO to throw us off the scent. Who knows where it might end. We've had one murder, we don't want anymore, do we?'

'It's a last resort,' said Whaffham. 'If you want me to sanction putting an officer's life at risk I need to have a damned good reason, and I need to give it considerable thought. You speak to David Fletcher again, and you explore all other possibilities first, then you come back to me. By then I will have made my decision.'

* * *

'Well, that didn't go too badly, did it?' asked Sarah as they made their way back from Whaffham's office.

'I suppose he's a bit less crabby because he doesn't have anyone breathing down his neck here,' said Henderson. 'He seems to like you.'

She laughed. 'Beginner's luck, I guess,' she said. 'I'm sure I'll step out of line before too long.'

'Oh, I have no doubt about that,' said Henderson, well aware of how often Sarah spoke out of turn.

'There's something I've been thinking about,' he went on.

'Yeah, go on.'

'No offence, but it's technical stuff.'

She tried to look suitably offended. 'I'm not a complete dunce when it comes to technology. Go on, ask me. I might just surprise you with an answer.'

'The problem is, I'm even worse with this stuff. I wouldn't know if you were telling me a load of old bull anyway,' he said, with a wry smile.

'If you don't ask you won't find out.'

'When we were in Miriam's flat there was no computer or laptop, right?'

'Right, but David Fletcher said she didn't have a laptop, and didn't we decide all that sort of stuff must have been stolen?'

'But there was no broadband router. I don't recall even seeing evidence of a telephone line.'

'So maybe she did it all with a mobile phone; even you must be aware you can get online with one of those.'

'But Fletcher said her mobile phone was ancient, only good for texts and calls.'

'Oh, yes, that's right, he did,' agreed Sarah. 'I see what you mean; you can't get online with one of those, so how did she create this dating profile?'

'Correct,' said Henderson, 'and that leads us to another question. If she had no internet access, or computer equipment, at home, where else could she have done it?'

'Work?' suggested Sarah.

'But we've already been there, haven't we?'

'Yes. We were told she doesn't use a computer at work.'

'That doesn't mean she doesn't have access to one,' said Henderson, as they walked into the main office.

'That's true enough,' agreed Sarah, 'but we didn't think it was important because we didn't know about the profile then.'

'I want someone over there today. No, better still, I want you to go over there. Take Parrott with you.'

'But what about the warrant?'

'I'll get someone else to sort that out. I want to know if Miriam ever used any of their computers to get online, maybe in her lunch break. Check if she had access to emails on there as well; we're going to look pretty stupid if there's a trail of emails leading to her killer.'

Parrott was hovering at Henderson's shoulder.

'I've managed to track down the solicitor who handled Fletcher's divorce,' he said.

Henderson sighed. 'Don't tell me, they quoted "data protection" and wouldn't tell you anything.'

'Actually, they were very helpful,' said Parrott. 'Especially when I told them Miriam had been murdered.'

'Thank goodness, someone's on our side. What did they say?'

'It was David Fletcher's suggestion to use unreasonable behaviour as the reason for the divorce. He said he wanted to make it as easy as possible for his wife to make a new start.'

'And did they think it was all above board?'

'Apparently he was very upset about the divorce, and was still in prison when it happened, but he gave them the impression he was one hundred per cent genuine about wanting to make life easy for Miriam.'

'Everything seems to be backing up his story,' said Sarah.

'It looks that way, doesn't it?' said Henderson. 'I still want to speak to him this afternoon, though.'

* * *

'I don't think you need to worry about going back into uniform,' said Sarah, as Parrott drove them to the animal shelter.

'I don't?'

'Not a chance,' said Sarah. 'You seem to be the only one making any progress, so the boss is hardly going to boot you out.'

Parrott's pleasure was obvious as his shy, boyish smile briefly lit up his face. 'That's good to hear,' he said. 'I just wish I could make some progress with those damned burglaries.'

'Don't stress about it,' said Sarah. 'Try to push it to the back of your mind. You'll be surprised what might happen if you let your subconscious work at it behind the scenes.'

'You reckon?'

'Ask the boss,' said Sarah. 'There have been many occasions when he's phoned me in the middle of the night because something has just occurred to him, and every time it has been when he wasn't consciously thinking about a case. Just try it and see.'

* * *

As soon as they walked into the reception area and announced who they were, Sarah could see they weren't exactly welcome. In fact, Miriam's friend Sonia seemed distinctly uneasy.

'I answered all the questions I was asked by the policeman who was here yesterday,' she said.

'Yes I know,' said Sarah, 'and we're really sorry to bother you again, but there are one or two more questions. I'm sure you'd like us to catch Miriam's killer, wouldn't you?'

'Well, yes, of course I would.'

'Did Miriam ever use any of the computers here?' asked Sarah.

'This is the only computer on the premises,' said Sonia. 'We are a charity, you know; we don't spend lots of money on fancy equipment.'

'Okay,' said Sarah, patiently, 'but I still need you to answer my question. Did Miriam ever use this computer?'

Sonia licked her lips. 'She worked out with the animals. She had no reason to use the computer. I'm not even sure she knew how to use one.'

'Oh, really? Why do you say that?'

'She had no time for computers or the internet,' said Sonia. 'She thought it was all a waste of time.'

'What about you?' asked Sarah. 'What do you think of the internet?'

'I think it opens a whole world of possibilities to everyone,' said Sonia.

Sarah waited to see if Sonia would add anything further, but she remained tight lipped.

'So what did you think about Miriam getting back together with David Fletcher?' she asked eventually.

'It was none of my business. Miriam was a mate, but she lived her own life, I didn't tell her what to do.'

'But you had an opinion?'

'I thought she was a fool, but it was her life.'

'You thought she could do better?' asked Sarah.

'You've seen the photo,' said Sonia. 'She was a sweet, kind, good-looking girl. David Fletcher was nothing but a thug. Of course she could do better.'

'You've met David, then, have you?'

'No, and I have no desire to,' said Sonia, confidently.

'That's a pity,' said Sarah, 'because if you had met him, as I have, you might have realised just how much he loved her.'

Sonia looked unimpressed. 'He was a violent man. He was convicted of assault.'

'He acted in self defence,' said Sarah.

Now Sonia didn't look quite so confident in her opinion. 'Yes, well, that's what he says, but he wouldn't have been convicted if he was innocent, would he?'

'So you thought she could do better for herself,' said Sarah. 'How do you think she could have gone about doing that?'

'They do these speed dating nights at The Seabrook Hotel,' said Sonia. 'There are usually some nice-looking guys there. I tried to persuade her to come with me.'

'That's run by that dating agency, Two's Company, isn't it? Don't you have to be a member and have a profile set up on their website?' asked Sarah.

Sonia said nothing, and suddenly became very interested in a small knot in the top of her desk, which she began to pick at with a fingernail. Sarah let her fiddle for a few seconds.

'Am I right, Sonia? Do you have to have a profile set up to go on the speed dating nights?'

'Yes,' muttered Sonia, without looking up.

'That was a "yes",' Sarah told Parrott, who was taking notes.

'Right, got it,' said Parrott.

'So, now we have a puzzle,' said Sarah. 'How did Miriam, a computer philistine, create an online profile, when,' she turned to Parrott, 'what was it Sonia said about Miriam's computer skills?'

'Err,' Parrott flipped back a page. 'Oh yes, here we are, "I'm not even sure she knew how to use one".'

Sonia continued to pick at the knot, but now Sarah reached for her hand and stopped her.

'So tell me, Sonia, how do you think Miriam created her dating profile?'

'I don't know.'

'I think you do,' said Sarah.

Now Sonia looked up at Sarah, and her face told Sarah everything she needed to know.

'Did Miriam actually know you had created a profile for her?'

'I just thought she could do so much better than him,' said Sonia.

'But you didn't actually tell her you had created a profile?'

'Well, no, I didn't think it really mattered. I just wanted to get her to go on one of these nights out. I thought it would be good for her, so I fixed it for her.'

'Has it ever occurred to you,' Sarah asked Sonia, 'that there are risks involved in doing anything online?'

'But it doesn't cost anything to set up a profile,' said Sonia.

'I'm not talking about what it costs.'

'I don't understand,' said Sonia.

'Then let me explain. You created a profile for Miriam, which showed her photograph and gave a description of her, a description which is completely at odds with everything we have heard about her. If the wrong sort of man saw that description, he could easily get the wrong idea.'

Sonia looked horrified. 'But I didn't post her address or anything.'

'That's true,' said Sarah, 'but what if one of these men recognised her, and already knew where she lived?'

'Oh my God. Is that what happened?'

'We don't know yet,' said Sarah, 'but it is a line of enquiry we are following.'

'Oh, God, what have I done?' asked Sonia, quietly.

* * *

'Well, it looks like David Fletcher is definitely in the clear,' said Sarah, as Parrott pulled away. 'When he says he didn't know about Miriam joining the dating agency, I'm sure he's telling the truth. How could he possibly have known, when even Miriam didn't know!'

'It's a bit of a coincidence,' said Parrott, 'but one of the burglary victims was a member of Two's Company.'

Sarah turned and stared at him. Something had been nagging away at her ever since she had left the dating agency with Henderson. Now she realised exactly what it was.

'How many of them?'

'Just the one,' said Parrott.

'You are sure it's just one?'

'Well, I can't cross my heart and hope to die, but I'm pretty sure. I can check as soon as we get back.'

'They were all out on dates, though, weren't they?'

'Every one of them. That's one thing I don't need to check.'

'If you were using an online dating site,' said Sarah, 'would you tell anyone?'

'I'm not with you.'

'Well, if it was me, I think I might be a bit embarrassed to tell anyone,' said Sarah.

Parrott stared at her.

'Keep your eyes on the road,' said Sarah.

He focused back on the road ahead. 'Are you suggesting what I think you're suggesting?'

'What do you think I'm suggesting?'

'You think there's a link between the dating agency, the burglaries and Miriam's murder?'

'It's worth having a look, don't you think? You've got all the names; it wouldn't take five minutes to do a search for their profiles, would it?'

CHAPTER FIFTEEN

'You do the search, I'll go and tell the boss,' said Sarah, as soon as they got back.

She found Henderson in his office.

'Have you spoken to Fletcher?' she asked.

'I'm sure he's as innocent as I am,' said Henderson, gloomily. 'He didn't know anything about that profile. He didn't even know there was a dating agency in town.'

'I'm not surprised to hear that,' said Sarah. 'Even Miriam didn't know about her profile.'

'What?'

'It appears Miriam wasn't interested in computers. If anything she seems to have thought they were the work of the devil, but her friend Sonia wasn't content with that. She created the profile without Miriam even knowing.'

'Why would she do that?'

'Sonia thought Miriam could do a lot better than David Fletcher, so she tried to get Miriam to go along to these speed dating nights. The thing is, you have to have a profile. Sonia knew Miriam either couldn't, or wouldn't create one, so Sonia created it for her, only she forgot to mention it to Miriam.'

'Does she realise she might have inadvertently introduced Miriam to her killer?' asked Henderson.

'She does now,' said Sarah.

'Bloody hell,' said Henderson.

'There's more,' said Sarah. 'It turns out one of our burglary victims was a member of that dating agency.'

'Oh, bloody hell, don't tell me there's a link and we didn't spot it.'

'We don't know yet,' said Sarah.

'We should have checked that earlier,' said Henderson.

'Why would we?' asked Sarah. 'Only one of them mentioned it, but I reckon that's not the sort of thing people boast about, so it's quite possible there are more. Parrott's looking for profiles as we speak. It could be a breakthrough.'

'It could also show we could have stopped Miriam's death if we'd checked this out sooner,' said Henderson, wearily. 'Let's go and see what he's found.'

* * *

They found Parrott studying the monitor at his desk.

'I've found two of them,' he said, without looking up.

'So that's three out of five burglary victims, plus Miriam,' confirmed Sarah.

'That still leaves two who aren't on there,' said Parrott. 'Maybe I should call the agency.'

'No, I don't want him alerted yet,' said Henderson. 'If this is the connection, he's got to be considered a suspect. Let's keep him in the dark for as long as we can.'

'Maybe the other two requested closure of their accounts,' suggested Sarah.

'Jesus Christ! How the hell did we miss this?' muttered Henderson, rubbing his eyes. 'Right!' he said, decisively. 'I want all five victims interviewed as soon as possible. I want to know how many of them had profiles on this dating site, if any of them had arranged dates, and who they dated.'

'That could take a while,' said Sarah. 'They'll probably all be at work. We'll be driving all over the place.'

‘In that case, telephone them,’ said Henderson. ‘We can worry about written statements later.’

Sarah looked at Polly. ‘Two each? First one to finish takes the fifth?’

‘You’re on,’ said Parrott.

‘Find me in my office when you’ve finished,’ said Henderson.

* * *

‘The two who don’t still have profiles on the site, did have them, but had them deleted after the burglary,’ said Sarah, leading Parrott into Henderson’s office.

‘So every one of them was on there?’

‘Yep,’ confirmed Sarah, ‘five burglary victims and one murder victim.’

‘We’ve got several names of men the burglary victims have been out with between them,’ added Parrott, ‘and there’s one, a guy called Jason Blackwell, who’s been out with every one of them. Three of them say they met him at one of the speed dating nights. I printed out his profile page.’

Parrott handed a sheet of paper to Henderson, who studied the face looking out at him.

‘I’m sorry, sir,’ said Parrott. ‘The woman who died, I should have—’

‘Stop right there,’ said Henderson. ‘I don’t want to hear you talking like that. If anyone should have seen it, it was me. I’m the one who was supposed to be supervising you.’

‘Yes, but—’

‘Do you want to fall out with me, Parrott?’

‘No, sir.’

‘Then don’t argue,’ said Henderson. ‘It’s my responsibility, not yours. But just to make sure you get proper supervision from now on, I’m going to ask DS Southall, here, to be your mentor.’

‘Oh, right, thank you, sir,’ said Parrott, looking nervously at Sarah.

‘I take it you have no objection?’ Henderson asked Sarah.

‘It’ll be a pleasure,’ said Sarah, flashing a smile at Parrott. ‘And I’ll start by pointing out the fact that we’ve only linked this man to the five burglary victims. As far as we know, Miriam didn’t meet anyone online, and didn’t date anyone apart from her ex-husband. As of yet, we have nothing to link this man to Miriam’s death, so you’re both wrong to claim guilt for her death.’

Henderson and Parrott both stared at Sarah.

‘Right, good point,’ admitted Henderson, not quite sure what else to say. ‘Now then, back to business. Sarah, I think we owe it to Superintendent Whaffham to let him know where we are with this, so you come with me. Polly, while we’re gone, I want you to see what you can find out about this Jason Blackwell.’

Polly couldn’t hide his smile. Until now Henderson had always addressed him as Parrott, he had never once called him Polly! ‘Yes, sir.’

* * *

‘How did this get missed?’ asked Whaffham, when they presented their findings.

‘It’s my fault,’ said Henderson. ‘I had a young DC on the burglaries, reporting back to me. I should have spotted it. I’m sorry.’

Whaffham studied Henderson’s face. He looked worn out and world weary. ‘You spread yourself too thinly, Don,’ he said. ‘You should have had a DS leading that case.’

‘With respect,’ said Henderson, ‘when my best DS went on maternity leave, I did request a replacement.’

‘And I got you one,’ replied Whaffham.

‘What you got me was an inexperienced DC. It’s not quite the same thing.’

There was an uneasy silence as Whaffham absorbed the truth in Henderson’s words.

'If I might speak,' offered Sarah, 'it could be argued that it was a line of questioning that could easily have been missed by many an experienced officer.'

'I'm not sure I'm following,' said Whaffham.

'If a woman's flat was burgled while she was out with a man, logic says that man can't be the burglar. She's provided his alibi before we even start to think of him as a suspect. Who he is becomes academic.'

Whaffham smiled a weary smile. 'I like your argument, Sergeant,' he said, 'but I doubt if anyone will accept it as a valid excuse for a woman losing her life.'

'But, so far, we have nothing to link this man to the murder victim,' argued Henderson.

'What about the dating agency?' asked Whaffham.

'At the moment it's just a coincidence. Miriam's profile was created by her friend. We have reason to believe she didn't even know she had a profile with the agency, and, consequently, we're pretty sure she never actually used it, so even if she did know Jason Blackwell, she didn't meet him that way.'

'But she could have met him some other way,' argued Whaffham.

'That's true,' Sarah conceded, 'but if he's the link, there's never been any violence before, and, as you know, there are the other differences between the murder and the burglaries.'

'I think I'd be skating on very thin ice if I use that as our defence,' he said, gloomily. His mood had darkened at the thought of having to face questions about how they had managed to let a killer slip through the net when they should have stopped him before it got that far. But, whatever anyone might have thought to the contrary, Whaffham was a realist. He knew they were only human, and mistakes would be made, no matter how careful they were.

'Well, let's not dwell on what might have been,' he said. 'Do we have enough to arrest this man?'

'I don't want to be the bearer of bad tidings,' said Henderson, 'but, on what grounds? Dating a lady from a dating agency? I don't think we'd get far with that one.'

'Oh, come on, Don, it's too much of a coincidence. It must be him. There must be something we can do!'

'I'm sorry, sir, we've got someone checking him out as we speak, but at the moment we simply have no grounds to arrest him. We can't even prove he's been anywhere near any of the victims' homes.'

'Can I make a suggestion?' asked Sarah.

Whaffham nodded. He was beginning to take a shine to Detective Sergeant Sarah Southall. She had ideas and wasn't frightened to put them forward. He liked that, just as long as she didn't get too full of herself . . .

'We know who Jason Blackwell is now, but he doesn't know we know. We can't arrest him, but Parrott will have found his address, so why don't we put a watch on him for a couple of days while we dig a bit deeper?'

'It makes sense, sir,' added Henderson. 'It will give us time to speak to the women who have been out with him.'

'But will it get us anywhere?' asked Whaffham.

'There's a bit more,' said Sarah. 'Remember we talked about sending me, undercover, to one of these speed dating nights? Well, we know who we're looking out for now, and we know Blackwell uses these nights to pick up girls. I think we should go for it!'

Whaffham felt vaguely nauseous as he considered Sarah's proposal, but he knew they didn't really have a better plan. 'I will allow this, but only because we know who our target is. Don, I insist there is a watch on DS Southall's home, and I want two undercover male officers at this event. Their brief is to keep an eye on our man and ensure DS Southall's safety. Can you guarantee that?'

'When we talked about this before I had planned the same sort of cover, so yes, I have men ear-marked to do that.'

'Good. Now when do you intend to mount this operation?'

'They're on Thursday nights,' said Sarah, 'which means the next one's tomorrow.'

Whaffham looked uncomfortable.

‘It’s either that or we have to wait another two weeks, sir,’ she explained.

Whaffham sighed. They couldn’t afford to wait. Like it or not, he had to commit to it. ‘Alright, let’s do it,’ he said. ‘Carry on, Sarah. Don, can I have a word before you go?’

‘You go on down,’ Henderson said to Sarah. ‘Tell Parrott and Grinder to get online and create profiles on that dating site. They’re going to need them to attend the speed dating night. I’ll catch you up shortly.’

Silently they watched Sarah until the door clicked shut behind her.

‘Sir?’ asked Henderson.

‘Now I understand why you value her so highly, I’m holding you responsible for Southall’s welfare. You make sure no harm comes to her.’

‘I’ll make sure the lads don’t let her out of their sight, and I’ll have two or three officers posted in the hotel lobby and out in the street. I’ll also be out there myself co-ordinating things.’

‘Let me know if you need more officers and I’ll find them for you.’

‘I think we can cover it,’ said Henderson, ‘but I’ll let you know if we’re short.’

‘Right. Good luck,’ said Whaffham.

As Henderson made his way back to his office, he wondered what had got into his boss. He must have sanctioned undercover operations before, and yet he seemed almost nervous about this one, which was pretty straightforward really. It’s not as if they were going into battle with a band of armed warriors, was it? They were confident this guy wasn’t actually going to be alone with Sarah, so the risk was minimal. It was more a case of observing his behaviour and seeing who his next victim might be. If they were really lucky, Sarah might even get a chance to exchange a few words with the guy. Anyway, if there was anything dodgy going down, they would have plenty of backup on hand.

CHAPTER SIXTEEN

When Sarah got home, she was surprised to find her husband Kenny's car parked in their drive. She couldn't remember the last time he had come home from work this early; it had become a rare occurrence since their daughter was born.

'Hello, stranger,' she said. He was standing in the kitchen, leaning against the counter, eating what appeared to be a bowl of breakfast cereal. Mouth full, he merely grunted a greeting in return.

'Where's Dad?'

'He's upstairs, bathing the baby.'

'Her name's Laura,' corrected Sarah.

'Yes, so I understand.'

Sarah noticed his right hand was bandaged.

'What have you done to your hand?'

'Don't you ever listen to anything I tell you? I cut the back of my hand at work. It's been like this for months.'

Now Sarah felt both foolish and guilty as she recalled he had indeed told her about the injury weeks ago.

'Shouldn't it have healed by now?'

'It was, but it got a bit infected when I caught it again.' He continued shovelling cereal into his mouth.

‘Oh, right, I see. Actually, I’m glad you’re here, because there’s something I need to tell you. D’you remember that guy I work with whose wife died?’

‘Grinder, wasn’t it? You spent a lot of time looking out for him.’

‘That’s right, I did. Someone had to stop him falling apart.’

‘And, so, what about him?’

‘Well, he’s never been quite right since she died. He’s never really got over it. Sometimes I think he sees me as a sort of replacement for her.’

‘What’s that supposed to mean?’

‘It’s a bit of a joke at work. They say he’s been missing me while I’ve been away.’

‘Is that it? Some bloke at work has a thing about you?’ Kenny had stopped eating now, the loaded spoon halfway to his mouth.

‘Well, that was it,’ she said, nervously, ‘but it’s escalated.’

‘What do you mean “escalated”?’

‘He stopped me in the car park. He thinks he’s the father of our baby.’

Kenny didn’t say a word; he just kept staring at her.

‘Well, say something,’ she urged.

‘What am I supposed to say to that? Is it true?’

‘Of course it’s not true!’

‘So why are you telling me?’

‘I thought it would be better if you heard it from me, and not from someone else.’

‘Are you telling me this is common knowledge?’

‘No, I don’t think so,’ she said, ‘but it’s possible someone might have heard him talking to me. I don’t know! He’s off his head. He might have told someone for all I know. I just don’t want you to hear it from someone else.’

‘But why would he think that?’ insisted Kenny. ‘Doesn’t he know how you make babies?’

‘Yes, of course he does.’

‘So why would he think the baby’s his, Sarah? What are you telling me here?’

‘I’m telling you he’s imagining something that didn’t happen.’

‘Why would he do that?’

She had really been hoping Kenny would have trusted her and accepted what she was telling him without all these questions.

‘When you were away just before the Christmas I fell pregnant, we solved a big case. You know what it’s like, we all go down the pub, sink a few drinks, get hammered. And this was just before Christmas so we made it our Christmas party too. We all booked rooms because we were nearly all too drunk to drive home, but they didn’t have enough rooms so we had to share.’

‘And you shared with Grinder?’ asked Kenny, angrily.

‘No-one else would, so I had to.’

‘I see,’ said Kenny, grimly. ‘So you slept with him?’

‘Nothing happened,’ she said. ‘I put him to bed, and I slept in a chair. He could barely stand up. He was way too pissed to do anything. You know I wouldn’t do something like that.’

Kenny looked away from her and pulled a face but passed no comment.

‘I promise you nothing happened,’ she said again.

Slowly he raised the spoonful of cereal to his mouth and chewed thoughtfully, gazing at the window as if he’d never seen it before. Sarah was confident she could usually read Kenny’s thoughts, but on this occasion he was giving nothing away, and she began to wish she’d kept it all to herself. After what seemed like a very long silence she felt she had to say something, although she couldn’t be sure what might happen next.

‘So is this your starter,’ she asked, nodding her head at the bowl of cereal, ‘or are you rushing off out again?’

‘I’ve actually got a night off,’ he said, with a sigh, ‘but if this is going to be an interrogation after what I’ve just heard, I’m definitely not stopping.’

'Well, what do you expect?' said Sarah, exasperated. 'I feel like I'm single again. You're never here. You seem to do nothing but work, and when you do eventually come home you sleep in the spare room. Don't you think it's time you helped out with looking after our daughter?'

'In case you hadn't noticed, babies cost money. It makes more sense that I do the overtime to bring in the extra money we need,' he said. 'And as for the sleeping arrangements, I thought you would appreciate the fact I'm not waking you, or the baby, every night when I come home.' He placed the now empty cereal bowl and spoon in the sink. 'And as for helping out, I thought that's what the old man was here for.'

'But it's not fair he should be looking after a baby at his age.'

'And whose fault is that?'

'What's that supposed to mean?' snapped Sarah.

'What do you think it means?' he answered, angrily. 'You were the one who wanted to have this baby.'

'We agreed—'

'No, Sarah, you agreed, not me.'

'But you always wanted children.'

'Yeah, until I got to forty,' he said. 'After that I felt I was too old and too set in my ways. God, how many times have we had this conversation?'

'It's not my fault I didn't get pregnant sooner.'

'I know that,' he said, more gently now, 'and you know I've never blamed you. As far as I was concerned it was just one of those things that was never supposed to happen. I mean, it's not as if we didn't try, is it?'

Sarah knew this was true. He had never, ever blamed her, and they had certainly put plenty of effort into trying, especially when they were younger!

He spread his arms in appeal. 'But I told you, when I got to forty, I had accepted we'd never have any kids. Didn't we agree we had a pretty good life anyway, and without kids we had the freedom to do whatever we wanted?'

She couldn't argue with this. 'Well, yes, we did, but—'

'I thought we had agreed we just couldn't have kids and that was it; yes, it was disappointing, but it wasn't the end of the world,' he continued. 'We were comfortable. I could look at all my mates stressing out about money, and trying to keep their wife and kids happy, and I told myself that, in a way, I was the lucky one. I had none of that pressure to deal with. Life was great, and I was really happy, and then, right out of the blue, you dropped this bomb on me. Suddenly, the life I thought I was going to live and enjoy was snatched away. I was going to become just like them, except they had fifteen years start on me.'

'I hate to tell you this, Kenny, but a marriage is about two people, it isn't all about you!'

'You're certainly right about that,' he said, angrily. 'But then it never has been about me, has it?'

Sarah sighed. 'Oh, no, not this again.'

'Oh, yes, this again,' he said, his voice getting louder. 'Because it's always been all about you, and your precious career!'

'Keep your voice down, Dad will hear,' she hissed.

'I don't care what he hears,' said Kenny. 'If he's honest he'll know I'm right. D'you think he really wants to be here every day looking after a baby at his age? Of course he doesn't, he's her bloody grandfather. He should be able to dip in and out of her life when he feels like it, not be stuck with her 24/7. He's only here now because of your selfish desire to have your baby and your career. You want your cake, and you want to eat it, and you expect everyone else to bend over backwards to make sure you can do it.'

'That's not true!'

'Yes, it is, Sarah, and you know it!' He picked up his car keys.

'Where are you going?'

'Out!'

'But you can't stay away from our baby forever, it's not her fault!'

'Your baby,' said Kenny, brushing past her, 'not mine.'

'What's that supposed to mean? If you're referring to Grinder—'

'I was quite happy the way things were, when we could both do whatever we wanted,' he said as he stormed out, the front door slamming closed behind him, quickly followed by the muffled sound of his car starting, then the engine noise fading away as he drove off. Sarah stared at the cereal bowl and spoon in the sink, and wondered was she really so selfish?

Her father shuffled into the room, not sure quite what to say. 'Has he gone back to work?'

She swung round to face him, a half-hearted smile on her face. 'Yes, I think so,' she said, then corrected herself, 'well, actually, I'm not sure where he's gone.'

'I couldn't help but catch a few words,' he said.

'Yes, I'm sorry,' she said. 'It's been a bit difficult. He's finding it hard.'

'Yes, so I heard,' said her dad, with a sad little smile. 'I just want you to know I'm happy to help out for as long as you need me. If I was at home I'd only be sitting there on my own, missing your mum, wondering what to do with myself. I'd much rather be here, making myself useful.'

'Where is she?'

'I've just put her down, but she's not asleep yet if you want to see her.'

'Yes, I will I think, but first I need to ask a favour. I know I said I wouldn't be working nights, but I've got to work tomorrow evening.'

'But that's my cards night!'

'Yes, I know,' she said, 'and I am really sorry, but it's important.'

Freddie sighed in disappointment. 'Why can't Kenny do it?'

'I don't think he'll be around,' she said. 'I think he said he would be working.'

Freddie knew very well Kenny had said no such thing, but Sarah looked as though she might burst into tears.

'Alright, I'll do it,' he said, reluctantly. 'I suppose the cards will still be there next week.'

'I am sorry.'

The faint sound of crying drifted through the room from the intercom.

'You go on up and see to her,' said Freddie. 'I'll phone Jim and make my excuses for tomorrow night, and then I'll find us something to eat from the freezer.'

* * *

By nine o'clock that evening, Freddie, having had enough of the awkward atmosphere in the house, made his excuses and went up to bed, leaving Sarah downstairs on her own. She poured herself a glass of wine, settled in her favourite armchair and opened their laptop. She couldn't attend the speed dating night without becoming a member of Two's Company, so that was her plan for tonight.

She booted up the laptop and then opened the web browser. She was one of those people who always closed every window behind her, so that when she next opened the browser she would be presented with the search engine home page. So she was not at all prepared for the page that greeted her.

'Jesus!' she exclaimed in surprise, almost spilling her wine. 'Who the hell's been watching this stuff?'

But, of course, there could only be one answer. She knew very well that Freddie was a technology philistine who had never taken to home computers, and she doubted he would even know how to switch the thing on. It had to be Kenny, but what was he watching this stuff for? She had known him for twenty years, and in that time he had never given her any indication that he was even remotely interested in pornography.

She tried to convince herself it must be one of those cases where an innocent search had produced a result that was anything but innocent, but a quick look at the history soon dispelled that optimistic theory. There was no doubt about it, whoever it was had been looking for some pretty specific stuff.

The very idea that Kenny had been watching porn made her feel quite uneasy. She knew they had grown apart these last few months, and she couldn't remember the last time they had shared a bed, but surely that couldn't be the reason for this. She quickly closed the browser window and erased the history, as if that would somehow convince her it had never happened. Then she turned to the task she was supposed to be doing, and tapped in the address of the Two's Company website.

She clicked her way through to the 'new member sign-up form' and stared at the page. It was only now she realised she hadn't really thought this bit through. It sounded simple enough, but how should she describe herself? She could hardly say she was a 37-year-old new mum with a grumpy husband, could she? Then she had a bright idea. Miriam's profile had sounded quite good, maybe she could use that as a template and make a few adjustments.

She opened a new window and typed in Miriam's name. Within a couple of seconds she was informed there were no members with that name. Sarah sighed in frustration. Damn! If Miriam's profile was gone she would just have to try and find another one she could copy and adapt.

* * *

Next morning Sarah was awakened as usual by the hungry cries from the cot at the foot of her bed. As she carried her noisy little bundle downstairs she noticed the spare bedroom door was ajar just as it had been when she had gone to bed last night. Hushing the baby she pushed the door open enough to peer inside, but the room was empty, and the bed clearly had not been slept in.

CHAPTER SEVENTEEN

'I'm sure you must all be aware we had something of a breakthrough yesterday,' began Henderson. He pointed to the latest photograph to be added to their board. 'For anyone who doesn't know, this is Jason Blackwell. At this stage we know he's linked to the five burglaries—'

'So, is he the PKN?' asked Grinder, triumphantly. 'I told you from the start he was our man, didn't I?'

Henderson glared at Grinder. 'At this stage all we know is that he has dated all of the burglary victims.'

'Well, there you are then,' said Grinder.

'We also know he was with each of the victims on the nights their homes were robbed,' said Henderson, patiently.

'He can't have been,' said Grinder.

Henderson sighed. Grinder was definitely beginning to get on his nerves. 'Perhaps, DS Boulting, you know something we don't. Would you like to share?'

'Well, he can't have been in two places at once, can he?' argued Grinder.

'Which is exactly why we can't bring him in,' said Henderson. 'He has an alibi for each of the burglaries, because he was with the victim, every time.'

Grinder looked puzzled. 'How does that work, then?'

'Have you ever heard of an accomplice?' suggested Henderson.

'How do you know he has an accomplice?'

'I don't, but if he's involved in these burglaries, he must have one. As you just said, he can't be in two places at once, can he?'

'Can't we bring him in and ask him?' asked Grinder.

Henderson had a feeling of déjà vu.

'If we had a half decent reason we would,' said Sarah. 'But as far as I know, meeting someone online via a dating agency and asking them out isn't a crime, and, as we just said, he has an alibi for each of the robberies.'

'Never mind the burglaries, does he have an alibi for the murder?' insisted Grinder.

'On what grounds would we be asking that question?' asked Sarah. 'We have no evidence that he even knew Miriam existed, and nothing to suggest he's been anywhere near the crime scene.'

'So, you're just going to let him do it again?'

'Perhaps you should be leading this investigation,' said Henderson, testily, 'as I obviously have no idea what I'm doing.'

'I'm not saying that.' Grinder realised he was digging a big hole for himself. 'It's just that if we're so sure this guy's a murderer . . .'

'But that's the thing,' said Henderson. 'We're not sure he's a murderer. If anything, we're pretty certain he's not a murderer. You're the only one who seems keen to convict him.'

'I just don't see why we can't question him.'

'There are things called procedures,' said Henderson. 'You should be aware of that.'

'Yes, but—'

'When we have a good reason to question Mr Blackwell, in connection with the murder,' Henderson snapped, 'I can assure you he will be brought in here so fast his feet won't touch the ground, but until such time, he is being kept under observation, and you will keep well away from him, do I make myself clear?'

Grinder's face had reddened. He would have liked to have carried on the argument, but he wasn't going to do it here, in front of the others, and especially not in front of Sarah.

'Do I make myself clear?' repeated Henderson, menacingly.

'Yes, boss,' said Grinder.

'Good. Perhaps I can carry on now, unless you have some objection?'

Grinder decided maybe he had pushed his luck far enough and kept quiet.

'As I was saying,' said Henderson, addressing the room, 'we have a suspect for the burglaries, who is also potentially a suspect in the murder case. However, because there are several differences in the MO, I'm not convinced he's our man. There again, we've got bugger all else to go on at the moment, so he's going to be our focus for a day or two. He's under 24-hour surveillance at the moment, so we know what he's up to, and we have an undercover operation going down tonight. We think our man may be selecting his burglary victims through speed dating nights at The Seabrook Hotel. These events happen on Thursday nights. The more observant among you will have noticed that today is Thursday, so, tonight, DS Southall, DS Boulting and DC Parrott will be attending undercover. The rest of us will be deployed in and around the hotel. We're not expecting any trouble, but we'll be there just in case. I'll give each of you more specific details about your roles later.'

He looked around the room for Parrott.

'Ah, there you are, how much did you find out about our man last night?'

'Not much more than an address, sir, then I was told to go home.'

'Yes, of course,' said Henderson. 'Well, I'd like you to get back onto that this morning.'

'Yes, sir.'

'Right, you all know what you need to be doing for now. Unless something important crops up, I'd like everyone to be here at six thirty this evening. Is there anything else?'

* * *

It was just before 7.30 that evening when Sarah made her way into the hotel lobby. She had thought about dressing up for the occasion, but as she wasn't actually hoping to attract anyone, she had settled for a simple jacket, blouse and trousers ensemble. She felt she looked neat enough, without attracting too much attention. A large sign informed her 'This way to Two's Company' and she followed the direction down a corridor to a small reception room.

'Hello. My name's Alicia, I'm your hostess for this evening,' announced a pretty young woman sitting at a desk in the centre of the room. 'Can I have your ticket, please?'

Sarah produced the ticket she had printed from the membership site. She realised each ticket bore a number, and Alicia quickly found the matching number on her list and ticked it off.

She directed an artificial smile at Sarah. 'Is this your first time?'

'Yes it is.'

'Okay, well there's no need to be nervous. Just relax and try to enjoy yourself.' She pointed to a door behind her. 'Go through into the next room and get yourself a drink,' she instructed, handing Sarah a numbered counter. 'You're number six. When the bell goes, take your place at table number six, choose a name and write it on the card on the table, then place it so anyone coming to the table can see it.'

'What do you mean "choose a name"?' asked Sarah. 'I've already got a name.'

'Not everyone likes to use their real name in here,' explained Alicia. 'It's a security and privacy thing, just in case you find someone gets a bit too familiar. They won't know your real name.'

'But they'll know my face. Don't you think they might remember that?'

Alicia had to think about this, but slowly she realised what Sarah meant.

'Oh, yeah, I see what you mean,' she said. 'I hadn't thought of that.'

'Never mind,' said Sarah, 'maybe everyone else is as vague as you.'

'D'you think so?'

Sarah rolled her eyes. 'Not really, Alicia. I would imagine you're one of a kind.'

'Oh, thanks,' said Alicia, with a warm smile, genuinely pleased to be considered so special. 'Now, where was I?'

'You were telling me what goes on inside,' Sarah reminded her. 'We got as far as I have to write my name on the card.'

'Oh, yeah, that's right. You have a minute or two to get settled, then the bell will ring again and you'll be joined at the table by your first partner. Then you will have five to ten minutes to get to know your partner. When the bell rings again, your partner will move off, and you will be joined by the next one. And that's how it goes until the end.'

'How many men will that be?'

Alicia quickly scanned the list before her, as if she didn't already know the answer.

'Nine,' she said.

'What if I find I don't like someone?' asked Sarah.

'Everyone deserves a few minutes,' said Alicia. 'No-one's really that bad, and it's not as if you have to have sex with any of them. Well, not unless you want to, of course,' she added, coyly. 'If you really don't like someone, try to remember what my mum used to say.'

Sarah waited for the punch line, but it wasn't forthcoming.

'And what did your mum used to say?' she asked.

'Eh? Oh, yeah, she used to say, if you want to make a rainbow you've first got to have some rain.'

'Really? How deeply philosophical of her.'

'Yeah, she was clever like that.'

* * *

Sarah followed Alicia's directions and made her way through the door into what was obviously a small function room. A waiter stood behind a bar, so she made her way over to him.

'Yes, madam, what can I get you?'

'I'd like a gin and tonic, please.'

As she waited for her drink, she looked around the room. As she cast her eye around, she spotted Polly studying a painting hanging on the wall on the opposite side of the room. She thought he actually looked quite attractive, and could easily imagine him leaving here with several phone numbers. Several hungry-looking women had already taken their places at their tables, and more than one had their eye on the young detective. She looked again at one particular woman. She could only see the back of her head, but even so Sarah felt there was something familiar about her. And then, as the woman turned towards her, she realised who it was.

'Oh, bloody hell, what are you doing here?' she muttered under her breath. She quickly turned away and took a large sip of her drink, but deep inside she was sure she had been spotted. Sure enough, just a few seconds later there was a tap on her shoulder, and reluctantly she turned around.

'My God, so it is you!' said her sister. 'What on earth are you doing here?'

'I could ask you the same.'

'Well, as a single woman in her prime, I'm here looking for a man to service my needs, as I often do,' said Mandy. 'But what's your excuse? When you told me about that guy from work you slept with, I had my doubts, but here you are, right out in the open. Perhaps you're not such a dark horse after all?'

'I didn't sleep with him, and will you keep your voice down,' hissed Sarah. 'God forbid anyone hears you blabbing about that.'

'But what are you doing here?' asked Mandy. 'If you just want a bit of nooky on the side, I can give you the names of one or two men who'd be only too happy to help. It would be far more discreet.'

‘I’m not looking for a bit of “nooky on the side”, as you put it,’ said Sarah, tetchily. ‘I’m a married woman.’

Mandy gave her a sympathetic look, ‘As are half the women here tonight.’

‘What?’

Mandy cast a practised eye around the room. ‘There are probably more married women here than singles.’

Sarah looked around in surprise, ‘Really?’

‘Oh yes, you’re in good company, but I warn you, the competition will be fierce.’

‘Look, I know you find it hard to believe, but I am genuinely not looking for a new husband.’

‘Nor are any of these, darling. All they’re hoping to find is a single, virile, young stallion, who’s looking for the same thing as them: temporary relief from their dull, boring lives, with no strings attached.’

‘But my life isn’t dull and boring.’

‘No, of course not.’

‘It’s not! If you must know, I’m here undercover with a couple of colleagues.’

‘Oh, how exciting!’ squealed Mandy, clapping her hands excitedly.

‘For God’s sake calm down, Mandy, you’re drawing attention to us,’ snapped Sarah.

Mandy nodded towards Parrott, who was still studying the same painting. ‘Is he with you?’

‘What? Why would you think that?’

‘Because he’s been staring at that painting for at least fifteen minutes. Only a policeman could show that much interest in something so dull. Anyone normal would be able to see it’s total crap in less than fifteen seconds. Anyway, I’ve been watching him, he looks round every time someone comes in, and he seemed to let out a sigh of relief when you came in, as if he was waiting for you.’

‘Look, you’ve got to promise me you’ll keep quiet about this,’ said Sarah.

‘Of course I will, as long as you admit he’s with you.’

‘Alright, I admit it, but you promise you’ll keep quiet.’

‘Scout’s honour,’ said Mandy, with a mocking salute. She looked across at Parrott again. ‘He is rather nice, your young man, isn’t he?’

‘You can forget about that,’ said Sarah. ‘For a start, he’s not my young man, plus he’s on duty, and he’s got a job to do. He doesn’t need you distracting him. Besides, you’re way too old for him.’

‘Oh, you think so, do you?’ She gave Sarah a wicked grin, but before she could respond the first bell rang.

‘Got to take my place now,’ she said, rushing off. ‘See you in the bar afterwards. We can compare notes.’

Sarah cursed quietly to herself as she took her place at table number six. Of all the people she didn’t need to be here tonight, she should have known her sister was probably the one most likely to appear. This situation was just made for her and her appetite. She was awoken from her thoughts by the sound of a chair scraping back, and a man sat down across the small table from her.

‘Good evening, Sarah,’ said a familiar voice.

Sarah couldn’t believe her ears. She’d known Grinder was here, and that there was a possibility she would have to spend time talking to him, but getting him first? How did that happen? She wondered if the evening could have got off to a worse start.

‘Can’t you read? It’s Melanie,’ she snapped, pointing at the card on the table.

‘But I already know your real name.’

‘We’re supposed to be under-bloody-cover,’ hissed Sarah. ‘Why can’t you play the part?’

‘I don’t need to play a part when it comes to you, Sarah,’ said Grinder.

‘What?’

‘You know what I’m talking about,’ he said. ‘I told you the other day. Whenever you’re ready, I’m waiting.’

‘And I told you, I’m not interested,’ she said, firmly.

'But what about our baby? She should be with her real father.'

Now Sarah placed her elbows on the table and leaned menacingly towards him. 'Have you gone deaf, or have you got a bloody screw loose?' she asked.

'There's plenty of room for the two of you at my house,' he continued. 'You could move in tomorrow.'

'You're not hearing anything I'm saying, are you?'

'I'll never forget that night we spent together.'

'What do you mean, you'll never forget it?' she said, astonished. 'You were too pissed to even remember which room we were in, how could you possibly remember anything about it?'

'It was the best night of my life,' he said. 'You were wonderful.'

'It's a figment of your imagination,' she said.

'And then nine months later, along comes little Laura.'

'This is complete bollocks,' she said, but her anger was slowly turning to alarm. Apart from anything else, this whole operation was in danger of going tits up.

'I just want to do the right thing by my daughter,' he said.

'Right now, Graham—' she knew people rarely used his Christian name — 'the right thing for you to do would be to shut up. I think you need to go home, I honestly do. You're sick. You need to go and see someone. You've got a real problem.'

He reached across the table for her hand.

'Err, no touching allowed, sir,' said a firm voice from behind him. It was the barman, who obviously doubled as a bouncer and seemed to be keeping an eye on proceedings.

'It's alright,' said Grinder, 'we know each other, we're a couple.' He reached for her hand again, but she drew it back out of his reach.

'Are you alright, miss?' asked the bouncer, who could see Sarah was visibly shaken. 'Is this man bothering you?'

For a second or two Sarah couldn't decide what was best, but then she felt she had to do something.

'I'm afraid he is, yes,' she said.

'I'm going to have to ask you to leave, sir.'

Grinder looked round at the man. 'Look, pal, why don't you piss off and do something useful like pour yourself a drink?'

'Come on, sir, let's go,' said the barman. 'We don't want to make a scene and spoil the evening for everyone, now do we?' He placed a precise grip on Grinder's shoulder, and suddenly Grinder was as meek as a lamb. The barman leaned down and whispered into his ear, 'That's a pressure point,' he explained, very quietly. 'I can make it hurt a whole lot worse if you want me to, or you can come quietly with me. You decide.'

'Alright, alright,' said Grinder. 'I'll come with you, just take your hands off me.'

'I don't think so,' said the barman, 'not until we're outside.'

Grinder got slowly to his feet, apparently being supported by the barman. A few heads turned their way. 'There's no need to be alarmed,' announced the barman. 'This gentleman's been taken ill. I'm just helping him from the room.'

Sarah was deeply impressed with the way the barman had handled the whole situation. What could have developed into a nasty scene that would have certainly made them conspicuous, and almost certainly blown their cover, had been dealt with expertly. She looked around. It seemed as if no-one was paying her any attention. With any luck they might have got away with it.

She wondered about Grinder. He really was taking this whole 'father of the baby' thing way too far, and she wondered what she should do about it. She didn't really want to get Don Henderson involved, but what else could she do? She would have to consider it, although she had no idea how exactly she would explain it to him.

She took a couple of deep breaths, and absently brushed her hand across the front of her blouse and touched the brooch she was wearing, the one that had a microphone concealed in it. Her stomach lurched as she realised it was still switched on from the earlier test. There was no need to worry how she was going to explain the situation to Don Henderson. He must have heard the whole thing over the radio . . .

'Sarah,' said Henderson's voice in her earpiece. 'There seems to be some sort of fault with your mike, I didn't catch any of that conversation with Grinder. Can you switch it off and then back on again, please. Perhaps it'll fix it.'

She switched the mike on and off a couple of times, and wondered if she had really been that lucky. The mike had been fine when they'd tested it earlier.

She tried to get her mind back on the job, and looked around the room. Then she cursed quietly to herself. There seemed to be plenty of men here, but there was no sign of the one they wanted to see. Jason Blackwell wasn't here. She wondered if perhaps they had got it all wrong, and this wasn't how he found his victims. Maybe it was a coincidence that he had been out with all those women.

And then the bell sounded. There was the sound of chairs scraping on the floor, and a few seconds later a new man sat down opposite her.

* * *

Out in the hotel car park, Don Henderson was sitting in his car, slowly being enveloped by the increasing darkness as the night drew in. He had radio contact with everyone should the need arise, but they had decided against using open mikes. Blackwell was the focus of this operation, and if he approached Sarah, she was to switch her mike on so Henderson could hear what he had to say.

Henderson was deep in thought. He had been concerned about Grinder for a while now. Once a steady, if unspectacular, pair of hands, he had become increasingly argumentative and even obstructive at times, but this latest escapade had taken the biscuit! Tomorrow morning he was going to have to sort the man out once and for all.

His thoughts were interrupted by the passenger door of his car opening unexpectedly, and suddenly someone was sitting next to him.

'At least it's not raining,' said Whaffham, as he settled into his seat.

Henderson looked across at him in surprise.

'Sir? I wasn't expecting to see you tonight. You didn't say you were coming.'

'Relax, Don, I haven't come to check up on you. I was just on my way home and thought I'd drop in to see how it was going. To be honest, I was worried about Southall.'

'She's fine, sir. We're in radio contact, we've got plenty of bodies on the ground, and our man hasn't turned up yet.'

'D'you think he will?'

'The surveillance team have just told me he's on the move, so, fingers crossed, he's on his way here.'

'You seem to be very relaxed about this,' said Whaffham. 'Do you trust her?'

Henderson looked at his boss as if he were mad.

'Who, Sarah? With my life,' he said.

'I didn't mean is she honest. I mean, is she headstrong?'

Henderson smiled. 'She has a strong opinion about some things,' he said, 'and she's not frightened to say what she thinks, but I don't think that's a bad thing. Certainly I have no problem with it.'

'But can she keep her head?'

'I'm not sure I understand what you're driving at, sir.'

'What's her decision-making like? Would she take an unnecessary risk?'

'She's not a fool, if that's what you mean.'

Whaffham sighed. 'I'm not making a very good job of this, am I? Can I be honest with you, Don?'

'Honesty always works for me, sir.'

Whaffham sighed again. 'I had a DC once. I think she would have been quite like Southall. She was bright, hard working, and had her own opinion. I think she could have gone far, but she was too headstrong.'

'What happened? Did she quit?'

'We had an undercover operation. It was a bit more risky than this one. We knew there was a possibility of firearms being used against us, so everyone was under very strict instructions about what they should, or shouldn't, do. Of course we had a firearms team with us, and they went in first, and we were to stay put until they gave us the all clear. Unfortunately, my young DC decided she would ignore those orders. She thought she knew better, you see, and so she made the decision to do her own thing.'

'Ah, right,' said Henderson. He thought he could guess where this was going. 'Did she get hurt?'

'Worse,' said Whaffham. 'She rushed in without being given the all clear. As she went in, she met the man the firearms team had missed, coming out. He shot her dead.'

'Ah, I see. I'm sorry, sir.'

'Oh, it was her fault, no doubt about it, but now, whenever I have to give the go-ahead to these undercover operations, I always worry the same thing might happen again.'

'I can imagine,' said Henderson. 'I think anyone would worry after something like that.'

'So, what about Sarah? Is she headstrong enough to think she knows better?'

'No,' said Henderson. 'If it was to go pear-shaped, I'm sure she would be only too happy to suggest how we could have done things differently, but she wouldn't ignore her orders like that.'

'Good. That makes me feel a little better anyway.'

They sat in silence for a few minutes, and Henderson found himself wondering about the man sitting next to him. He often came across as someone who was only interested in promoting his own career and presenting the right image at all times, but over the last couple of days he had shown he was also quite capable of being reasonable and understanding of just how difficult their job could be. And now he'd just demonstrated he was very human too. Henderson was surprised to find he thought maybe his boss wasn't such a bad bloke after all.

'Right,' said Whaffham. 'You don't need me here taking up space. I'll get off home and let you get on. Give me a ring later and let me know how it went.'

'That could be late, sir.'

'It doesn't matter. I'd still like to know. I have a phone by the bed.'

* * *

Over the next hour Sarah exchanged more or less the same meaningless chat with a bewildering number of men. In the beginning she had been surprised to find how many of them seemed to be interested in her. She had never considered herself of particular interest to anyone apart from Kenny, and she wasn't too sure about him right now, so it was quite unexpected. However, by the end she had come to realise most of them were only interested in one thing.

Sarah's final suitor was none other than Parrott. She breathed a sigh of relief as he sat down; at least he wouldn't be trying to talk his way into her knickers. As he sank into his chair, he gave her a lopsided grin. 'This is a bit of alright, isn't it?'

'I'm glad you're enjoying yourself,' she said. 'I'll never consider my life to be dull and boring again.'

'Maybe you're just not entering into it with the right spirit.'

'Is that right?' asked Sarah.

'Just go with the flow, and it's a bit of fun,' advised Parrott.

Sarah gave him an indulgent smile. 'Go with the flow? Ha! I think if I went with the flow here I'd probably drown in a sea of boredom. Don't think you'll find every undercover job you go on is going to be this much fun.'

'Where did Grinder go?' asked Parrott.

'He wasn't feeling well, so the boss suggested he left early,' she said, surprised and relieved that Parrott didn't seem to have noticed the earlier incident.

'It's a bummer, Blackwell not showing,' said Parrott. 'Does anyone know where he is?'

'Apparently he's in a pub just down the road, hustling at the pool table. It seems he's rather good.'

'It's a bit weird he should be there and not here,' said Parrott. 'I thought he was supposed to be a lady's man. D'you think he knew we were going to be here?'

'How could he have known?'

Parrott pulled a face. 'Yeah, good point,' he conceded. 'So I suppose this was all a waste of time and we didn't really learn anything, then?'

'Oh, I don't know,' said Sarah. 'One nice man explained to me that this is really just a place for people looking for sex, without complications. He pointed you out as a classic example of the type.'

Parrott blushed.

'Oh, God,' she said. 'Is he right? You're supposed to be working!'

'Hey, look,' argued Parrott. 'You told me to play the part, and that's what I'm doing. I can't help it if one or two of these women like me.'

'You haven't really—'

'To be honest, I'm thinking about keeping my membership going and becoming a regular down here,' he said. 'I had no idea I would be so popular. It seems I'm in demand.'

'In demand?'

'Apparently, half the married women in this town come here looking for a bit on the side.'

'Where exactly did you get this information?' asked Sarah, suspiciously.

Parrott nodded his head towards Mandy. 'That blonde over there,' he said. 'She calls herself Mandy.'

'You like to prey on married women, do you?' she asked disapprovingly.

'I wouldn't call it preying, exactly,' he said. 'I'm talking consenting adults. That word "prey" makes it sound creepy.

I just happen to like older women, and, as it happens, a lot of them are married. If they're looking to pull, who am I to disappoint them? Anyway, Mandy isn't married.'

Sarah closed her eyes in despair. 'Oh, no, don't tell me you've arranged to see her again.'

'Why? Do you know her?'

Sarah wondered if she should admit Mandy was her sister. Would it make things difficult for her and Parrott working together?

'I know who she is,' she admitted. 'And I know she must be nearly old enough to be your mother.'

Parrott smiled. 'Actually she is old enough, if she'd had me at eighteen.'

'Well, then, she's far too old for you.'

'On the contrary, she's just the age I like,' he said. He gazed across at Mandy, as if to make sure she was real. 'She's pretty fit, too.'

Sarah felt rather uncomfortable discussing her sister like this, but she knew that most men viewed her in the way Parrott did. 'She gets around, you know.' As soon as the words left her mouth, Sarah thought this was actually a terrible thing to say about her own sister, but, there again, it was the truth.

Parrott studied Sarah's face. 'What's going on?'

'Sorry?'

'How come you're so concerned about who I sleep with?'

'I just think a good-looking young man like you could do a lot better, like someone your own age, someone you could settle down with. I'm looking out for you, that's all.'

'Look, you might be my immediate senior at work,' he said, indignantly, 'but that doesn't make you my mum.'

Sarah suddenly realised what she must sound like. She liked Parrott, and she didn't want to fall out with him, yet here she was telling him how to run his life.

'Of course, you're right, it's none of my business,' she said, hastily. 'I'm sorry. I shouldn't be poking my nose in.'

'Yeah, at least that's one thing we can agree on.'

The awkward silence that followed was broken by the sound of the final bell ringing to signify the end of the evening.

'Come on,' said Sarah, 'we've wasted enough time for one night. Let's get out of here and go home.'

Once the final bell had been rung, and it was obvious they weren't going to set eyes on Jason Blackwell, Henderson radioed his thanks to everyone and told them to go home. Once Sarah was sure Parrott had gone, she made her way to the bar. She could do with a drink.

She found Mandy perched on a bar stool, flirting with the barman who she obviously knew well enough to be on first name terms with.

'Aha!' she said to the barman, when she spotted Sarah. 'Here's my little dark horse sister. Get this woman a gin and tonic.'

Sarah pulled a stool up to the bar and settled next to Mandy.

'So, how did you enjoy your first speed dating experience?' asked Mandy.

'I didn't. Some of those men need lessons in subtlety. It's much too in your face for me.'

'One or two of them are rather like pigs at a trough,' conceded Mandy, 'but you have to take the rough with the smooth.'

Sarah took a large slug of her gin and tonic, as if it would take the taste away.

'I think I'd rather steer well clear of the trough, if you don't mind,' she said.

Mandy laughed. 'Listen to little miss prim and proper! It's not always that bad. The best-looking guys weren't here tonight. Mind you, that young detective of yours is quite something.'

'Isn't he a bit young for you?'

Mandy patted her arm sympathetically. 'How on earth can two sisters, who were brought up in the same household, have such totally opposite views?'

'I have no idea,' said Sarah. 'Maybe we're not really sisters and Mum and Dad just told us that.'

She looked around the bar, but apart from one couple getting up close and personal in a far corner they were the only two here.

'How often do you come here, Mandy?'

Mandy thought for a moment. 'I'm not sure. Once or twice a month?'

'So you're a bit of a regular, then?'

'I know my way around.'

'Are many of the guys regulars?'

'A few.'

'What about this one?' She placed Blackwell's photo on the bar in front of her sister.

'Jason,' said Mandy, straight away. 'I don't remember his surname.'

'So you know him?'

'We're acquainted.'

'What does that mean?'

'What do you think it means?'

Sarah was shocked to think of her sister with Blackwell. God, if he's the killer . . .

'Don't you ever worry that one of these men might not be who he says he is?'

Mandy looked at her sister as if she were simple. 'Oh, come on, Sarah, you could meet anyone, anywhere, and you would have no idea if they're who they say they are. You, of all people, should know that. There are conmen everywhere. It's all a bloody gamble.'

'That's rather a reckless way of looking at it, isn't it?'

'I'm a big girl now, and I enjoy my life,' said Mandy. 'I meet life head on, and deal with the consequences come what may. I always have, and I always will. I'm not prepared to start questioning everything just in case things aren't quite as they first appear. Are you suggesting Jason is some sort of conman?'

'Let's just say he's a person of interest,' said Sarah.

'Really? He's always seemed a perfect gentleman to me.'

Now Sarah was genuinely horrified. 'Has he been to your house? Does he know where you live?'

'No, he doesn't know where I live, but he will know on Monday. He's picking me up and taking me for dinner.'

'I don't think that's a good idea. You can't do that,' said Sarah.

'What on earth is wrong with you?' asked Mandy. 'You can't tell me who I can and can't go out with.'

'You won't take him back to your house, will you?'

Now Mandy was getting irritated. 'You're not going to tell me who I can sleep with, either.'

'But you don't understand—'

'No, you're the one who doesn't understand, Sarah. I'm not some lost little girl who's impressed because you've got a badge. I'm an adult who's quite capable of making her own decisions. I think this conversation is over. I'm going home. I suggest you do the same and stop poking your nose into my affairs.'

She slid gracefully from her stool and gathered her things together.

'Wait,' said Sarah. 'You can't print any of this.'

Mandy was clearly appalled at the idea. 'I wasn't going to,' she said, then her training kicked in and she seemed to pick up a scent. 'Is this to do with that murder?'

'You know I can't talk about that,' said Sarah.

'Jason's not a suspect, is he? You must be mad if you think he had anything to do with that!'

'I won't talk about this,' said Sarah, 'and remember our agreement. If you print any of it I—'

'—could lose your job. Yes, I know,' said Mandy. 'Don't worry, I won't tell a soul, but you just wait until you arrest the wrong man; I might find it hard to resist writing that one!'

CHAPTER EIGHTEEN

Sarah thought Henderson seemed a bit off with her when he arrived just before the 7 a.m. briefing next morning.

'There's no sign of Grinder yet,' she told him.

'That's because, when I sent him home last night, I told him I want to see him in my office at eight. I want to know why he was ejected from an undercover operation. It's just as well Blackwell wasn't there, because if he had been, Grinder's actions could easily have blown the whole thing.'

Sarah's heart sank. This was probably going to get seriously embarrassing. She thought she'd got away with it last night, but if Grinder was to tell Henderson what they were arguing about . . .

'Ah, yes, about that,' she began.

'I don't want to hear any excuses on his behalf. You've spent the last three years covering for him. This time I want to hear it from him,' he snapped. 'You can give me your version of events afterwards.'

Henderson was usually pretty even-tempered and rarely, if ever, snapped at Sarah. He really was annoyed.

'What did Mr Whaffham say when you called him last night?' she asked.

'Let's just say he wasn't exactly thrilled to know he'd authorised all that overtime for nothing,' said Henderson.

'I suppose he gave you a bit of grief, then?'

'You suppose correctly,' he said, curtly.

Sarah had gone home worried sick about her sister last night, but by the time she had woken this morning, she had decided that maybe they could use Mandy's stubbornness to their advantage. However, she decided now may not be the best time to suggest her plan to Henderson. Perhaps later, when his mood had improved, he might be a bit more amenable to her idea.

* * *

Henderson kept the briefing so short that Sarah wondered why they had actually bothered, but although it was short, no-one was under any illusions when it had finished. According to Henderson, their progress had been woeful so far, and he thought last night's escapade had been a fiasco. Sarah thought it was rather unfair to blame anyone for last night. It wasn't their fault Blackwell hadn't turned up, and as for the fiasco he was referring to, that was surely down to her and Grinder. However, she couldn't disagree with his assessment that they had some serious catching up to do, and she wasn't surprised when he told them they would all be expected to work over the weekend.

As the team made their way from the briefing room, Henderson stalked off to his office, closing the door firmly behind him. Sarah could take a hint, so she left him to it and took the mikes and earpieces back to the tech department.

* * *

It was 8.30 when Henderson asked Sarah to join him in his office. Grinder was nowhere to be seen, and nervously she wondered what exactly he had told the boss.

'Take a seat, Sarah,' said Henderson. He was obviously not a happy man.

She sat in the chair he had indicated, and nervously waited.

'Grinder tells me he was arguing with you about the way this investigation is being handled, is that right?'

Sarah couldn't quite believe what she was hearing. 'Err, well—'

'I want you to understand I appreciate your loyalty in backing me up, but that was hardly the best place to get into an argument, was it?'

She had been caught totally off guard and couldn't quite catch up with him. She had expected to be trying to explain why Grinder thought he was the father of her baby, and now she had to try and guess what Grinder might have said instead.

'The thing is, he just started ranting—'

'The whole thing could have gone tits up,' said Henderson. 'Thank God Blackwell didn't show. Can you imagine how I would have explained to Whaffham how two of my officers had got into an argument and blown their cover? Jesus, he'd have us all back out directing traffic!'

Sarah was quickly recovering from her surprise. This wasn't the conversation she was expecting, but she still hadn't figured out how she would explain the real argument to Henderson, so she thought it would be best to play along.

'I'm sorry. I won't try and make excuses. I was in the wrong; it was very unprofessional of me.'

For a moment it seemed as if Henderson had a lot more to say about the matter, but then he seemed to change his mind.

'Well, I suppose none of us is perfect,' he said. 'We all make mistakes, right?'

'I probably make more than my fair share,' she admitted.

'You certainly did in this situation,' he told her, 'but I hope this is a lesson learned and we can put it behind us. Like I said, I appreciate loyalty, and I back you up because I know you'll always back me up.'

'Of course I will,' she said. 'You've always stood by me, even when I've let my mouth run away with me.'

'We've worked together a long time now,' said Henderson. 'I think we're friends as well as colleagues. That warrants even more loyalty as far as I'm concerned.'

Sarah thought Henderson was making rather a big deal out of this, and rather overstating the loyalty thing; consequently, she wasn't quite sure what he was driving at, or how to respond, so she said nothing and instead tried to read his face, but he was a blank canvas, giving nothing away.

'So, what are we going to do today?' she asked, eventually.

'Well, if Jason Blackwell won't come to us, we'll have to go to him,' he said. 'We know his address, so I suggest we pay him a visit.'

* * *

They were standing outside the front door to Blackwell's house.

'Am I supposed to believe he lives in a bedsit?' asked Henderson.

'I thought you would have guessed from the address,' said Sarah. 'Most of the houses around here are shared student houses; they're all divided up into bedsits.'

'But it's a bit cheap and cheerful for a bloke who likes the ladies, isn't it? I mean, would you be impressed if he brought you back here?'

'I wouldn't be impressed if he took me back to the Ritz,' said Sarah, 'but then I'm not the impressionable sort, and he's definitely not my type. It is a bit weird, though, isn't it? You'd think he'd have somewhere better than this.'

'There again,' said Henderson, 'if my sole intention was to get inside a woman's home, I suppose I wouldn't need a fancy pad to bring them back to, would I?'

'You think this is just somewhere to sleep?'

'It's got to be. He's not a student, is he? Come on, let's go and ask him.'

Sarah rang the bell and, after a couple of minutes, an untidy-looking youth came to the door, struggling into a coat.

'We're looking for Jason Blackwell,' she said, waving her warrant card in his face.

The youth zipped up his coat, yawned expansively, then pointed down the hall. 'If you mean Mr Smooth and Creepy, his room is the one on the right back there.'

'Is he in?' asked Sarah.

'I don't know, and frankly, I don't care.'

'You don't like him?' asked Henderson.

'He's not exactly one of the gang, if that's what you mean. Look, I'd love to stop and chat, but I have to go.'

He rushed past them.

'So he's not exactly Mr Popularity around here,' said Henderson, as they closed the front door behind them and made their way to Blackwell's room.

Sarah knocked on the door. There was a brief sound of shuffling from the other side of the door, and then it opened and Jason Blackwell stood before them, a sly grin on his face.

'Jason Blackwell?'

'Yep, that's me. And you are?'

'DS Southall and DI Henderson,' said Sarah, flashing her wallet. 'We wondered if we could come in and have a word.'

He stepped back and opened the door for them. 'It's not exactly roomy, but if you don't mind a squeeze.'

Sarah could see he wasn't joking; the room certainly couldn't be described as spacious.

'I'd offer you a drink,' said Blackwell, 'but as you can see, I don't exactly have the facilities in here, and I'm not using the kitchen. Those mucky bloody students have never heard of washing up.'

'It's a bit spartan, isn't it?' asked Henderson.

'It's somewhere to sleep,' said Blackwell. 'But enough of that, what can I do for you?'

'Your name has come up in one of our investigations,' began Sarah. 'I'm sure it's a coincidence, but it would help us if we could eliminate you from our enquiries.'

‘What am I supposed to have done?’

‘No-one said you had done anything,’ said Henderson. ‘There have been a handful of burglaries—’

‘I promise it wasn’t me, guv,’ interrupted Blackwell, with a broad grin.

Henderson stopped briefly to show he didn’t think the situation called for humour before continuing. ‘And we’re just trying to ascertain the movements of the victims. We believe you may have been with one or two of them when their flats were broken into.’

Blackwell grinned again. ‘I could well be guilty of that, if they were women,’ he said, smugly. ‘I do like my lady friends.’ He reached for the drawer in his bedside cabinet. ‘Have you got dates?’

Sarah could see Henderson was as surprised as she was. They hadn’t expected Blackwell to be quite so co-operative.

She read out the first date, and he thumbed through his diary, found the page he was looking for, and handed it to her.

‘There you are. I was having dinner with a lovely lady called Mary Quinnan.’

Sarah read the entry. ‘We’ll have to check this with the restaurant.’

‘Be my guest. They’ll confirm I booked the table for eight thirty and we were there until about ten thirty.’

‘Then what happened?’ asked Henderson.

‘I escorted the lady home, of course.’

‘And then what?’

‘And then I came back here.’

‘You didn’t go into the house with her?’

‘I never have sex with a lady until the third date,’ said Blackwell, looking pointedly at Sarah. She would have loved to slap that smug face, but she kept her cool.

‘Oh, really?’ said Henderson.

‘I’ve got a theory, you see,’ explained Blackwell. ‘On the first date the lady’s a bit nervous, not sure if she wants to or not. On the second date she’ll have decided, but I don’t push it, and give her a chance to change her mind. Third date, it's a home run, every time.'

'What if you don't get a third date?' asked Sarah, challengingly. 'Does that annoy you?'

He shrugged his shoulders. 'Why would it? There's plenty more fish in the sea.'

'Do you mind if I check your diary against my list?' she asked.

'Go ahead.'

'You are a busy boy, aren't you?' she said, as she thumbed through the book.

'I must have something they like, I suppose,' he said.

And so it went on for a further ten minutes. Jason Blackwell seemed to be completely at ease, to the point of being vaguely amused, as Sarah studied his diary and made little notes on her list. Henderson's questions were all fielded with confident ease.

'What are these numbers?' asked Sarah. 'There's a number after each first date.'

'Ah, yes,' said Blackwell, looking slightly uncomfortable for the first time. 'They're scores.'

Sarah looked horrified. 'Scores?'

Now he was grinning again. 'Yeah, you know, out of ten.'

'What do you score them on?'

'Ah, now that would be telling.'

'So tell.'

'It's just a bit of fun, to remind me if I thought they were worth going out with again. I meet a lot of women, you know? I can't remember what they're all like, so I rate them after the first date, for reference purposes.'

'What's the difference between those scored in red and those scored in blue?'

'The colour of the ink in the pen.'

'Sorry?'

'I just pick up the nearest pen,' said Blackwell, 'sometimes it's a red one, sometimes it's a blue one.'

Sarah stared at him.

'Honest, red, blue, black, green, it makes no difference, it's just a score.'

Sarah looked disgusted, shook her head, and muttered to herself as she went back to her scribbling. This just served to make Blackwell's grin even wider.

'You don't seem to have any entries in this diary for the weekends,' she said a few minutes later.

'I don't do dating at the weekends,' said Blackwell, with a huge grin, 'that's when I'm off recuperating and building my strength up for the week ahead.'

'What do you mean "off recuperating"?' asked Sarah.

'I go away for the weekend.'

'Can I ask where?'

'Down on the coast. Bognor, if you must know.'

'Can anyone verify that?'

'Look, am I being accused of something? I think I've been pretty helpful and co-operative so far, but there's a limit, and I think we've reached it.'

'No, you're not being accused of anything,' said Sarah. 'Should you be?'

'Then I think we're done,' said Blackwell, but the cheeky grin was gone now.

* * *

'Smug bugger, isn't he?' said Henderson, as they walked back to their car. 'Why do women go for blokes like that?'

'I have no idea,' she said. 'All I wanted to do was slap him!'

For the first time that morning Henderson laughed. 'He's not your type, then?'

'Certainly not,' she said. 'But if that diary's for real, he must tick a lot of boxes for a lot of women, although he doesn't seem to be able to keep them for long.'

'I don't think he's looking for long-term partners,' observed Henderson. 'He's only got one thing on his mind, and it's not finding a wife for himself.'

As they reached the car she spoke again. 'I thought he was ready for us, didn't you?'

'Sure he was. He's far too bloody sure of himself. I reckon he knew we were likely to find him, that's why he's got everything written down like that.'

'He seems to have covered all his bases though. He's got an alibi for every occasion.'

'Maybe,' said Henderson, 'but I've no doubt he's involved in this up to his neck.'

'In that case he must be working with an accomplice,' said Sarah. 'He keeps the women occupied while the accomplice is in their home, but what about the murder? We can link him to all the burglary victims through that diary, but if that's a record of all his victims, why is it there's no mention of Miriam?'

'I haven't figured that one out yet,' admitted Henderson, 'but then I've yet to be convinced it's the same bloke.'

* * *

As they got back to the police station and climbed from the car, Sarah's phone started ringing.

'I'll catch you up,' she said, as she fished the phone from her bag.

Henderson carried on walking but raised a hand to indicate he had heard her.

'DS Southall,' she said into the phone.

'It's Phil from the tech department. I've checked all the equipment you used last night, just as you requested, and I can't find any faults with any of the microphones or earpieces. If your boss reckons he couldn't hear properly, tell him from me he needs to buy some cotton buds and clean his ears out.'

'Are you sure?'

'Is Kermit a frog? Of course I'm sure. You people are always blaming the equipment, but 99.9 per cent of the time it's the operators that are at fault, and that was the problem this time.'

'But he said he couldn't hear me. He said everything sounded fuzzy.'

'Did you have something in front of the mike?'

'No.'

'Then it would have been fine.'

'But it can't have been.'

'Did you test it before you started?'

'Yes.'

'And was it working?'

'Yes.'

'And was it working when you finished?'

'Yes.'

'Well, now it's passed all my tests with flying colours as well.'

'But it can't have.'

'Look, Sarah, I don't want to be funny, but how would you feel if you presented me with a load of evidence and I started to question it all? I'm guessing you wouldn't like it, because that's your area of expertise, isn't it? Well, microphones and earpieces are my area of expertise. Do you get my drift?'

'I'm sorry, Phil, I didn't mean to suggest you don't know what you're talking about.'

'But that's exactly what you are suggesting. Trust me, all the equipment works fine. Now, I don't know about you, but I've got better things to do than sit around talking to someone who doesn't accept what I say.'

Before she knew it, the line was dead. She thought about what she'd just heard. If that microphone was working then Henderson must surely have heard the argument with Grinder, and if that was really the case then he must think it quite possible that she had slept with Grinder, and little Laura was the result. If so, when he went on about loyalty earlier, was he telling her that her secret was safe with him? And what about Grinder? Had he really told him they were arguing about the case? Come to think about it, where was Grinder? Henderson hadn't mentioned what had happened to him. Should she ask, or would it better to let sleeping dogs lie?

Oh, God, what a mess!

* * *

Sarah had been going through the notes she had scribbled from Blackwell's diary.

'I don't know if anyone mentioned it, but my sister was there last night,' she said.

'Really?' said Henderson, looking up from the report he had been reading. 'Is that where she usually catches her prey?'

'That's makes her sound like some sort of predator!' protested Sarah.

'I thought you told me she was.'

Sarah thought for a moment.

'I don't think I put it quite like that, but I suppose it can't be denied she has an appetite.'

'She must have been surprised to see you there.'

'She thought I was looking for a bit on the side,' said Sarah.

'Are you?'

'No, I'm not!' said Sarah, shocked that he should ask such a thing. 'I'm a happily married woman.'

Henderson didn't look convinced and, to be honest, Sarah wasn't sure she was even convincing herself.

'Yes, well, that's alright then,' he said. 'Anyway, you didn't tell her who we were after, did you?'

'Of course not,' said Sarah, indignantly.

'So what did you tell her?'

'Not much really, just that we were there on business, and to make sure she didn't blow my cover.'

'And did she?'

'No, she was very well behaved actually.' She didn't think he needed to know about her sister and Parrott.

'Good,' said Henderson, and turned his attention back to the report he had been reading.

'The thing is,' she continued, 'I went for a drink with her in the bar after you sent us all home.'

It was obvious she had something to tell him, so Henderson stopped reading and leaned back in his seat.

'It turns out Mandy goes to this speed dating night once or twice a month. She knows Blackwell. She says he's nearly always there.'

Now she had Henderson's full attention. 'Does she know anything about him? Maybe she can fill in some of our blanks.'

'According to my sister, we're well off the mark. Jason Blackwell couldn't possibly be a murder suspect. In fact she was so adamant we must be wrong she told me we must be mad! That was just before she stormed off in a huff.'

'Christ! So she does know who we're looking for! I'm not going to read all about this in the local paper, am I?'

'Has she ever betrayed my confidence?' asked Sarah, testily.

'Well, no, I suppose not,' agreed Henderson. 'But can she be relied upon if she's upset . . .'

'I think so. But I've got an idea that I'm pretty sure will guarantee her silence.'

'Okay, let's hear it.'

'It turns out Mandy has a date with Blackwell on Monday night.'

'Jesus!' said Henderson. 'You can't let her do that.'

'Actually, I can't stop her. And, believe me, I have tried,' admitted Sarah. 'That's how she guessed he must be a suspect.'

Henderson couldn't hide his frustration. 'Oh, for God's sake, Sarah!'

'I'm sorry, but she's my sister! I couldn't just sit there and ignore the fact she's having dinner with a possible murder suspect and not say anything.'

Henderson cast his eyes to the window across the office and heaved a sigh. 'Shit! Now what do we do?' he muttered, quietly.

Sarah had some sympathy for her boss. Although Blackwell was their only suspect, they didn't have a single shred of concrete evidence that linked him to the murder. It was frustrating for everyone, and especially for Henderson. Even so, he seemed to be giving her an unusually hard time this morning.

'If you'll just let me explain,' she said, wearily. 'I might have an idea that will help us, and guarantee to keep Mandy quiet.'

Henderson bristled at her tone, but he knew he had been giving her a rough time, so he bit his tongue.

'Okay,' he said. 'I've got nothing right now, so let's hear this idea.'

'I've had another look at those dates against his diary entries. Remember he had this theory about how to guarantee having sex with his dates?'

'Third time lucky, wasn't it?'

'Yes, that's what he said, but he doesn't get lucky quite as often as he'd like us to think, because in quite a few cases he only gets to the first date, and then doesn't date them again.'

'Yes, but like he said, there are plenty of fish in the sea.'

'Most of which are discarded after the first date,' said Sarah. 'Only the select few get a second date, and even less of those get to three.'

'So, he has a selection process,' said Henderson. 'I know you find it distasteful, but there's not actually a law against it.'

'But what is his selection criteria?'

'I have no idea,' admitted Henderson, 'maybe they have to laugh at all his jokes.' He had absolutely no idea where she was going with this, and he was rapidly losing interest.

'And there's the thing,' she said. 'We've been assuming this diary of his is all about sex. But suppose that's just what we're supposed to think? What if he's not selecting them for sex, but for something else entirely?'

'Such as what?'

'Well, what if that first date is designed to figure out whether or not they're worth robbing?'

Suddenly Henderson was very interested in Sarah's idea. 'Go on.'

'No-one gets a second date unless they score at least an eight.'

'Is that a red or a blue eight?'

'Now that's where it gets interesting,' she said. 'All our victims scored a red eight or nine on the first date, and were taken on a second date soon after.'

'What about the blues?' asked Henderson.

'I was only specifically looking for our victims,' she said, 'but I'm pretty sure there weren't too many blues who scored that high.'

'So you think he's assessing them on the first date, and if they're worth robbing they get scored in red, and then get taken for a second date.'

'Exactly, and while they're on that second date, someone else gets inside their home and takes whatever they can carry.'

'But how do they get into the victim's home?' asked Henderson, absently.

'Sorry, I haven't figured that one out yet,' said Sarah.

'One step at a time,' said Henderson. 'I think you could be onto something here. But how does this keep your sister quiet?'

'She told me she had been on a date with him, so I looked for her in his diary. She has a second date on Monday.'

'Jesus!' said Henderson. 'Did you find her score?'

'She got a red ten!'

* * *

The silence was broken by Sarah's phone.

'It's the surveillance team,' she said to Henderson. 'Blackwell's on the move. He's getting into a car.'

Henderson was clearly irritated. 'What bloody car? I thought he didn't have a car. How the hell did we miss that?'

Sarah put her hand over the mouthpiece of the phone. 'We checked, there isn't a car registered to him with the DVLA.' She listened to the caller again. 'He's driving out of town, what do you want them to do?'

'Follow him,' said Henderson, 'and get that registration number. If it's not his car, I want to know who it belongs to.'

'Did you get that?' asked Sarah, into the phone.

She scribbled the number onto her notepad.

'Get Parrott to trace that number,' said Henderson.

* * *

Fifteen minutes later, Parrott knocked on Henderson's door and leaned inside.

'It's not Blackwell's car, sir,' he said. 'It belongs to a Gillian Bowden. She lives in Bognor.'

'Bognor? That's bloody miles away. Is it reported stolen?'

'Err, no, sir, and it's taxed and insured, all above board.'

Henderson scratched his head. 'Okay, Parrott, thank you.'

He watched absently as Parrott left the room and closed the door.

'We've been watching Blackwell for days,' mused Henderson, 'and he hasn't used that car once. He hasn't been anywhere to collect the keys either, so he must have had it all the time.'

'He said he likes to go to the coast at the weekends. Maybe Gillian Bowden is another one of his women,' suggested Sarah. 'Perhaps he's persuaded her to let him borrow her car. Should we stop him?'

'No, I don't think so,' he replied, thoughtfully. 'He's the only lead we've got at the moment. Tell them to keep following him. Let's see where he takes us.'

'Do you think we flushed him out?' asked Sarah. 'What if he's doing a runner?'

'I don't think so; he didn't look bothered this morning when we spoke to him, did he?' said Henderson. 'And he had a holdall on the bed. Maybe you're right about this woman being one of a harem, and he's off to Bognor for the weekend. We'll just have to wait and see.'

'If you're right, he'll be back on Monday,' said Sarah, confidently.

'You sound very sure.'

'I am. He's got a date with my sister, remember?'

'Yes, of course. What are we going to do about that? Can you stop her?'

'My sister isn't the sort to take advice from the likes of her little sister. She told me I have no right to suggest who she can or can't sleep with.'

'But if he's a killer . . .'

'I know she's my sister, but she's also a journalist, remember? We have an agreement that we never discuss my job, and if I do ever let anything slip, it's top secret and she can't print it. That way she never has to face the dilemma of should she publish what she's heard because it's in the public interest. But this is a murder. It's a big case for us, but it would be a huge story if she could get hold of it.'

'Yes, but—'

'She's still a very competitive journalist. You know what they're like. If I confirm Blackwell's our chief suspect, she wouldn't consider the risk to herself, she would probably see it as the perfect opportunity to interview him.'

'But it's her life on the line!'

'Her exact words the other night were, "I meet life head on, and deal with the consequences come what may. I always have, and I always will." Trust me, she wouldn't think twice about it.'

'Bloody hell, Sarah. Have you thought about what you are going to do?'

'I've thought about very little else since she told me, but I did come up with one idea that might work for her and for us. You'd have to get permission from above though.'

'Go on,' said Henderson, 'what's your plan.'

‘We let Mandy go on the date, but we put someone in her house while she’s out, and we keep tabs on her all the time she’s with Blackwell.’

‘But you said she will just use it as a chance to interview him. Why would she go along with it?’

‘I thought maybe we could offer her the chance to write an exclusive after the event,’ suggested Sarah. ‘Let her interview us so she gets an inside story. Would Whaffham go for that?’

‘He won’t be keen on using a civilian as a decoy,’ said Henderson, ‘but there again, he’s usually keen on publicity if it shows us in a good light, and especially if that light shines favourably on him.’

‘Is that a yes or a no?’

‘I don’t know,’ said Henderson, ‘we would have to ask him, but let me think about it over the weekend.’

‘Don’t you think that’s leaving it a bit late?’

‘The less time he has to think of a reason why we can’t do it, the more chance we have of getting the go-ahead,’ said Henderson, ‘and I really do need to think about it first.’

CHAPTER NINETEEN

It was 10 a.m. on Saturday.

Henderson was in his office, sitting at his desk, reading and waiting. He was waiting for Sarah to let him know if her sister was prepared to help them out, he was waiting for Parrott to give him some background information on Gillian Bowden, and he was waiting for the surveillance team to let him know what Blackwell was up to.

He had just finished a call to his equivalent rank at Bognor, explaining why he had a surveillance team watching a house in their town. To his surprise this had gone rather better than expected, and once he had explained the case he was working on, and why his team had ended up in Bognor, he was even offered assistance. He had declined at this stage, but had agreed that he would call in the Bognor boys should it become necessary to effect some sort of intervention. His hunch was that Jason Blackwell had actually told them the truth about spending his weekends by the coast. He suspected the man led a double life, and that he actually lived with Gillian Bowden at the weekend.

He was reading through the information they had on Blackwell: it had taken a couple of days to gather, and it wasn't a great deal. They knew he was twenty-four years old, and that he'd been born and raised in Newcastle. When he left school he'd started an apprenticeship at a small boat-builders yard, but when the company went bust, he seemed to fall off the radar for a while, until he turned up at an address in Portsmouth three years ago. Since then he had moved around the south coast, changing his address every six months or so, until he had moved further inland to his current bedsit four months ago. And that was about it.

There was a driving licence photograph included, and now Henderson studied it. He had met Blackwell, and knew what he looked like, but frankly he thought this photograph could have been anyone. It was all stuff to make any detective suspicious, and Henderson was now becoming quite convinced Blackwell was their burglar, but it was looking increasingly unlikely he was a murderer. Not for the first time he felt they were focusing on the wrong man.

His thoughts were interrupted by a knock on the door. He had left the door wide open as he often did. He saw it as a sign to everyone that he was here too, and they were welcome to come and talk if they felt the need. On this occasion it was Parrott who had the need.

'Yes, Parrott, what can I do for you?'

Parrott stepped into the office and handed him a couple of printed sheets of paper. 'You asked me to check out Gillian Bowden,' he said.

Henderson ignored the notes and focused on Parrott. He could read the details later.

'So what have we got? Anything I should know?'

'Gillian Bowden,' recited Parrott. 'Thirty-five years old, has lived at sixteen Cathedral View, Bognor, for the past three years. Has owned the car Blackwell's driving for the past two years. Works part time as a librarian, doesn't have a criminal record.'

Henderson considered for a moment. 'Does she own the house or rent it?'

'Rents it.'

'Does she have any other income? I can't imagine a part-time librarian's salary would amount to enough to cover the rent and living costs.'

'Yes, I suppose she must have, but I haven't found it,' said Parrott.

'You realise where she fits into our scenario with this profile?'

'Yes, she looks like a potential victim, that's why I thought I should come and show you what I've got so far.'

'What about before she moved to Bognor? Where was she? What was she doing?'

'I haven't found anything,' said Parrott.

'What? Nothing?'

'Not a sausage, but I haven't finished yet, I just thought you should know what I've got so far.'

'Okay. If you can't find anything, try calling Bognor,' suggested Henderson. 'She's on their doorstep, so maybe they know her.'

When Parrott had gone back to his work, Henderson glanced through the notes, but apart from a few minor details there was nothing here the young detective hadn't already told him. He thought about the possibilities. What if Gillian Bowden was about to become Blackwell's next victim? If she was, should he alert Bognor? There was one big difference between Gillian and the other victims; he had stayed the night with Gillian, and he had told them he liked to spend his weekends by the coast. On balance he thought he was probably correct in his earlier assessment that Gillian Bowden was a part of Blackwell's other life.

Now his thoughts were interrupted by Sarah's arrival.

'Did you speak to her?' asked Henderson.

'Morning, Sarah, how are you today?' she replied.

'Sorry,' he said, guiltily. 'So how are you this morning?'

'I'm fine, thank you very much.'

'So, what did she say?'

'She says she'll think about it.'

'What exactly does that mean?'

'I think it means she will help us, but she wants to keep me guessing as a punishment for the other night.'

'D'you really think she will?'

'Well, she said she'll come in Monday morning to speak to the boss, so, unless he really puts her back up, I think we're in.'

'I'm sorry to nag,' said Henderson, 'but this is so important.'

'Yes, I know. I do understand. Have I missed anything?'

'Not really. He doesn't appear to have moved since he arrived at Gillian Bowden's last night.'

Sarah nodded her head at the notes in Henderson's hand. 'Anything I should know?'

'Gillian Bowden,' he said, passing the notes to her, 'it seems she has the perfect victim profile.'

Sarah looked up sharply. 'Do you think she is?'

'I don't think so. He's spent the night with her; he's never done that with any of the others, and he did tell us he liked to spend his weekends by the sea. I reckon he's leading some sort of double life, and this is his second home.'

'Do you think she is his partner?'

'I believe so, but there seems to be a gap in her history. Parrott's looking into it now.'

'Anything else?' asked Sarah.

'I finally got some proper notes on Blackwell,' said Henderson. 'It turns out he's twenty-four years old.'

'You're kidding me,' said Sarah. 'Thirty-four more like.'

'Yes, I thought he looked older,' agreed Henderson. 'Apparently he grew up in Newcastle.'

'Are you sure?'

'That's what it says here. Born and raised in Newcastle, left school to start an apprenticeship in a boat-builders—'

'Hang on,' said Sarah. 'You said he was twenty-four. If he started an apprenticeship, he must have been what, sixteen? That's just eight years ago. I'm afraid I find it hard to believe that a man can have totally lost his accent in the space of eight years. We're talking about a Geordie accent. It just wouldn't happen, would it?'

Henderson smacked his palm against his forehead.

'That's it!' he said. 'I knew there was something wrong about this, but I couldn't see what it was. And it's so damned obvious now you've pointed it out.'

'He's not from the north, is he?'

'No, he's definitely southern counties,' agreed Henderson. 'So, if that much is bullshit, the chances are this whole thing is just a huge pile of it.'

'Do you want me to start again?' she asked.

'Start with the boat-builders,' he said. 'There's a bit of a gap between then and when he appeared in Portsmouth three years ago.'

'Fake identity?' asked Sarah.

'It looks that way,' agreed Henderson, 'but if it is, what's he hiding, and why? See if his photograph comes up with a match against the prison database.'

* * *

'I think you need to see this,' said Sarah, rushing into Henderson's office. 'You were right about the boat-builders. The reason they went bust is because there was an accident, and they were found to be negligent. An apprentice was killed.'

'Don't tell me,' said Henderson, 'his name was Jason Blackwell.'

'Exactly! Jason Blackwell was an eighteen-year-old apprentice. He was working under a boat when the support gave way and he was crushed to death. The company was found to be negligent in just about every way possible.'

'And when was this?'

'Six years ago,' said Sarah.

'Right,' said Henderson. 'Find out who was released from prison anywhere from six to eight years ago.'

'There will be hundreds,' said Sarah.

'The person we're looking for would have been aged between twenty-five and thirty,' said Henderson. 'That should narrow it down a bit. Get Parrott to give you a hand, he's good at that sort of thing.'

'Can I ask a question?'

'Of course,' said Henderson, 'what's on your mind?'

'Where's Grinder? I know he is a pain in the arse, but he's good at this stuff, too. We could do with his help but he doesn't seem to be here.'

'Yes, well, after his escapades the other night, and because he seems to be determined to undermine the way I run this investigation, I suggested he take a few days off,' said Henderson. 'I thought it would get him off your back, too.'

'Off my back?'

'Well, you were arguing with him the other night, weren't you?'

'Oh, yes, I see what you mean.'

'I could have gone down the disciplinary road,' said Henderson, 'but I thought I would try this way first. He'll be back in a couple of days, and hopefully he will have learned a lesson and won't be such a pain in future. In the meantime, I'm afraid you will just have to cope. Use Parrott, he's a good lad, and he's keen.'

As she walked back to her own desk, Sarah was feeling guilty. What was Henderson playing at? She was quite sure he knew exactly what she and Grinder had been arguing about, and if that was grounds for him to have been suspended from duty, how come she was still here? Fair enough, she had wanted Grinder to stop hassling her, but if he got suspended it would ruin his record, and possibly end up doing even worse. Maybe she should go round and see him. Perhaps they could sit down and talk things through and clear the air.

She decided if she was going to enlist Parrott's help she might as well sit with him in the main office.

'How are you doing?' she asked him as she slipped into place at the next desk.

'I can't find any trace of this Gillian Bowden. She just seems to pop up, out of nowhere, three years ago.'

'Now that's interesting,' she said. 'Because our friend Jason Blackwell died eight years ago, and then he popped up, out of nowhere, three years ago in Portsmouth.'

Parrott looked confused. 'Sorry?'

'A young lad called Jason Blackwell was killed in an accident eight years ago,' she explained. 'The man we call Jason Blackwell has stolen his identity and is born again, so to speak. Perhaps your friend Gillian has done the same thing.'

'Wow! D'you really think so?'

'It's got to be a possibility,' she said. 'They seem to be a couple, and if one's a fake, perhaps the other one is too.'

'This is a new one on me,' said Parrott. 'I've heard of this sort of thing before, but I've never actually had to deal with it. Where do I start?'

'The boss has asked that you help me find out who Jason Blackwell really is. How about we do that first, and then I will help you find out who Gillian Bowden really is. Deal?'

'Sounds good to me,' said Parrott, 'what do you want me to do?'

'We're going to start with prison records. We're looking for a man released between six and eight years ago, aged between twenty-five and thirty.'

'Okay, cool,' said Parrott, and began tapping away at his keyboard.

* * *

'Here you go, this one looks promising,' said Parrott. 'Jonathon Bowden. Born 10th of June 1982. Twice convicted of conning money from women, he was released 10th of June 2009. Current whereabouts unknown.'

'I take it there's a photograph?' asked Sarah.

Parrott moved his mouse and clicked to enlarge the image. 'Oh, yes. Bingo!' he said.

She jumped from her seat and peered over his shoulder. 'That's him. No doubt about it. Well done, Polly. Where was he born, does it say?'

'Croydon.'

'Huh,' she said, 'I knew it. Newcastle, my arse. I'll go and tell the boss.'

Two minutes later, she was back with Henderson in tow. He looked at Parrott's monitor and then clapped a hand on his shoulder. 'Well done, Parrott, good work. Bit of a coincidence, don't you think, he's a Bowden, and he spends his weekends with a Bowden?'

'Do you think she is his wife?' asked Parrott.

'I didn't think he had a wife,' said Sarah. She turned to Henderson, 'I thought you said she was his girlfriend?'

'I was just guessing, based on him saying he spends most weekends by the sea.'

'Perhaps she's his sister,' suggested Parrott.

Henderson turned to Sarah with a big smile on his face. 'There, you see, I told you he was good at this stuff.'

'I never doubted it for a minute,' she said, with a smile of her own, 'but don't distract him any further, we've still got to confirm exactly who she is. Maybe she's into this new identity idea, too, and her name isn't Bowden at all.'

'Okay, I'll let you get on. Send that stuff about Jonathon Bowden through to me, Parrott, and I'll try and figure out where we go from here. I think I need to make a call to Bognor as well.'

'Right,' said Sarah, as Henderson headed back to his office, 'you might have beaten me to that one, but I did tell you where to look. Now let's see how good you are on your own.'

Parrott laughed. 'No problem,' he said. 'I'm on a roll. I'll beat you this time as well.'

'Don't get too cocky,' she said. 'And don't forget who the boss is around here.'

* * *

An hour later Parrott sat back in his seat, stretched, and looked up at the ceiling. 'This is doing my head in,' he said.

'I found her birth certificate, so I know she's real. But then when she gets to eighteen she disappears. Now I'm running out of places to search, and I haven't found one more single bloody thing about her, until she suddenly reappears three years ago. How can someone disappear for fourteen years?'

'Yes,' agreed Sarah, 'she does seem to have reappeared from nowhere. I have to admit I'm all out of ideas on this one. Let's go and ask the boss if he has any suggestions.'

They struggled wearily from their chairs, stretching and yawning as they did, and made their way over to Henderson's office. The door was still open, so Sarah leaned against the door post to speak to him.

'We're banging our heads against a brick wall here, boss. We'd appreciate some ideas if you have any.'

'What's up?'

'We know where Gillian is now, and we know where she was until she was eighteen, but there's a gap of about fourteen years where she seems to disappear.'

'It seems to be all the rage with this family, doesn't it?' said Henderson, 'but don't lose sleep over it. The guys at Bognor are going to interview her on Monday morning. I'll ask them to see if she can fill in the blanks.'

'How come they're doing the interview?' asked Sarah.

'Politics and good old-fashioned courtesy,' said Henderson. 'It's their patch, and they have offered support to our surveillance team. It just seemed the right thing to do. Besides, it'll take hours for us to get there and back. They know what questions we want answers to, and I can add more if we think we need to.'

'Oh, right. So what do you want us to do now?'

'Have you tried the brother?' suggested Henderson.

Sarah looked questioningly at Parrott, whose face had turned a deep shade of red, and then back at Henderson. 'Brother? What brother?'

Henderson smiled a knowing smile. 'And there I was thinking my team knew what they were doing,' he teased. 'I searched a bit deeper into the prison records. According to them, Jonathon Bowden has a brother called Jolyon. He was a regular visitor when Jonathon was inside. With all these new identities flying around, it might be a good idea to check that out.'

Sarah looked at Parrott. 'Come on, the boss has spoken. I bet you a tenner he's right.'

'Oh no, I'm not betting on that,' said Parrott, with a grin, 'he's the boss, of course he's right.'

Henderson smiled indulgently. 'Keep saying things like that, Parrott, and you'll go far.'

* * *

'What is it with this bloody family?' asked Parrott, in exasperation, half an hour later. 'There is a brother, but now I've no idea where the hell he is.'

'How come?'

'He's disappeared off the sodding radar too. I can find him five years ago because, conveniently for us, he also has a criminal record. He did eighteen months for breaking and entering.'

'So you know where he was living back then?'

'Yeah, somewhere in the great outdoors. He is listed as no fixed abode, and as far as I can tell he must still be living on the street.'

'Shit!' said Sarah. 'What's the matter with these people?'

'Problem?' Henderson had arrived behind them, unheard.

'We've got a brother who was nicked for breaking and entering five years ago,' explained Sarah, 'but he was living rough. As far as we can tell, he still is, so we have no idea where to find him, or even if he's still alive.'

'They're a slippery lot, these Bowdens, aren't they?' said Henderson.

'As a bucketful of eels,' agreed Sarah.

'Look, it's Saturday afternoon, it's four o'clock and you two look dead on your feet,' said Henderson. 'It looks as if

Blackwell is settled for the weekend, so I think things should be quiet enough here. We've no reason to think this brother, Jolyon, has anything to do with this, so maybe we can leave him for now. Let the guys from Bognor ask Gillian if she can shed some light on his whereabouts when they speak to her on Monday. In the meantime, I suggest we call it a day and come back on Monday morning ready to start afresh.'

'Sounds good to me,' said Parrott.

'And I'm not going to argue,' agreed Sarah.

'Right, that's settled, then,' said Henderson. 'Get on your bikes and clear off.'

CHAPTER TWENTY

Grinder's house was hidden away down a bumpy lane, behind a small church. Sarah appreciated peace and quiet as much as anyone, but as she climbed from her car she found the deathly silence that settled around her quite unnerving. She stood in the lane and looked around. There was no movement anywhere, not even a bird flitting around. It seemed almost unnatural.

It had been a long time since she had visited the house, and it seemed so different from how she remembered it that she briefly wondered if she had come to the wrong place. Then she realised why it seemed so different. It had been Grinder's wife who had been the life and soul of this place. She had been the gardener, keeping everything neat and tidy, and making sure the creepers that grew up the sides of the house were clipped back from the windows.

Now, three years of neglect had allowed weeds to take over the lawn. The vibrant flower beds she remembered were home to nettles and brambles, and the creepers had taken advantage of their freedom and almost covered the windows completely.

She crunched her way up the gravel drive to the front door and rang the bell. She couldn't hear it ringing inside, so she rapped hard with her knuckles and waited. She gave it a minute, then lifted the flap of the letterbox and peered inside. The hall carpet looked as if it hadn't seen a vacuum cleaner in months.

'Grinder! It's me, Sarah,' she called through the flap, then she knocked again. She waited for another couple of minutes, but still there was no reply. She thought he must be out, but she was also concerned about the state of the house. It was common knowledge he had struggled to come to terms with the death of his wife, but the state of the house suggested he was probably struggling a lot more than anyone realised.

She knew she ought to get home, but she felt compelled to investigate further. If what she had seen so far was anything to go by, Grinder needed help. She couldn't just ignore the state of this place. He was a colleague and had been for years. It was her duty to look out for him whatever differences they might have.

She followed what should have been a path round the side of the house and stopped at the first window. It was so dirty she had to use a hand to wipe an area to look through. Gazing inside, she could see what should have been a neat and tidy dining room. What she saw was a table and chairs buried under a layer of dust that must have been half an inch thick.

Almost afraid to pry any further, she made her way around to the back of the house and peered through the kitchen window. A small mountain of dirty plates and assorted mugs filled the sink. On a small table to one side a half empty bottle of what looked like vodka and an empty glass told its own sorry story.

'Oh my, Grinder,' she muttered to herself, 'this is not looking good, mate, not good at all.'

She felt a wave of guilt at the realisation she was intruding on his private grief, but then, at the same time, she was glad she had come. He was obviously struggling much more than anyone realised, and the way they all treated him could only be making him feel worse still. Then she was hit by an even bigger wave of guilt when she recalled how she had treated him earlier this week.

She stepped back from the window and made her way around to the front of the house, and out to the lane to her car. Then she had an awful thought. He was obviously in a bad way; what if his suspension from duty had been the final straw? Suppose he'd done something stupid? But, if he was here, his car would be here, wouldn't it?

She ran back into the garden and across to the rickety garage. There was no lock so she pulled open the door and looked inside. She breathed a sigh of relief. The car wasn't there. He must be out somewhere. Just to be sure, she went back to the front door and pounded on it as hard as she could. Then she fished her phone from her pocket and dialled his number. She could hear it ringing inside. It rang half a dozen times, and then the answer machine clicked into life.

'It's Sarah,' she said to the machine. 'I'm just calling to see if you're alright. If you need anything, just let me know. The boss says you'll be back at work in a few days so 'bye for now, see you in the week.'

She took one last look up at the house as she slipped the phone back in her pocket, then turned and trudged to her car.

CHAPTER TWENTY-ONE

Sarah opened her eyes, eased herself into a sitting position, and looked at the clock. It was 8.30 on Sunday morning. She stared forlornly at the untouched pillow next to her. Yet again Kenny had chosen not to sleep with her. Not that she was really surprised; they had had yet another ferocious argument last night and he had stormed out of the house around nine o'clock. She was quite sure he had not returned. She feared they were in danger of reaching the point of no return in their relationship, and she wasn't sure she actually had the will to keep holding on. Maybe their marriage had reached its sell-by date, as so many did. Perhaps it was time they faced up to the reality of the situation.

She suddenly realised there was no sound coming from the cot at the foot of the bed, and in a panic she rushed from the bed, but the cot was empty. Still not really fully awake, she ran to the door, but as she swung it open she heard the familiar sounds of a baby gurgling happily and her dad singing one of his tuneless songs. She grabbed a dressing gown and made her way downstairs and into the kitchen.

'Thank goodness,' she said. 'I woke in a panic, wondering where she was.'

‘Well, I thought you could do with a lie in,’ said her father. ‘Unfortunately, this little one doesn’t know it’s Sunday. She is still awake at six, expecting to be fed. I was awake anyway, and you were dead to the world, so we decided to let you sleep. We can manage just fine, can’t we?’ He tickled the baby’s chin and she gurgled again.

‘I don’t know what I would do without you,’ she said, sadly.

‘Yes, well, someone has to help out around here. That husband of yours doesn’t seem interested.’

‘Look, about that—’

‘I would have to be deaf not to have heard you two arguing last night. Honestly, I don’t want to get involved, but I really think you need to sort yourselves out. This is not the right atmosphere in which to bring up a child.’

‘You heard all of it?’

He shook his head sadly. ‘More or less. Like I said, I think you two need to sit down and talk. Not shout at each other, but actually talk.’

Sarah didn’t know what to say to that. He was right, she knew he was. She was saved by the sound of her phone beeping to announce the arrival of a text message. She looked at her father.

‘Go on,’ he said, wearily, ‘you’d better see what it is. It might be important.’

She picked up the phone and found the message. Her expression changed from curious to perplexed as she read it for a second time, then she closed the phone and put it down.

‘What’s the matter?’ asked Freddie. ‘You put that phone down as if it was red-hot.’

‘What? No, it’s nothing, just one of those annoying spam messages.’

‘That’s the problem with those fancy mobile phones,’ said Freddie. ‘They seem to be a magnet for nuisance calls. Isn’t there some sort of law against it?’

‘Not for one-off calls,’ she said. ‘It has to be persistent, repeat calls.’

She decided she needed to divert his attention away from her phone. 'I fancy a nice cup of tea, can I get you one?'

* * *

By early afternoon, Sarah had fielded another four text messages from Grinder, each one a little more worrying than the previous. She hadn't replied to any of them so far, but now Freddie and the baby were both taking a nap, she felt it was time to do something about it.

Sarah re-read the message she had created, and then, satisfied it was both polite and firm in tone, she clicked send. She had told him that if there was something she could do to help him, she would, but otherwise could he please stop texting her. She had already resolved to do something to help him, although she wasn't quite sure what form that help would take. Maybe she should bite the bullet and raise the subject with Henderson and see what he suggested.

Two minutes later, her phone beeped again. It was a reply to her message. It appeared Grinder wasn't going to be fobbed off. Yes, there was something she could do to help: she could bring the baby and move in. There was plenty of room at his house . . .

'Oh, God, this is getting ridiculous,' she muttered. Then her phone beeped again. This time, he insisted he would do anything to keep her happy. Hadn't he already proved that?

She stared at this last message and wondered what it was supposed to mean? Exasperated, she thought the only thing he had proved was that he was rather disturbed and in need of help, so she sent him another message saying 'turning my phone off now, so stop texting', then she switched off her phone and admitted to herself that she really had no choice. She would talk to Henderson in the morning.

* * *

Sarah had resisted the temptation to switch her phone on until she was sitting in her car on Monday morning. She had half expected to find dozens of text messages waiting for her, but there was only one. It said 'I've tried so hard to make you happy. I can't believe you're choosing him over me. I hope you're happy now.'

Sarah thought it rather ironic that Grinder should think she and Kenny were getting on so well, at a time when she was thinking their marriage had reached the end of the line. But then, if it meant he was going to stop hassling her, she really didn't care what he thought. She had enough problems to deal with at home, she didn't need more waiting for her at work.

CHAPTER TWENTY-TWO

It was 7.15 when Sarah finally eased her car into the car park. She thought being fifteen minutes late wasn't that bad, considering she had the baby to deal with. The fact was, she'd often been much later before having the baby, so this was actually quite impressive.

'Well, well, if it isn't Detective Sergeant "Late Again" Southall,' said the desk sergeant, looking pointedly at the clock, as she pushed her way through the back doors. 'You should have taken your full entitlement of maternity leave if you're not ready to come back on time.'

'It's good to see you too, Bill,' said Sarah. 'I knew something was missing last week, but I couldn't work out what it was. Now I remember: sarcasm. If you must know, I couldn't afford to take the full entitlement. Anyway, I'm only fifteen minutes late.'

'Late is still late,' said Sergeant Bill Reed, affably. 'DCI Whaffham likes everyone to be in for the morning briefing at seven.'

'Yes, well, unless someone with a very large mouth tells him, he's not going to know, is he?'

'It won't be necessary for anyone to tell him, he's already here.'

'What? Why didn't you warn me?'

'It's not my place to go around warning people. It's your responsibility to know what time you're supposed to start work, and to make sure you're here. If you didn't already know, the DCI is a stickler for time-keeping.'

'Oh, great,' said Sarah, wearily. 'That's my biggest weakness.'

'Really? I can't say that I've ever noticed,' said Reed, sarcastically. 'It'll have to improve when you're back in uniform.'

'I'm not going back into uniform,' she said.

'I wouldn't bank on that if I was you. Not only is he in early, he's also in a shit mood; his face was black as thunder when he walked in here.'

'Why? What's happened?'

'There was another burglary over the weekend.'

'What? Was it the same MO?'

'I don't know, but it would explain why he's in such a shit mood, wouldn't it? If I was you, I'd stop chatting, get up those stairs and think of a damned good excuse for being late.'

Sarah pulled a face and headed for the stairs, Reed's voice drifting after her.

'And, by the way, welcome back DS Southall, late as ever.'

'Thank you, Sergeant Reed,' she muttered, 'as big an arse as ever.'

She rushed up the stairs and through the doors into the incident room. As she entered, every head turned her way. She looked to the front of the room, expecting to see Henderson, but there was no-one there.

'Where's the boss?' she asked Parrott.

He nodded his head towards Henderson's office. 'He's in there, waiting for you with the DCI.'

DCI Troy Whaffham was perched on the edge of Henderson's desk, a scowl creasing his face. Henderson was looking distinctly uncomfortable on his left.

'Well, good morning, DS Southall,' said Whaffham, his voice heavy with sarcasm. 'Thank you so much for joining us.'

'I'm sorry, sir, I—'

'Spare us the details,' he said, raising the palm of his right hand to stop her. 'I'm really not interested in your domestic problems. Just close the door so we can get started.'

She caught Henderson's eye with a questioning look, but all she got in return was the slightest shrug of the shoulders and a tiny shake of the head.

Whaffham turned to Henderson. 'Isn't there another DS?'

'DS Boulting is off sick,' said Henderson. 'He'll be back in a day or two.'

'Right then,' began Whaffham, 'I'm sure you must both be wondering what I'm doing here this early in the morning, so I won't beat about the bush, I'll come straight to the point. In my opinion, this department is a shambles. We've got an unsolved murder and a string of petty burglaries. Now, I think my priority would be the murder, and yet you, DI Henderson, have chosen to focus on the burglaries. Can you explain why?'

'At the moment we have no leads in the murder case,' began Henderson, 'but, as I explained the other day, we have a strong possibility for the burglaries. We also believe there's a link between the cases, which is why we arranged surveillance on Jason Blackwell.'

'That would be the ongoing surveillance that you and DS Southall persuaded me to sanction, the same ongoing surveillance that's cost a small fortune in overtime, is that right?'

'Yes, sir.'

'And what did your surveillance operation reveal?'

'Blackwell drove down to Bognor and spent the weekend with a woman called Gillian Bowden,' said Sarah.

'And that's it?'

'We've also been looking into Blackwell's background,' said Henderson. 'It turns out his real name is Jonathon Bowden, or it was when he came out of prison in 2009. The very fact he's changed identity makes him even more suspicious as far as I'm concerned.'

'What was his crime?' asked Whaffham.

'He's a conman. He wins ladies' hearts, and then bleeds them dry.'

'What about this woman he spent the weekend with? Is she a victim?'

'I think he leads two lives, and she's the weekend one.'

'Is he still down there?'

'Yes, sir. We believe he will return this morning.'

'So you know for a fact that your only suspect has been miles away all weekend?'

'Yes, sir.'

'Well then, if your main suspect has been away for the weekend, perhaps you can explain how there's been another burglary?'

'Oh, Christ!' exclaimed Henderson. 'I haven't seen the crime reports yet. Why didn't someone tell me before?'

'Because it's not the sort of thing that would normally be reported to an off-duty DI heading a murder case,' said Whaffham.

'Yes, but if we'd known—'

'Did you ask anyone to notify you?' asked Whaffham. 'No, you didn't. You were so sure your man Blackwell was responsible for it all, you took your eye off the ball. Frankly, I'm bloody disappointed, Don. So far these two investigations have produced bugger all. You've made no progress with the murder, and you're not doing much better with the burglaries. You keep telling me there's a link, but where is it? You've pinned all your hopes on Blackwell. Yes, I'll grant you, if he's changed his name he's almost certainly up to no good, but, as far as these two cases are concerned, I think you've latched onto the wrong man.'

'I think that's a bit harsh, sir,' said Sarah.

'Oh, you do, do you?' said Whaffham, the threat clear in his voice.

'We had good reason to suspect Blackwell,' she continued. 'He's linked to all the victims.'

'Not quite all. You've got no link to the murder victim, have you?' snapped Whaffham. 'And he's also got a bloody good alibi for each of the burglaries, or have you forgotten that?'

Sarah thought silence was probably the best response.

'I need to be able to trust my DI, and his right hand, to run an effective team,' said Whaffham. 'Right now, I don't think that's the case. I've got a boss who's demanding answers. I've got the press hounding me. Should I tell them half our officers have spent the weekend in Bognor on a jolly?'

'It was only two officers,' said Sarah.

Whaffham slammed his fist on the desk. 'That's not the point, and you know it!' he roared, his face reddening. 'It was a waste of time and money, and it will not happen again. I want you both to know, if this bloody shambles isn't sorted out, and soon, there are going to be some changes around here. Do I make myself clear?'

'Yes, sir.'

He had been holding a folded sheet of paper in his left hand, and now he tossed it onto Henderson's desk. 'Right then, pull your fingers out and get on with it.' He stormed from the office, banging the door closed behind him.

Sarah experienced an involuntary intake of breath as Whaffham slammed the door, and then there was a sudden stillness in the room. Neither of them spoke for a full minute until Sarah let her breath out.

'I think that was uncalled for,' she said.

'I think he made his point, though, don't you?' said Henderson. He picked up the sheet of paper, unfolded it and read it.

'Does he do that often?' asked Sarah.

'I've not seen him go off on one like that before,' said Henderson, 'but you can hardly blame him, can you? He's right. We've had a week on this murder and we've got sod all in the way of leads. The burglaries have been going on for a damned sight longer and we're not doing much better with them, and what we have got looks to be all wrong. If it's the same guy doing them all, it can't be Blackwell, can it?'

'But it could still be his accomplice,' suggested Sarah.

Henderson sighed. 'Mind that straw you're clutching hold of doesn't snap.'

'Look,' said Sarah, 'I don't care what he says, Blackwell's in this up to his neck.'

'But even we don't really believe he's the murderer, do we?' said Henderson. 'I'm sorry, but Whaffham's right, we allowed one man to become the focus to the detriment of everything else. We need to go back over everything and see what we've missed. Come on, let's go and break the good news to the others.'

'I don't suppose there's any point in asking him if we can follow my sister tonight, is there?' asked Sarah, as Henderson reached for the door.

'Absolutely none,' he said.

He made his way to the front of the room.

'Right, listen up everyone. I've just had my balls thoroughly chewed by the DCI. He thinks we've messed up this murder investigation, and I have to say it's difficult not to agree with him.' There were some discontented mumblings, but he continued speaking over them. 'So, we're going to go right back to the beginning. I want everything looked at again, evidence, photos, statements, you name it, I want it checked.'

'What are we looking for?' asked a voice.

'If we knew that we wouldn't need to check again, would we?' said Sarah.

'Whatever we missed the first time round,' said Henderson. 'I want as many pairs of eyes as possible checking everything. Sharp eyes, please, we need to start making progress, and soon.'

When he finished speaking he handed the sheet of paper to Sarah.

'What's this?'

'The address of the latest robbery. Take Parrott and check it out, please.'

* * *

'It's not the same MO,' Sarah told Henderson when she got back. 'I reckon this is the work of some sort of copycat.'

'In what way is it different?' he asked.

'Well, for a start it happened over the weekend. That's a first; the others have all been Tuesday, Wednesday or Thursday.'

'Where was the owner at the time?' asked Henderson.

'She was away for the weekend.'

'So she was out of the house; that's consistent,' said Henderson. 'What's missing?'

'Jewellery, iPad, laptop and some cash.'

'That's a match,' said Henderson.

'Yes, but you haven't heard the best bit. None of her underwear is missing.'

'No trophy taken? Now that is different,' said Henderson.

'Are we sure Blackwell has been in Bognor all weekend?' asked Sarah.

'The car didn't move from Friday evening, and half an hour ago he got a taxi to take him to the train station. From the ticket he bought, it looks as if he's coming back here. The boys are sure he hasn't left that house all weekend. He's even been spotted looking out of the windows a couple of times.'

'That's it, then. It's got be some sort of copycat. What about the sister?'

'The Bognor detectives are going to interview her this morning.'

'What about Mandy tonight?' asked Sarah.

'What?'

'I think we should ask if we can follow her.'

'Are you serious?' asked Henderson. 'He distinctly said no more surveillance.'

'Yes, but that was when he thought we had the wrong man. This proves we could still be right.'

'You really think he'll go for that?'

'We can ask, can't we?'

Henderson was pretty sure they'd be wasting their time, but they had nothing to lose by asking, did they?

* * *

'So let me get this straight,' said Whaffham, twenty minutes later. 'You're proposing we use your sister as a decoy, by sending her on a date with a man who we think might be, but probably isn't, a murder suspect, in the hope we might catch a burglar. Is that right?'

'We don't really think Blackwell is the murderer, sir,' admitted Henderson, 'but we can't be sure.'

'You've changed your tune about that, haven't you?'

'Pretty much,' agreed Henderson. 'Like you said, what do we really have to link him to the murder? There again, even though we've spoken to him, we now know he's using a fake identity, and we can't ignore the fact he wouldn't be the first murderer to have been interviewed and overlooked.'

Henderson figured Whaffham couldn't really argue with that one.

'And tell me again,' continued Whaffham, turning to Sarah, 'why would your sister be interested in doing this?'

'Because she's a journalist,' said Sarah.

'And does she know about this plan?'

Sarah thought this probably wasn't the time to admit she had already spoken to her sister. 'Er, not yet, sir, no.'

'Thank God for small mercies,' he muttered to himself, before addressing Sarah again. 'Remind me, which newspaper is she with?'

'The local,' said Sarah.

'Ah, yes, I remember,' he said. 'Isn't she the one who wrote that piece about our incompetence over these burglaries?'

'Yes, sir, I'm afraid she is,' admitted Sarah. 'But she's done as we've asked, and not commented on the progress of the murder investigation. She's only reported what we've told her.'

'I'm supposed to be grateful that she's followed accepted protocol for a murder investigation, am I?'

Sarah couldn't respond to that, and he knew it.

'So what makes you think she'll write anything positive about us this time?' he continued.

'We offer her a carrot in the form of an exclusive in-depth story about the whole investigation, once it's over, of course.'

'I don't know,' he said. 'I'm not sure I can trust a journalist who's attacked us before. I think we'd be risking our reputation. And I'm not happy about the risk involved in this operation. What if it goes wrong and something happens to her? She'd have a monster of a story then, wouldn't she?'

'But we'll have plain clothes officers watching,' said Henderson. 'They wouldn't let her out of their sight.'

'But if, as you now seem to agree, this man's not the murderer, it's a lot of trouble to go to for a burglar, isn't it? Especially when we now have reason to believe he's not responsible for that either.'

'We'll have people at the house,' urged Henderson. 'If we're right about the accomplice, we'll catch him. It might not be the murder case solved, but it would be a big feather in our caps if we could catch the burglar, wouldn't it? You said yourself, it's making a mess of our crime figures.'

'And Mandy would be obliged to put the record straight,' added Sarah. 'She's a great one for allowing people to explain their side. She's always done it before.'

At last, it seemed they may have found something that appealed to Whaffham.

'I'm sure she could be persuaded to do a piece about the improvements you've made since you've been here,' suggested Sarah.

Whaffham spun slowly round on his chair. He was thinking. Sarah was convinced he was going to say yes.

'Whose idea was it to try to appeal to my vanity?' he said, swinging his chair back round to face them. He gazed from one to the other but they both managed blank stares.

'I hate to disappoint you but, whatever you might have heard to the contrary, I'm not actually interested in having someone write a puff piece about me.'

Inwardly, Sarah cursed herself. It had been a stupid idea. It wasn't as if she could guarantee such a thing anyway.

'The answer's no,' said Whaffham. 'I understand your concern for your sister, but if she chooses to go on a date with this man Blackwell, that's her choice. If we had proof she was in some sort of danger, I wouldn't hesitate to say yes, but there is no evidence he's actually a threat, is there? And how would it look if it ever got out that we had a team protecting an officer's sister without good reason? She would probably have a field day with a story like that herself. No, I'm sorry, I can't allow it.'

* * *

'I thought that went better than expected,' said Henderson, as they made their way back down the stairs.

'Better?' asked Sarah, in surprise. 'What do you mean, better?'

'Well, I thought he was quite reasonable about it; he didn't shout at us, did he?'

'If he hadn't calmed down he would have had a coronary by now,' said Sarah. 'But it doesn't help Mandy much, does it?'

'I'm sorry,' said Henderson, 'and I know you're disappointed, but he is right when he says we've got no reason to think she'll be in danger from Blackwell. No-one has ever suggested he was violent, have they?'

'But what if she takes him home?'

'Again, we've got no evidence to suggest he's a danger to her safety, have we?'

'I suppose not,' agreed Sarah, reluctantly.

They said nothing more until they were back in Henderson's office, then Sarah decided it was time.

'There's something I need to talk to you about,' she said, but as she spoke, his phone began to ring.

'Hang on a tick,' he said, reaching for it, 'let me get this.'

Sarah quietly cursed. Why did his phone have to ring now? She walked quietly from the room and left him to his call.

Five minutes later he called her back in.

'That was Bognor on the phone letting me know they've spoken to Gillian Bowden.'

'Wow! They don't hang about, do they?'

'They moved in as soon as they were sure Blackwell had left town.'

'And?'

'She confirmed Blackwell had been there all weekend, that he stays most weekends, and that he has permission to use her car.'

Sarah was struggling to hide her disappointment. 'Is that it? What about his real name? What about his brother?'

'She claims Blackwell's never mentioned a brother and says she's never heard of either Jason, or Jolyon, Bowden.'

'Well that's not much help, is it?'

'It's the best they could do,' said Henderson. 'I asked them to tread carefully. Let's be honest, we've got nothing definite on Blackwell, so it's not as if we've got grounds to question her about him really, is it?'

'So what grounds did they use?'

'They'd had a call from us about a man driving her car. We've been cracking down on car theft, and the suggestion was that her car may have been stolen.'

Sarah pulled a face.

'Of course, if you've got any better ideas . . .' said Henderson.

'No, I haven't,' she admitted with a sigh. 'Like you said, we don't really have grounds to be asking her anything.'

'I'm glad you agree,' said Henderson. 'It's bad enough having Grinder telling me I don't know how to do my job.'

'Yes, about Grinder. I need to—'

Henderson's phone was ringing again, and, automatically, he snatched it up.

'Henderson.'

Sarah quietly cursed to herself once again, but the urgency in Henderson's voice caused her to forget about her own problem.

'You're sure about this? Jesus!' he said. He turned to her, pointed to the notepad on his desk and made a writing motion with his hand.

'Yes, straight away. What's the address again?'

He repeated the address out loud, and Sarah scribbled it down on the pad.

As he put the phone down, Henderson spoke. 'You can forget about Blackwell being our murder suspect. There's been another one over the weekend. Come on, let's go.'

As they left Henderson's office to cross the incident room, Parrott waved a hand and headed towards them, clutching a sheet of paper.

'Sir, I've got something here you might find interesting,' he said.

'It will have to wait for now,' said Henderson, almost running in his haste. 'Get your coat. I want you to come with us.'

Parrott rushed back to his desk, dropped the sheet of paper, grabbed his coat and phone, then took off after them.

'Where are we going?' he asked, running to keep up with Sarah, as they followed in Henderson's wake.

'There's been another murder,' she said.

CHAPTER TWENTY-THREE

With their arrival at the scene, there must have been a dozen people working in the house, but once again Sarah was struck by the hushed atmosphere. She thought whoever had coined the expression 'a deathly hush' had got it spot on. Although she often said she would like 'a nice juicy murder to investigate' when things were quiet, it was just a figure of speech. The truth was, if she never had to go within ten miles of another murder scene she would be one very happy lady.

'We've got to stop meeting like this, Don,' said the forensic-suited pathologist examining the body. 'If you really want to see me, you could just call in at my office, you know.'

'Good morning, Christine,' said Henderson, with a grim smile. 'I'll try to bear that advice in mind.'

'I hope this isn't going to become a habit,' she said, still on her hands and knees leaning over the victim.

Henderson sighed. 'You and me both,' he said. 'Trust me, I'd much rather be trying to find Mrs Dingley's lost cat than doing this sort of thing.'

The pathologist sat back on her heels and looked up at him from behind her face mask.

'Perhaps you should go back into uniform, luv,' she suggested. 'They get to do that sort of stuff all the time.'

'Now it's funny you should mention going back into uniform,' he said. 'My boss has suggested I might be doing just that if I don't start making some progress with the first murder. I can't wait to hear what he's going to say now we've got a second.'

'Oh dear, poor you,' she said, sadly. 'And I'm afraid I'm not going to be much help with this one either.'

So, what have we got?'

'Sally Stewart, thirty-five years old, strangled with a silk scarf, same as the last one,' she said.

'Any guess at a time of death?'

'I can't say for sure, but I would guess at between twenty-four and thirty-six hours ago.'

'So it could have been Saturday night?'

'I'll have a much more accurate idea when I've got her back to the lab.'

'Do you think it's the same killer?'

'Would you rather there were two to catch?'

'That might give us a bit more chance,' he said. 'So far we've got nowhere trying to catch one.'

'Sorry,' she said, 'but as far as I can tell, at this stage, you've still only got one to catch.'

'Surely there must be something,' he pleaded.

'Well, there was this note,' she said, handing him a plastic evidence bag. 'It was under the victim's left arm.'

Henderson took the bag, read the note, and passed it on to Sarah.

'I have no idea what that means, but I suppose it's better than nothing,' he said.

'I hope you're happy now,' Sarah read out loud. 'I wonder who that refers to.'

'That'll be your starter for ten,' said Christine, taking hold of the victim's right hand. The hand was closed in a fist and she began to prise the fingers open gently.

'Is that it?' asked Henderson. 'Can't you give us a real lead, something we can follow up?'

'Sorry, luv, I can't give you what isn't here. Ooh! Hang on, what have we got here?' She was looking closely at the hand. She took a small pair of tweezers and poked them into the fist. 'I think you may be in luck,' she said, raising the tweezers for them to see.

'What is it?' asked Sarah.

Christine held it closer to her own eyes. 'I would say it's a shirt button, and there's enough fabric torn off to suggest it's come from a pale blue shirt!'

'So maybe it's not the same person,' suggested Sarah. 'Last time the killer was careful to make sure there wasn't a shred of evidence anywhere. This would seem to be a bit careless by comparison, don't you agree?'

'Speculation is a job for you clever detective people,' said Christine, with a wry smile. 'I'm a scientist. I just deal with facts.'

'Talking of science,' said Henderson. 'When's the PM?'

'How does nine o'clock tomorrow morning sound?'

'A long way away,' said Henderson. 'I suspect Whaffham will have kicked my arse all over the shop by then. You couldn't do it this afternoon, could you?'

'Sorry, no can do, but for you, I can do it tonight, say at about six, if you'd prefer.'

'That's an offer I can't refuse,' said Henderson.

'I didn't know you were open to offers,' she said, with a wicked grin. 'What a shame. If only I'd known before.' She cast an experienced eye over Parrott. 'What about your new young detective? Is he open to offers?'

Parrott had been standing slightly off to one side, trying hard not to look out of place. He had more or less succeeded so far, but now he couldn't hide his embarrassment.

'Take note, Parrott,' said Henderson. 'Dr Morgan sometimes gets fed up handling dead bodies and would love the opportunity to get someone with some life left in them on that big table of hers. As the youngest and fittest here, you will no doubt be elevated above me in the pecking order. In order to protect your dignity, I suggest you never visit her lair without a chaperone.'

'Well, if you're going to spoil my fun, I'm going,' she said, with a grin. 'I'm going to take this body with me and leave you detectives to do some detecting.'

* * *

An hour later, a thorough search of the house had revealed nothing in the way of clues, but from what they had learned about the victim, it seemed her profile was going to be much the same as the previous victim. This was the last scenario Henderson wanted, but it was more or less what he had expected. He had a pretty good idea how DCI Whaffham was going to react when he reported back. It wasn't going to be pleasant.

CHAPTER TWENTY-FOUR

Sergeant Bill Reed was waiting for them when they got back to the station.

'Ah,' he said, 'just the people I'm looking for.'

'This isn't a good time, Bill,' said Sarah.

'I know where you've just been, and I know you're not in the mood for jokes right now,' said Reed, soothingly, 'but I might actually have some good news for you.'

'I doubt that,' said Henderson, 'unless someone has walked in and confessed to two murders.'

'Sorry, I can't help you with that, but we might have found your burglar. He's currently waiting to be interviewed.'

'Well, I suppose that's better than nothing,' said Henderson, 'but I'm afraid I'm already booked in to be sacrificed to appease the crime-figure gods.' He turned to Sarah. 'You can handle this, can't you?'

'Yes, of course,' she said.

'Parrott, you've done the most work on that case,' said Henderson, 'so you can help Sarah interview the suspect. I'll get the ball rolling upstairs and then go and face the music.'

'Good luck,' said Sarah as her boss headed for the stairs.

'Is it really that bad?' asked Reed.

'With two murders and virtually no clues, what do you think?' replied Sarah, gloomily. 'But at least if we can put these burglaries to bed, we might earn a few brownie points in our favour. Alright Bill, what's the story?'

'A sharp-eyed PC spotted a kid trying to sell some jewellery down at the market. He stopped him, searched him, and found several different pieces. When questioned, the kid couldn't explain where he got them from, so he was brought down here. When I pointed out to the kid that two of the pieces were from a recent burglary, he started to brag about how many he had carried out and how clueless we had been to stop him. That's when I thought he might be of interest to you.'

'Where is he?'

'In cell number four, getting used to the idea of being locked up,' said Reed.

'Right, give us ten minutes,' said Sarah, 'and then have him brought to interview room one. Has he asked for a solicitor?'

'He's a bit of a smart arse, reckons he doesn't need one,' said Reed.

'Yes, well, we'll see just how clever he is in a few minutes.'

* * *

Sarah had deliberately kept the teenager waiting for a good ten minutes. He had been left in the interview room on his own, totally unaware that Sarah and Parrott were watching him on CCTV. He was sitting with his feet on the table, leaning back in the chair, balancing it on two legs.

'Look at him,' said Sarah, 'if you cut him in half I bet you would find the words "teenage arrogance" running all the way through, just like a stick of rock.'

'He doesn't look like the sort who could repeatedly outwit us,' observed Parrott. 'He can't be our man, can he?'

Sarah sighed. 'It doesn't look likely, does it?'

'What if he insists he's guilty?' asked Parrott.

'Then we have to prove he isn't,' replied Sarah. 'I hate it when we get time-wasters like this.'

She stared at the monitor for a few more moments, and then an evil grin broke out on her face.

'What?' asked Parrott. 'Why are you grinning like that?'

'I have a plan. I'm pretty sure we can get him to admit the truth, and it won't take long.'

* * *

Sarah marched into the interview room ahead of Parrott, sweeping the boy's feet off the table as she passed.

The boy, taken by surprise, crashed forward in the seat.

'What the f—'

'Watch your language,' snapped Sarah. 'This is a police station, not a holiday camp. This may be how you behave at home, but it's not how you're going to behave here. You will sit in your chair properly, and you will watch that foul mouth of yours. Do I make myself clear?'

The boy was initially shocked, but a self-satisfied smirk gradually took over his face as he regained his composure. He appeared to think he had scored a point.

Sarah sat down opposite the boy and waited while Parrott set up the machinery to record the interview. Then she did the introductions and again gave the boy the option to call a solicitor, but again he refused.

'I can manage,' he said, 'I don't need no solicitor.'

'Can you tell us your name?' asked Parrott.

'I don't think I have to.'

'Okay,' he said, 'so where do you live?'

'Around.'

'How old are you?'

'How old d'you think I am?'

'From your attitude, I would guess about eleven or twelve,' said Sarah.

'Piss off, missus, I'm eighteen!' snapped the boy, angrily.

'There, that wasn't so hard, was it?' said Sarah.

'I don't have to tell you nuffink, I know my rights.'

'Oh good,' she said, 'that'll save us some time in the long run.'

Parrott placed four plastic evidence bags, each containing a different item of jewellery, on the table in front of the boy.

'What can you tell me about these?'

The boy looked at the bags, and then looked at Parrott as if he was stupid.

'They're bits of jewellery.'

'That's correct,' said Parrott, 'they're the bits of jewellery found in your pockets. We would like to know where you got them from.'

'I dunno, I've never seen them before.'

Sarah pointed to the two bags nearest to her. 'Didn't you see these two on Saturday night?'

She waited for the boy to answer, but he just grinned at her.

'What's happened? Cat got your tongue? I heard you had been bragging about how clever you were, about how many burglaries you had committed, and about how the stupid police couldn't catch you. And yet, here you are. Not so clever now, are you?'

'It was getting boring. If I hadn't given you this chance, you would never have caught me.'

'Oh, I see. You've done us a favour. How very public spirited of you,' said Sarah.

'So, are you admitting to all ten?' asked Parrott.

The boy smiled. 'I could have just gone on and on,' he said, 'but I had to give you a chance.'

'Cocky little sod, aren't you?' said Sarah. 'The thing is, we know what you're doing, Philip.'

The smile rapidly disappeared from the boy's face.

'Oh, sorry,' she said, 'were we supposed to be so stupid we couldn't even identify you? You're Philip Lumley, you're eighteen years old, and you live at 82 Sussex Court. Is that right?'

The boy stared at her but said nothing.

'It's alright, you don't need to answer, we know it's right.'

Parrott slid a sheet of paper across the table. The boy looked at it, but didn't read it.

'This is a report from our forensics people,' explained Parrott, 'it tells us they found your fingerprints at the scene of a crime on Saturday, the same place you stole the jewellery from.'

'Yeah, well, like I said, you would never have caught me if I hadn't left you a clue.'

'Who are you trying to impress, Philip?' asked Sarah.

'I don't need to impress anyone.'

'But I think that's what you're trying to do,' insisted Sarah. 'I think you're looking to make a name for yourself, to get some attention. And what gets attention faster than anything? Notoriety, that's what.'

'I dunno what you mean.'

'Well, let me explain. You see, I think you're trying to impress someone. I reckon you've heard there have been some burglaries lately, and you've heard that the police don't have a clue who is behind them. Am I right so far?'

'It's not just me, everyone knows you lot don't have a clue.'

'Is that so?' said Sarah. 'That just goes to show you can't believe everything you hear. Anyway, as I was saying, I reckon you've heard all this stuff about these burglaries, and you figured if you did a burglary of your own and got caught, you could claim responsibility for all of them, and show everyone just how clever you are.'

'But I am responsible for all of them.'

'So would you like to tell us about all the others?' asked Parrott.

He gave Parrott a wide smile. 'I thought you knew about them all.'

'What about the people who got hurt?' asked Sarah.

The smile vanished instantly. 'What? I've never hurt no-one.'

'But if you've carried out all these burglaries you must have,' insisted Parrott.

Sarah gave Philip her best icy smile. 'And then there's the murder,' she said. 'Now that really will make you notorious. There's nothing more notorious than a murderer.'

She sat back and smiled at the boy, whose eyes widened so much she thought they might pop.

'Murder?' he cried, his voice now an octave higher as he began to panic. 'Now wait a minute, you can't pin that on me. I haven't murdered no-one. I haven't hurt no-one!'

Sarah leaned back in her chair and watched the arrogant teenager of a few minutes ago morph into a terrified kid. It wasn't long before the tears started.

'Right,' she said, eventually, 'are you sure you still want to claim responsibility for all the burglaries?'

'No, no. I only did the one on Saturday. I thought—'

'If one thing's clear, Philip, it's that you didn't think,' she said. 'You're lucky we do actually know how to do our jobs. That's how we know you did one burglary on Saturday, but you didn't do any others. My advice to you would be to be careful what you wish for.'

* * *

By the time Sarah and Parrott had finished with Philip Lumley it was close to 6 p.m. While Parrott finished off the paperwork, Sarah went to find Henderson. She reappeared just as Parrott was tidying up.

'What's going on then?' asked Parrott.

'Not much right now,' said Sarah, 'the boss has gone to watch the post- mortem. He suggested we might as well all go home. He thinks it will be better to wait until the morning when we've got some decent forensics to go on.'

'How did he get on with the DCI?'

'Not very well. DCI Whaffham seems to be one of those guys who expect miracles. It's a pity, I was hoping he might allow me to set up a surveillance operation for tonight, but he's got enough on his plate as it is, and I don't want to make things any worse . . .'

'What surveillance operation?'

'My sister has a second date with Blackwell tonight.'

'I thought he was out of the picture?' said Parrott.

'For the murders, perhaps, but I'm still convinced he's behind these burglaries, even if it's an accomplice that actually breaks in.'

'Well, I'm not doing anything tonight, if that's any help.'

Sarah studied Parrott's face for a moment. 'Are you serious?'

'Sure I'm serious. I met your sister, remember?'

'You do realise what you would be getting into? This would be a completely unauthorised operation.'

'Yeah, I understand that, but this is your sister, right? If it was my sister, I'd be worried about her, too. I know there will only be two of us, but that's better than nothing. At least we can try to keep her safe.'

'It would be risky watching Blackwell because if he spots me, he'll recognise me,' said Sarah. 'Anyway, I'm not sure we need to worry about that side of it so much; he's never hurt anyone before, and they will be in a public place, so there's no reason to think he will this time. What I'm more concerned about is Mandy's house.'

'You think someone will try to break in while Mandy is out?'

'That's one thing,' she admitted, 'but until we actually catch the murderer, I'm not ruling out the possibility that he is in some way involved. For that reason, I want to make sure he's not alone with her in that house.'

'Wow! Have you spoken to her about this?'

'What do you think? You've met her, do you really think she would put up with me telling her who she can take back to her house?'

Parrott smiled. Yes, he had met her, and he knew exactly what Sarah meant; if he was any judge, she certainly wasn't the sort who would allow her sister to tell her what she should do.

'Right,' said Parrott, decisively. 'What have you got in mind?'

'Well, as I'm her sister, Mandy has entrusted me with a spare key to her house. I was planning on waiting inside, just in case someone tries to join me. Perhaps you could be outside somewhere close by, maybe in a car. We won't have radios, but we can keep in touch with our phones.'

'That sounds like a plan.'

'I'm not sure we could actually call it a plan. That rather implies a lot of thought has gone into it. This is very much Hobson's choice; it's about the best we can do in the circumstances.'

'I know it's none of my business, but don't you have a baby? I mean, I'm sure I could keep an eye on the house for you if you need to be at home.'

'You're right, it is none of your business,' said Sarah, firmly but gently, 'but you don't need to worry about the baby; I have helpers, one of whom is my dad. As soon as I mentioned Mandy, and how I thought her house might be broken into, he was only too happy to help out.'

'Okay, you're the boss,' said Parrott. 'What time, and where?'

CHAPTER TWENTY-FIVE

It was just after 9 p.m. Parrott was sitting in his car, parked at the side of the road about fifty yards from Mandy's house. He had been in the same place when Blackwell had arrived to collect Mandy. He had slid as low as he could in his seat as Blackwell had driven down the road, staying there until he heard the car drive back the other way. He was satisfied he was far enough away not to attract attention, but close enough to see the front of the house and to spot anyone approaching from either direction.

Sarah had been in the back of his car when Blackwell had arrived. Like Parrott, she had slid down in her seat until the car had gone, and then five minutes later she had slipped from the car and made her way to Mandy's front door.

Inside the house, Sarah waited patiently in the darkness. It had taken a while for her eyes to become accustomed to the lack of light, but now she could see quite well. She was, however, feeling particularly weary, and, concerned she might actually fall asleep, she had chosen to keep moving from room to room, never keeping still long enough to get comfortable. They had no radios, but had worked out a system whereby Parrott would send her a text if he saw anything even vaguely suspicious. So far there had been nothing, and she hoped he, too, was still awake.

She had just climbed the stairs and was standing on the landing. Mandy had not closed the curtains at the landing window, and Sarah stared out at the night sky, idly wondering how it was her life appeared to be falling apart. What had happened to her and Kenny? They had been drifting along quite happily, hadn't they? Or maybe the fact they were drifting was the problem. Was Kenny right when he said it was all down to her selfishness?

Her thoughts were interrupted as she slowly became aware of a noise. It was a faint, almost scratching sound. She thought she should know what it was, and then suddenly she realised: it was a key being inserted in a lock. Someone was letting themselves into the house!

Her initial thought was that Mandy had come home early, perhaps with Blackwell, but that thought was immediately dismissed when she heard the front door open and then close, but no lights were switched on. Mandy would have switched all the lights on as soon as she came through the door, and anyway, whoever had come in was obviously trying to make as little noise as possible. This couldn't possibly be Mandy.

She stood stock still and held her breath. She had the distinct impression that whoever was downstairs was doing the same thing, waiting and listening. After a couple of minutes she was sure she could hear movement downstairs, and a few seconds later there was the familiar noise of creaky hinges as Mandy's dining room door was pushed open.

Sarah was rarely indecisive in these situations, and had been known to rush in and tackle people twice her size before now, but on this occasion she hesitated. She was sure the intruder would hear her if she tried to get down the stairs, and if that happened the element of surprise would be lost. With a head start, there was a good chance the person would be out through the front door before she got anywhere near it. And where the hell was Parrott? Why hadn't he texted a warning? He was supposed to be her backup, but now she had to wonder if he had fallen asleep. Worse still, had he been spotted and taken out somehow.

She decided she should text him. If he didn't answer, at least she knew for sure she was on her own. Very carefully, she reached down and drew her phone from her pocket. Just as she began to type, the phone flashed to announce an incoming text. It was on silent, so there was no sound to give her away, but such was her surprise that she dropped the phone, which landed with a dull thud on the thickly carpeted floor. Once more she found she was holding her breath, and then she sank slowly to her knees to get the phone, but in that same instant the intruder burst from the dining room, sprinted across the hall, threw open the front door and was gone.

Grabbing the phone, Sarah ran down the stairs and out of the house as fast as she could. Cursing loudly, she ran up the short drive to the road, desperately looking both ways, but there was no sign of anyone anywhere, running or otherwise.

* * *

Sitting in his car, Parrott was wondering how much longer they would have to wait before anything happened. He was bored out of his mind and had just sent a text to Sarah to see if she was as bored as he was. He was waiting for a reply when a figure suddenly appeared outside Mandy's house. At first he couldn't make out who it was as the figure looked up and down the road. Then she started gesticulating at him, and he realised it was Sarah. He leapt from the car and ran up the road to join her.

'What happened? What are you doing out here?' he asked her.

'Have you been asleep?' she snarled.

'No I bloody well haven't,' he said, indignantly. 'I just sent you a text to see if you were as bored as I was. I couldn't have done that if I was asleep, could I?'

'Are you sure? Someone came in through the front door. They must have come past you.'

Parrott looked at Mandy's house. As she had come out through the front door, Sarah had flicked at the switches just inside it. Now there was a light over the front door, and another one at the back corner of the house showing a path down into the garden.

'Where does that path go?' demanded Parrott.

'Down the garden to her garage, of course,' said Sarah.

'And is there a back gate?'

There was a brief stunned silence before she spoke.

'Err, yes. There's a lane. It's how everyone gets to their garages.'

'And so,' said Parrott, rather self-righteously, 'it would be a simple matter for someone to walk down the lane, come through the back gate, walk up the garden path, and access the front door, which, I should point out, is at the side of the house and not the front, making it completely hidden from my view.'

Sarah looked suitably mortified. 'Look, I'm sorry, this is my fault. I should have remembered the path. I jumped to the wrong conclusion. I had no right to accuse you of being asleep. I really am sorry.'

Parrott allowed her to stew in her guilt for a few seconds, then he gave her a little smile before he spoke.

'It's a good job I don't hold grudges against people who piss me off, or it would make our working relationship very difficult.'

'Yes, thank you. You're doing me a favour here, and I've been so ungrateful. I am sorry, really.'

'Well, whoever was in there will be long gone by now,' said Parrott, 'so there's no point in making a big deal of it. The fact is we've lost them. Did you get a look?'

'No, I was upstairs and it was too bloody dark. They'd only been there a couple of minutes. I was just about to text you when your text arrived. It made me jump and I dropped my damned phone. Talk about a stupid amateur . . .'

'I won't tell anybody if you won't,' said Parrott, with a conspiratorial wink.

'Oh well, at least we've learned something from this,' said Sarah. 'Whoever it was definitely had a key. That confirms your theory about means of entry.'

'But how do they get hold of a key every time?'

'Yes, that's a very good question, but at least it gives us something to work on. I really appreciate your help tonight, and I'm sorry I bit your head off, but I think you'd better get off home now.'

'What about you?'

'I'm going to stay here and wait for Mandy. I need to tell her what's happened, and she needs to know she must change her locks.'

* * *

'What on earth are you doing here?' demanded Mandy, when she got home and found Sarah waiting for her.

'I did tell you about doing surveillance tonight.'

'You told me it wasn't going to happen!'

'Yes, well, officially it didn't happen.'

'Are you under a lot of stress? Only you don't seem to be making much sense,' said Mandy.

'We were forbidden from doing the surveillance, so I persuaded a colleague to come along and help me watch your house.'

'Surely you don't still think—'

'Mandy, someone was here, in your house. They had a key.'

'But that's not possible. The only person with a key, apart from me, is you!'

'I'm sorry, but that's obviously not the case. You need to get your locks changed as soon as you can.'

'But this can't be true. There must be some mistake.'

'Mandy, listen to me. I was upstairs, and someone opened the front door with a key. I scared them before they could actually steal anything and they ran away, but it happened exactly as I told you it would.'

'But you said Jason Blackwell was behind it all. Well, he can't be because he's been with me all night.'

'We think he's a decoy,' explained Sarah. 'He keeps you out for a few hours while his accomplice comes to your house.'

Mandy was struggling to take this in. She had been convinced she was right about Blackwell not being involved, but now she wasn't so sure.

'So, how was your date?' asked Sarah.

'Actually he was a perfect gentleman,' said Mandy. 'Well, almost.'

'Why do you say "almost"?'

'Well, it started out very well. He held the door open for me, and was every inch the gentleman at first.'

'And then what happened?'

'A gentleman would switch his mobile phone off and not look at it. Jason actually fielded a text message at one point.'

'What time was this?'

'Oh, I don't know, about nine thirty?'

'Have you any idea what it was about?'

'No, but whatever it was it seemed to spoil his night. He wasn't the same after that.'

'In what way?'

'I was sure he was coming back here afterwards; he was giving me all the right signals, and I was looking forward to it, but he wasn't the same after that text message. He was distracted, like he had something on his mind. And then, to really spoil my night, he sent me home in a taxi!'

'What happened to his car?'

'He said he wasn't sure he had enough petrol and didn't want to risk running out. God, it's not even two miles from the centre of town to here!'

'So you don't think that was true?'

'Good God, no! I've been around long enough to know when I'm being dumped.'

'I hate to say it,' said Sarah, 'but this behaviour is almost exactly what I had expected. The first date is to learn what you're worth, and the second is to keep you out of the way while the accomplice steals your goodies.'

'But how did he get a key, sis?'

'I'm not sure. Was there any point during your first date when he could have had access to your handbag?'

'I couldn't say for sure,' admitted Mandy, 'but it's quite possible I might have gone to the loo. Would that give him enough time?'

'Probably. I'm beginning to think he's been doing this for a long time, so the chances are he's got it down to a fine art.'

'What happens now?' asked Mandy. 'Will I be safe tonight?'

'I think I scared him sufficiently to stop him returning for a while, but it wouldn't hurt to bolt the doors and use the security chain. And get those locks changed tomorrow!'

* * *

It had just started to drizzle as Sarah trudged away from Mandy's house to where she had left her car. She was so tired she could barely think, and it was a relief to see her car up ahead. What a pain it would be if she had to find some other way home. It's not as if—

She stopped walking and stared up to the sky. Of course! How could they have been so stupid? She grabbed her phone and quickly thumbed through the contacts until she found the right one. She reached her car and climbed inside, listening impatiently as the phone rang, and rang, and then finally a voice thick with sleep answered.

'Hullo.'

'Polly? It's Sarah. I didn't wake you, did I?'

'Oh no,' he said, caustically, 'I always sound like this when I'm wide awake. D'you know what the time is?'

She looked at the clock on her car dashboard, and was quite shocked to find it was well past midnight.

'Oh, God,' she said, 'I didn't realise it was so late. I'll let you get back to sleep. I'm sorry, I didn't mean to annoy you.'

'Hang on,' said Parrott, irritably. 'You've made sure I'm awake now, so you'd better tell me why you called. If you think I'm annoyed now, imagine how much worse I'm going to be if you don't!'

'Oh, right, okay. The thing is, we both missed something tonight.'

'Don't expect me to think,' said Parrott. 'Someone just woke me up from a deep sleep, remember?'

'Yes, of course.'

'Just get to the point.'

'When Blackwell picked Mandy up tonight, he had Gillian Bowden's car.'

'Yes, and . . .' said Parrott, impatiently.

'He came home by train.'

There was a momentary silence from Parrott's end of the phone.

'Bloody hell, yes, of course,' he said.

'Someone must have driven that car up here later in the day,' said Sarah.

'It has to be his accomplice, right?'

'That would be my bet,' agreed Sarah.

'So, does that mean Gillian Bowden is his accomplice?' asked Parrott.

'It has to put her in the frame, and it certainly suggests she knows a lot more than she's letting on.'

'Right. So what do we do now?'

'Now, we get some sleep,' said Sarah. 'We'll speak to the boss in the morning and see what he suggests.'

* * *

It was after 1 a.m. when Sarah eventually got home. As usual there was no sign of Kenny, and she felt a deep unease at the thought of her dad having to deal with the baby on his own. They had all known her job might create problems for them, but this was far worse than she had envisioned. She knew they couldn't go on like this; she was going to have to insist Kenny pull his weight. The only other alternative she could see was for her to quit her job, but that would be her last resort.

As so often happens, the weariness that was threatening to overwhelm her had disappeared with the surge of adrenalin that had come with the realisation they may have made a breakthrough, and now she needed something to do. She padded quietly upstairs, checked on her dad and little Laura, grabbed the laundry basket and carried it down to the kitchen. The kettle had boiled while she was upstairs, so she made herself a cup of tea and then turned her attention to the laundry.

As she flipped the lid back, she was surprised at how much was in there. By now, of course, she was well aware just how much washing could be generated by one tiny person, but she had made a point of catching up with all the washing on Sunday. How could they have created so much more in just one day? Then she realised there was a lot of Kenny's stuff in here. The cheeky sod must have sneaked home during the day!

'You have to be joking, mate,' she muttered, angrily. 'I'm damned if I'm doing your washing when you're never here!'

As she sorted through the basket, she tossed his things to one side, quickly building a heap of socks, underpants and tee shirts before she even started on her own stuff. Finally, at the bottom of the basket, under everything else, she came across a pale blue shirt which had been rolled up. She wasn't surprised to find a pale blue shirt; after all, Kenny had several of these, and often wore one to work when he fancied a change from tee shirts. In fact, now she thought about it, he had been wearing one when he stormed out of the house on Saturday evening. But how had it found its way to the bottom of the basket when everything else had been so obviously dumped on top? It was almost as if it had been hidden.

She fished the shirt from the basket and went to throw it after the rest of his washing, but something made her stop and unroll the shirt. She held it up in front of her, and suddenly she froze and her blood seemed to run cold.

She told herself this couldn't be true. There had to be a perfectly reasonable explanation for why a button had been torn off the shirt, didn't there? Then she thought about how evasive Kenny had been recently, and about how he never seemed to be at home. And hadn't she found that awful pornography he had been watching on the laptop? But this was Kenny. She had known him for twenty years. And she was a trained police officer.

She would have known, wouldn't she?

CHAPTER TWENTY-SIX

When Sarah got to work next morning, Parrott was at his desk. He'd obviously been there for some time.

'How long have you been here?' she asked.

'Someone woke me up last night and I couldn't get back to sleep,' he said. 'So I thought I might as well come in and have a look through last night's CCTV footage in the vicinity of your sister's house.'

'Did you find anything?' she asked, as she slipped off her coat.

He nodded at his monitor and clicked 'play'. 'I got this from the petrol station.'

On the monitor a figure, dressed from head to toe in black, could be seen running across the forecourt from right to left.

'Oh, good work,' said Sarah, watching over his shoulder. 'That's not far from Mandy's house. It can't be a coincidence, can it?'

'Yeah, but I was looking for Gillian Bowden. I can't tell for sure, but I reckon this is a guy by the way he's running.'

'But it is at the right time,' said Sarah, 'and whoever he is, he's heading away from Mandy's and running hell for leather. I mean, look at him go. Even if I had chased him I would never have kept up. It's a pity we didn't get a face, though.'

'Aha!' said Parrott, triumphantly. 'It's funny you should say that, because it just so happens I might have one.'

'You have? Fantastic!'

'I say I might have,' said Parrott, hands poised over his keyboard, 'because I'm not sure this is the same person. You agree it looks like a man running away, right?'

'Yes, I agree,' said Sarah, not quite sure where Parrott was going with this.

'Well then, here's where it gets confusing.' He clicked a couple of keys and a black-clad figure came into view, head bowed, approaching the camera. Then the figure looked directly at the camera. A look of panic crossed the face, and then it quickly looked away again.

'Someone didn't know there was a camera there,' said Sarah. 'Can you play it again?'

Parrott rewound the video and played it again.

'Stop it there,' said Sarah. 'Can you go back to that full face and blow it up a bit?'

Parrott pressed pause, rewind and then pause again. Then he clicked a couple of keys and the image grew in size.

'You see what I mean?' he said. 'I'm sure it's the same person, but now it's clearly a woman!'

'Well, well, well,' said Sarah. 'Now it's all beginning to come together.'

'What?' asked Parrott. 'Do you know her?'

'Well, yes, unless I'm very much mistaken, that's Gillian Bowden, isn't it?'

'Is it?' asked Parrott, in surprise. 'Are you sure?'

'Of course I am.'

'That doesn't look anything like her passport photograph.'

Sarah looked quizzically at Parrott. 'What?'

'Here,' said Parrott, sifting through the assorted papers on his desk. 'I've got it here somewhere. Ah, there you go.'

He handed Sarah a copy of a passport photograph. Although the photo had been taken several years ago, and the copy wasn't exactly the best quality, it clearly wasn't the same person. Sarah studied the photo for a few seconds, then looked at Parrott.

'You're quite sure you've been investigating the right person?'

Parrott managed to look confused and embarrassed at the same time.

'Actually I'm glad you brought that up,' he said. 'I did try to bring this to your attention yesterday, but then we all rushed off to the murder and the DI told me to leave it . . .'

Now he had said it, Sarah could clearly remember the moment, but before she could say anything he began to speak again.

'Remember I said Gillian Bowden had disappeared for fourteen years? Well, I checked with the Border Agency. Apparently what happened was she went travelling and didn't come back for fourteen years.'

'Well, I suppose it explains where she's been, but it doesn't help us, does it?'

'But it's not where she's been that's the interesting bit,' said Parrott. 'It's where she is now. When she came back, she went to Newcastle to live.'

'Yes, and now she's living in Bognor,' said Sarah, testily.

'Yes, so it seems,' agreed Parrott, 'but she's still living in Newcastle, too.'

'Maybe she has two houses.'

'Not according to any records I've found,' said Parrott. 'But what if there are two Gillian Bowdens?'

Sarah didn't say anything for a few moments. 'You must have the wrong Gillian Bowden.'

'That's what I thought at first, but I've done all the checks I can think of. I'm sure they're both the same person.'

'And if the real Gillian lives in Newcastle,' said Sarah.

'Then the one in Bognor must be an imposter,' finished Parrott.

Sarah stared at the image looking out at her from the screen. 'So, Gillian, who are you really?' she asked, softly.

Henderson had arrived now, so Sarah called him over.

'Parrott's been scouring CCTV footage from last night,' she said. 'I think you'll want to see this.'

'Why has he been watching CCTV? What happened last night?'

'Someone let themselves into my sister's flat while she was on her date with Blackwell. I gave chase, but I never was a sprinter.'

Henderson was nonplussed. 'You gave chase? What were you doing there?'

'It's a long story,' she said. 'Trust me, I'll explain later. Just watch the video.'

Henderson didn't look impressed, but he did as she asked.

'Are we sure that's the same person in both videos?' he asked, leaning forward to study the face.

'As sure as we can be,' said Parrott.

'It's the person we know as Gillian Bowden, isn't it?' asked Sarah.

'It would explain why none of the stolen stuff ever appears for sale locally,' said Henderson, then he seemed to realise what Sarah had implied. 'What do you mean, "It's the person we know as Gillian Bowden"? Am I missing something?'

Sarah nodded to Parrott. 'Go on; tell him what you told me.'

'The real Gillian Bowden lives in Newcastle, sir. This one is an imposter.'

'Are you sure?'

'Yes, sir, positive.'

Henderson looked at Sarah. 'So, what does this mean?'

'It means Blackwell's got to be up to his neck in these burglaries, and so is Gillian Bowden. We know he came home by train yesterday, and yet last night he picked up my sister in Gillian's car. A bit later someone flees from Mandy's house, and then, shortly afterwards Gillian is caught on CCTV running through town. It all points to her being his accomplice.

Perhaps the reason Blackwell goes there every weekend is so they can share the spoils and plan the next job.'

'Parrott, you've done a brilliant job to get us this far,' said Henderson, patting him on the shoulder. 'Now I want you to get onto the ANPR and get them to search for her car coming here from Bognor during the day yesterday, or going back last night. With this CCTV footage and proof she was on the road last night, we can get her picked up in Bognor and bring her in for questioning. We'll ask her about the identity theft when we've got her here.'

'Right, sir, leave it with me.'

'Sarah,' said Henderson, 'you come with me. We've got another murder briefing to hold, and when we get a chance you'd better fill me in on what happened last night.'

* * *

Sarah looked around the incident room. It was 11 a.m. and she and Parrott were the only ones in the room. Henderson was upstairs with Whaffham, trying to explain why they were getting nowhere with their two murders. In his favour he could also report what had happened the previous evening, and how Gillian Bowden had been picked up in Bognor and should be arriving for interview this afternoon. It was a bit of a consolation prize, but it was better than nothing.

'I've just got to pop out for a while,' she said to Parrott.

'You're not going to arrest the murderer all on your own and steal the limelight for yourself, are you?' he joked. 'Only after the way I helped you out last night, I think I should be there to share the glory.'

'No, of course not,' she said, a little too hastily. 'It's just personal stuff I can't get done outside normal hours. The boss is upstairs at the moment but I expect he'll be down in a few minutes. You can keep an eye on the shop for a while, can't you?'

'Yeah, sure, you carry on.'

* * *

Kenny worked in commercial aircraft maintenance, which, by its very nature, meant there could be periods of intense work followed by periods of relative calm. It was all about keeping the things maintained efficiently and quickly to ensure they were in the air as much as possible. A breakdown could mean an aeroplane being stranded and out of action, so it wasn't unusual for the guys to be forced to work overtime to keep the fleet in the air.

Sarah hadn't been anywhere near Kenny's workplace in a long time. She'd also missed the last two Christmas parties, and with the way things were between her and Kenny right now, his workplace wasn't exactly a hot topic of conversation, so she had been unaware his boss, Melvyn Charles, had a new, young, secretary.

Sarah guessed the secretary, who introduced herself as April, couldn't have been much more than twenty years old, and if Charles had wanted to ring the changes he had certainly succeeded. April, with her long blonde hair, gleaming smile, never-ending legs and gaping cleavage, was the complete opposite of the former secretary, who, she guessed, must have retired.

'If you'd like to take a seat, he'll be with you in just a moment,' said April.

Sarah had barely sat down before the door burst open and Charles rushed into the room.

'Sarah, this is unexpected,' he said, with a beaming smile and outstretched hand. 'How nice to see you.'

Sarah had met Kenny's boss at several of the company Christmas parties, and she knew him to be a charming and generous host, so the effusive greeting didn't surprise her.

'Good morning, Mr Charles,' she said, shaking his hand.

'What brings you here this morning?' he asked. 'Nothing wrong with Kenny, I hope.'

'Oh, no, it's nothing like that. Actually, it's a bit awkward.'

'Come through to my office,' he said, casting an eye toward his young secretary, 'it's a bit more private.'

He requested two coffees from April, and then ushered Sarah into his office and closed the door behind them.

'April's a lovely girl,' he explained to Sarah, as he led her over to his desk, 'but she's a little . . . inquisitive, I suppose you'd call it.'

'I suppose no-one's perfect,' said Sarah.

'No, quite,' said Charles, offering her a seat. 'Now then, what can I do for you?'

'I'm sure you must be aware there's been a spate of burglaries?'

'Yes, of course, it's a terrible business.'

'The thing is, we're a bit stuck for leads, but we're quite sure we're looking for a local man.'

Charles shifted uncomfortably in his seat. 'I'm not quite sure how I can help you with that.'

'Obviously this is a delicate issue, and if we're right, we don't want it coming out and causing a panic, nor do we want to warn off our suspect. So we're going to try to eliminate as many men from our inquiry as possible without actually confronting anyone. But we want to keep it really low key.'

'And how are you going to do that?' asked Charles.

'Well, for a start we can eliminate anyone who was working nights at the time. That's where you come in.'

'Isn't that a bit uncomfortable for you, Sarah? I mean, Kenny works here. You're checking up on your own husband!'

'I did tell you it was a bit awkward,' she said. 'But we decided, as I know you personally, it would be better if I came here rather than anyone else. I'm relying on your discretion, of course.'

Charles was quick to give her a warm smile. 'Well, you know you can rely on that.'

Sarah returned his smile. 'If I could just take a quick peek at your work records for the last two months? I've got a list of dates, I just need to know who was working nights, and who worked overtime on those nights.'

Now Charles' smile became a frown.

‘Well now, Sarah, I’m not sure I can do that,’ he said, uncertainly.

Sarah had half expected this response, but she also knew Charles wouldn’t want police officers swarming everywhere.

‘I can come back with a warrant and a search team, if you insist,’ she said, ‘but that’s not exactly low key, is it?’

The warm smile was gone for good now, and Sarah knew it was unlikely to return anytime soon, but it didn’t faze her. As a police officer she was used to having this effect on people.

‘I’ll do it for you on this occasion, Sarah,’ said Charles, unhappily, ‘but I want you to understand I’m not happy about this, and I don’t like being threatened.’

CHAPTER TWENTY-SEVEN

Although Sarah and Henderson had seen Gillian Bowden's photograph before, this was the first time they had seen her in the flesh, albeit on a CCTV feed from the interview room.

'She looks a bit different from the last time we saw her on camera,' observed Henderson.

'Yes, but she'd been running away then,' said Sarah, 'she's not out of breath this time, that's why she looks so cool and collected.'

'Well, let's hope she's not too cool and collected,' said Henderson. 'I could do with a result here, and sooner rather than later.'

'I can't imagine she can talk her way out of this,' said Sarah. 'We can prove she drove the car here, we have her on CCTV running away from the crime scene, and we have her driving back to Bognor.'

'That's not enough to prove she was inside your sister's house, is it?' said Henderson. 'What we really need is to find a front door key from one of the victims with her fingerprints on it, but I can't believe we're going to be that lucky.'

'We do have the identity theft in our favour.'

'Yes, that's true, but that's our secret weapon to use as we see fit,' said Henderson, looking at his watch. 'Anyway, it's no good standing here thinking about it, let's get started and see what happens.'

* * *

Twenty minutes later, Henderson and Sarah were beginning to understand why Gillian looked so cool and collected. She had managed to provide a very short answer for every question they had asked so far, but had given absolutely nothing away in doing so.

'We have this thing called ANPR,' Sarah told her now. 'It stands for Automatic Number Plate Recognition. There are cameras on all major roads that record the registration number of every car that passes. It's a really useful system because if we suspect somebody has driven a certain route, we can put the registration number of their car into the system, and it will tell us if we're right.'

Gillian stared impassively at Sarah, but said nothing.

'We know you drove up here from Bognor late yesterday morning. Can you tell me why?'

'Jason had left his mobile phone at my house. I knew he would be lost without it, so I brought it up to him.'

'That seems to be a lot of trouble to go to.'

'He doesn't have a laptop or anything like that. He uses his mobile phone to do everything. Like I said, he would be lost without it.'

Sarah slid a photograph across the table in front of Gillian, who looked down at it disinterestedly. A smile flitted briefly across her face.

'This is you,' said Sarah, 'caught on CCTV last night running through town. Where had you been? Where were you going?'

Gillian looked up from the photograph. 'I look distressed in that photo, don't I?'

'Were you distressed?' asked Sarah. 'What about?'

Gillian sighed. 'Jason had gone out and left me in that gloomy bedsit. He said it was business. I didn't want to stay there on my own, so I went for a walk around town, just to have a look around. At one point I passed this restaurant. It looked nice, so I stopped to read the menu. Then I realised Jason was inside, sitting at a table with a woman.'

'And this was a problem? I thought you said he was out on business.'

'I can assure you, the only business Jason was interested in with this woman was funny business. I was horrified to think he was cheating on me. I was so upset I ran all the way back to my car, jumped in and drove home. I expect your ANPR system, or whatever you call it, will confirm this.' She looked confidently, and defiantly, at Sarah and Henderson.

Henderson was going to handle the next few questions, so, as Sarah sat back in her seat to let him take over, she studied Gillian Bowden. There was something about this woman that wasn't quite right, but whatever it was, it was one of those intangible things she couldn't put her finger on. But her senses were alert; there was definitely something not right, and she intended to figure out just what it was.

'Why are you using a stolen identity?' began Henderson.

For the first time Gillian looked surprised by the question. It was just the briefest flicker of surprise, and it was gone almost straight away, but both Henderson and Sarah saw it.

'Well?' insisted Henderson.

'I don't know what you're talking about.'

'Oh, I'm sure you do.' Henderson produced a photograph and lined it up in front of Gillian. 'This young lady here,' he pointed to the photograph, 'is the real Gillian Bowden.'

'I expect there are at least half a dozen of us,' said Gillian. 'I expect there are several people with your name,' she nodded her head at Sarah, 'and hers.'

'Yes, I'm sure you're right,' said Henderson. He produced two documents and placed them side-by-side in front of Gillian. 'But I bet there aren't many people with identical names and identical birth certificates. It seems you and her,' he pointed to the photograph again, 'have the same parents as well as the same name. How do you explain that?'

At last Gillian didn't look quite so cool and confident. She licked her lips, eyes darting between Henderson and Sarah, but now she had nothing to say.

'Quite a coincidence, isn't it?' said Henderson. 'Here's another one. Last night Jason Blackwell took a lady called Amanda Albright out to dinner. It was their second date. While they were having dinner, someone used a key to gain access to Amanda's house. Does this ring any bells with you?'

Gillian licked her lips again but still said nothing.

'There are another five coincidences where Jason Blackwell has taken ladies out on a second date and, each time, while they have been on the date, someone has used a key to gain access to their homes. You see where I'm going with this, Gillian, don't you? I think you are Jason Blackwell's accomplice. On the first date, he assesses their assets, somehow gets a key or a copy of a key, then on the second date, while he wines and dines the ladies, you use the key to access their homes.'

'I don't know what you're talking about.'

'Yes, you already told us that, but the thing is, we don't believe you.'

'Anyway,' said Sarah, 'we haven't mentioned the woman who was murdered yet.'

Suddenly there was panic in Gillian's eyes.

'Murder? What murder? I never enter a house if there's someone in there. You can't pin a murder on me!'

'But you didn't know there was going to be someone in there, did you?' asked Henderson, slowly. 'You see, we don't think you intended to murder anyone. You didn't expect her to be there, did you?'

'I'm not saying another word without a solicitor,' said Gillian, determinedly.

'But we haven't charged you with anything yet,' said Henderson.

'I don't care what you do. I'm not saying another word without a solicitor.'

'I'm going to stop this interview now, and detain you while we make further investigations. When we do charge you, it will probably be for identity theft, fraud, six burglaries and a murder. Do you understand?'

Gillian glared defiantly at him. 'Go to hell!'

Henderson smiled patiently. 'Yes, I might well do that in the end,' he said, 'but at least I'll be cosy at home tonight while you're trying to get comfortable in your cell.'

* * *

It was just after 5 p.m. Sarah felt guilty that she was getting ready to go home when they had two murders to solve, but all their efforts to date had produced absolutely nothing. In fact, the trail was so cold, she was beginning to think whoever was responsible must have a pretty thorough knowledge of murder investigations.

She was just about to leave when she heard Henderson's voice calling across to her. 'Sarah? Have you got a minute?'

'Yes, sure.'

She walked across to his office, leaned against the door frame and looked enquiringly at him.

'Come in, and shut the door, please,' he said.

'What's up?' she asked, closing the door behind her.

He perched on the edge of his desk, folded his arms and studied her face. 'I know you're just heading off home, and I know you're tired, but I need to ask you a couple of questions.'

His body language spoke volumes, and she began to feel distinctly uncomfortable. 'Questions? What questions?'

'Do we have a suspect for the murders?'

'You know we don't,' she said, 'apart from Blackwell, of course, but he's not a serious suspect, is he?'

'That's what I thought,' said Henderson. 'So, why have you sent a shirt to forensics for testing?'

The blood drained from Sarah's face. Surely the results couldn't have come back already. And why had they sent them to Henderson and not to her?

'Oh God, if they've sent the results to you, it means they've bypassed me. That means—'

'What on earth are you talking about, Sarah? I haven't been sent any results. They telephoned wanting to know who the suspect is for their comparisons. The thing is, because I have no idea why this shirt has been sent to them, I was in the embarrassing situation of not being able to answer their question. I was hoping perhaps you could tell me what's going on. You can start by telling me whose shirt they're talking about.'

'Oh God, this is awkward. I knew I should have told you, but I wanted to be sure first.'

'Wanted to be sure of what?'

'The shirt is Kenny's.'

'Kenny's? Why the hell are you sending them Kenny's shirt?'

'I found it hidden in the bottom of our laundry basket,' she explained. 'We had a row Saturday night and he stormed off out. He was wearing this pale blue shirt. When I found it in the laundry basket last night, I noticed there was a button torn off.'

'Have you asked him about it?'

Sarah was squirming inside. 'I haven't seen him. I hardly ever see him. He just hasn't adjusted to having the baby around.'

'I'm sorry,' said Henderson, 'I never realised. I always thought you two were the perfect, happy couple.'

'Yes, well, happy couples spend time together, don't they?' she said, miserably.

'But even so, surely you don't think he's a murderer, just because there's a button missing off his shirt. You've known him for over twenty years, do you really think he's capable of murder?'

'I'm not sure I know anything about him anymore,' said Sarah, sadly, 'but it's not just the button missing off his shirt.'

'What else is there?'

'Someone has been watching pornography on our laptop at home, and I'm not talking tame stuff, Don. It's not me, or my dad . . .'

'Yes but—'

'I haven't finished yet,' she said. 'According to Kenny, the reason he's never at home is because he's working overtime. But I've checked where he works. He doesn't do half the overtime he says, and every time there's been a murder, or a burglary, he wasn't at work, and he wasn't at home. I actually have no idea where he was on any of those occasions. That's why I sent the shirt to forensics without telling you, or anyone else. This isn't a situation I want everyone to know about.'

Henderson was unsure what to say. He didn't know Kenny that well, but he thought it more likely he was having an affair than murdering random women. There again, perhaps this wasn't the time to voice such speculation. Her distress was clear on her face, and in her voice.

'I'm sure there must be an explanation,' he said.

'I wish I was as sure as you seem to be. If I could just get him to sit down and talk to me I would ask him, but he's just so evasive.'

'Where is he now?'

'Your guess is as good as mine. I have no idea. I know it's not proper procedure, and if I've caused trouble over the shirt, I'm sorry, I didn't mean to put you in a difficult position, it's just . . .' Her voice trailed off.

'Don't worry about that,' said Henderson. 'I'll feed them some old bull about how I've got so much on my plate I just forgot. I'm more concerned about you.'

'Me? Oh, I'll be fine,' she said. 'I just don't know what to do about Kenny.'

'I don't think you should do anything. When he comes home tonight—'

'I don't think that's going to happen,' she said. 'He sneaked in yesterday to dump his washing when he knew no-one would be around. I'm pretty sure he's avoiding all of us.'

'Well, whatever, I'm sure there will be an explanation for the missing button, but just to put your mind at rest I'll ask forensics to pull their finger out and carry on with testing the shirt.'

'Are you sure?'

'Yes, it's fine,' he said. 'Now you get off home and try not to worry. And try to get some sleep.'

* * *

Despite her assurances to Henderson that she was unlikely to see Kenny that night, just after nine o'clock, as she was finishing tidying up in the kitchen, Sarah heard the unmistakable sound of her front door opening and closing.

'Is that you, Ken?' she called.

There was no answer, but the familiar sound of his approaching footsteps told her it was him, and a few seconds later he came through the kitchen door. She had put a lot of thought into how best to handle this situation, should it occur, finally deciding warm and friendly was the best approach.

'Have you eaten?' she asked. 'I didn't do anything because I didn't know if you were going to be coming home, but I can . . .' She stopped as she took in his face. It was anything but warm and friendly.

'What's the matter?' she asked.

'You tell me,' he said, menacingly.

'I don't know what you mean.'

'Don't play games with me,' he warned. 'I'm not some thick kid you've just caught shoplifting. You've been checking up on me. I want to know why?'

Just for the briefest moment the colour drained from Sarah's face as she realised her strategy hadn't made allowance for this particular eventuality, and she couldn't think what to do. Then, just as quickly, her face coloured up with guilt, and she knew she was going to have a lot of trouble getting out of this one.

'It's not what you think. I wasn't checking up on you specifically.'

'Oh, really?' he said, the doubt clear in his voice.

'It's work, you know, I can't really talk about it.'

'You're going to have to do better than that,' he said. 'I understand you're not supposed to discuss cases with me; that's why I never ask. But when you come into my workplace, it's getting personal. I think in that case I have a right to know why.'

'I'm sorry. I think you're taking this the wrong way. It's not about you—'

'When my wife starts checking time-sheets, and dates, and times specifically for my shift, it is about me. So, I'll ask you again: why are you checking up on me?'

After the events of the last couple of days, Sarah was desperately tired, and running on a short fuse. All the promises she had made to herself that she wasn't going to allow this to turn into a slanging match were suddenly forgotten.

'Why are you being so aggressive?' she demanded, angrily. 'You don't come home for days at a time, and then, when you do finally arrive, all you want to do is argue!'

Kenny gave her a cold smile. 'I can always tell when you know you're in the wrong,' he said, 'because you avoid answering the question, and turn things around to make them all about you.'

'About me?' she snapped. 'This isn't about me. I've got used to you not being here, but what about your daughter upstairs? When are you going to spend some time with her? What about my dad? He's seventy years old, and here he is looking after a baby. When are you going to start coming home to do your share of looking after your daughter?'

'Don't come that self-righteous "it's-all-your-fault" crap with me, Sarah. I can't remember how many times I've told you I wanted a baby years ago, but not now, at my age. I warned you it would make things difficult if you intended to carry on with your job, but you insisted you knew better. And your dad's here because you put him on the spot. You asked him because you knew he wouldn't be able to say no, so don't blame me for that!'

'But you agreed—' she pleaded.

'No, Sarah, I didn't agree to anything,' said Kenny. 'You just did what you always do; ignore whatever I say, and carry on regardless.'

'But I do listen to you.'

'No, you don't. The fact we had this very conversation a few nights ago proves it. You only listen to me when I say what you want to hear. Even when you know I'm right, if it isn't what you want to hear, you ignore me.'

Sarah was in turmoil. This was supposed to be the night she finally got him to accept his responsibilities, but now she seemed to have completely lost control of the situation and it had escalated into something much bigger. On top of that, the way Kenny was talking was beginning to worry her. It was true she had always tended to do what she wanted, regardless of any objections he might raise, but now she was beginning to fear she may actually have taken him for granted once too often. She had a momentary flashback of all the good times they had had together, and she was reminded how much she loved him. This worried her, and frightened her.

'I'd still like to know why you were checking up on me,' he asked, interrupting her thoughts. His voice was cool and calm, not showing the slightest hint of anger.

She couldn't decide what to say. Dare she risk a lie, or should she tell him the truth?

'Come on, Sarah, this is a matter of trust.'

'I found your blue shirt in the laundry basket,' she began. 'It was at the bottom, as if it had been hidden. There was a button torn from it.'

'Yeah,' said Kenny, puzzled. 'And?'

'How did the button get torn off?'

'I was tired. I got careless at work and leaned too far over one of the machines. The shirt wasn't tucked into my trousers and I got too close to the rollers. It was a good job it wasn't my sleeve or it might have dragged my hand in. The emergency stop came on, but it was too late to save the button. It got torn off, along with a bit of the shirt.'

'So why hide it?'

'I didn't hide it. I knocked over the basket and everything poured out. I must have shoved the shirt back in first.'

Sarah didn't know whether she should believe this or not. The wife in her said believe it, but the detective in her wasn't so sure.

'What's the big deal with a shirt anyway? What's it got to do with you checking up on me?'

'A woman was murdered on Saturday night.'

'Yes, I read about it. Is that what you're working on?' asked Kenny, innocently.

'You were wearing that blue shirt on Saturday night.'

'No. I was wearing a blue shirt on Saturday night. I've got more than one, remember?'

'The murderer was wearing a shirt, just like that, and a button, and a piece of fabric, were torn from it.' She stared defiantly up at him.

'But I was wearing the one that was in the basket at work on Friday.'

It was as if there had been some sort of delay between the words leaving Sarah's lips and reaching Kenny's ears, but now he suddenly caught up and realised what she was implying.

'Now hang on a minute,' he said, incredulously. 'Are you suggesting . . . You're not serious, are you? You think I killed someone?'

She didn't seem able to speak. A stunned expression scarred her face, as if she suddenly realised just how absurd this idea was.

'Jesus effing Christ, Sarah. You've known me for over twenty years and you think I could do something like that? Bloody hell, you don't know me at all, do you?'

She could have backed down and admitted she had got it wrong, but her tiredness and frustration drove her to carry on with the accusations.

'What about the pornography on the laptop? After twenty years I didn't think you watched stuff like that, but it's there in the search history.'

'I don't watch bloody pornography on your laptop or anywhere else,' he snarled, no longer cool and collected.

'Well, someone's been watching it!'

'Maybe they have,' he said, 'but don't bloody look at me. If you've got records of when it was being watched, why don't you go and compare that with my work records?'

She was lost for words again. Why hadn't she thought of that?

'What? Don't tell me Sherlock Southall didn't think to check. But then I suppose it's much easier to jump to bloody conclusions and start heaving accusations my way, isn't it?'

Sarah seemed to have been struck dumb.

'I think we've probably reached the end of the line with this, don't you?' he was raging now.

'What do you mean?' she asked. 'The end of what line?'

'The end of us, of course. D'you know the worst thing of all?' He didn't wait for a reply. 'The worst thing is your hypocrisy. You don't trust me? Jesus, I can't believe it!'

'What's that supposed to mean?' she snapped.

'I'll tell you what it means. It means you're in no position to point the finger of trust at me, when I'm not the father of your baby!'

Sarah couldn't understand where this was coming from. 'Don't be so ridiculous. Of course you're the father of my baby.'

He shook his head vigorously. 'No. I can't be. I had a vasectomy just after my fortieth birthday!'

Once again Sarah was stunned into a brief silence.

'What?' she said, finally. 'You can't have. You have no right to do something like that without asking me first!'

'Oh yes, that's good, coming from you,' argued Kenny. 'What did you say to me when I said I didn't want you to have a baby?'

'What? What did I say?'

'You said it was none of my business. "It's my body, and I'll decide what happens to it," you said. How come that works for you, but not for me?'

'That's different.'

'No, it isn't different, Sarah. It's exactly the same. This is my body, and I decided what happened to it.'

Sarah felt helpless. This whole situation had got away from her, and she couldn't see any way back. She had realised they were drifting apart, but she hadn't realised there was already a gaping chasm between them. She was trying desperately to think of a way back from this.

'Alright. I'm in the wrong,' she said desperately, 'but I'm sure we can sort this out. I love you so much, Kenny, I'm sure we can get over this.'

He shook his head. 'No, I'm sorry, Sarah, it's much too late for that.'

'No, please—'

'I'm going to leave now,' he said, 'but before I go, seeing as you brought up the subject of online activities, I have a question for you. If you love me so much, why do you have a profile set up on the Two's Company website? And, before you ask, I only know because one of the lads at work uses the site and told me he'd seen you on there. He tells me it's a great place to go if you're looking for a bit on the side.'

'I can explain that.'

'Yes, I bet you can.'

'It was for work.'

Kenny slowly shook his head.

'Yeah, right, sure it was,' he said, as he turned and headed for the door. 'You're unbelievable, d'you know that?'

'No, really, it was!' cried Sarah, sinking into a chair at the kitchen table, but the only sound she heard in reply was the slamming of the front door.

* * *

Sarah had no idea how long she had been sitting at the table, but she slowly became aware of someone speaking to her.

'Here, drink this,' said her father, as he placed a mug of tea before her and perched on the seat opposite.

'Ha,' she said, a sad little smile on her face, 'a cup of tea, the good old British answer to every crisis, but I don't think it's going to help much with this one.'

'Drink it,' he said. 'I know it won't solve the problem, but it'll make you feel a bit better.'

'I suppose you heard it all?'

'I'm sorry,' he said. 'I didn't want to, but it's hard to ignore when two people are screaming accusations at each other.'

It was true they had been shouting, and of course it wasn't Freddie's fault, but this was just about the last thing Sarah needed to know. What must her father think of her?

'Is it true?' he asked.

'Which bit?'

'Any of it. I mean, if Kenny isn't the father of that poor little mite upstairs, who is?'

'He is the father!' she snapped.

'But, how can he be if—'

'He is, Dad, honestly. I think he's bluffing about a vasectomy.'

'Bluffing? Why would he do that?'

'Because he doesn't want her!'

'What?'

'The baby, Laura, he doesn't want her. He never wanted her. It was me. I insisted I wanted a baby.'

'So he was right, then? You did ignore what he said.'

'Well, yes,' she said, sobbing now, 'but I thought he'd come round once the baby arrived.'

Freddie let out a long sigh. 'Oh, luv,' he said, sadly, 'this is a bit of a mess, isn't it?'

'A bit of a mess?' she said. 'It's a bloody disaster! How am I going to manage if he doesn't come back?'

'You want him to come back, do you?'

'Well, of course I do,' she said. 'Why wouldn't I?'

'What about this online dating thing?' he asked.

'I had to create the profile for something we were doing at work,' she explained. 'Three of us did it so we could attend one of their meetings. It was a one-off to try and catch someone.'

Freddie didn't look convinced.

'Honestly,' she said. 'Ask Mandy if you don't believe me!'

'What does she know about it?'

'She's on there. She was there the night I went.'

'Knowing Mandy's involved is hardly going to put my mind at rest, is it? I know she's my daughter, and I love her to bits but, let's be honest, promiscuous is her middle name. Something like that would be right up her street, and if she's managed to get you involved too, she would regard that as a triumph.'

'Really, Dad, are you saying you don't believe me?' asked Sarah, 'because if you are, I think that's probably going to be one kick in the teeth too many.'

'Hey, listen, I'm on your side,' said Freddie. 'I'm just trying to understand why Kenny would make these accusations.'

'And you're suggesting he wouldn't make them if they weren't true?'

'No, I'm suggesting he wouldn't make them if he didn't think they were true. What you have to consider is why he would think that.'

'I've told you why. Why don't you believe me? Whose side are you on here?'

'Being on your side doesn't mean I have to think you're right about everything,' said Freddie.

'So you think I'm in the wrong? You think this baby isn't Kenny's?'

'You're trying to put words into my mouth,' said Freddie, disappointedly. 'You want to start an argument with me because you're angry and you want someone to take it out on, someone to hurt.'

'That's ridiculous.'

'Is it? I think, when you calm down later, you'll admit to yourself that I'm right, but by then it might be too late.'

'What do you mean?'

'Look, Sarah, I'm your father. If there's a problem I'm here to help you, and I always will be, regardless of why there's a problem. So, before you say something you regret,

I'm going to bed. I think you should do the same, but before you do, you might consider how you're going to manage if you push me away too.'

He rose from his chair and headed for the stairs. 'Goodnight, luv. I'll see you in the morning.'

CHAPTER TWENTY-EIGHT

Next morning, Henderson and Sarah arrived in the car park at the same time.

'If you don't mind me saying, you look terrible,' said Henderson, as soon as he saw her. 'Are you alright?'

Normally, Sarah might have taken issue with such a comment this early in the morning, but she knew her boss was right, and she could understand his concern; she had hardly slept last night, and as a result she didn't just look a frightful mess this morning, she felt like a mess, too.

'Bad night,' she said, trying hard not to sound upset. 'Not much sleep.'

'What was it? Did the baby keep you awake?'

'Yes,' she said, then immediately felt guilty. It really wasn't fair to lay the blame on the baby, who had somehow managed to sleep through everything. 'Well, no. Actually, I'd rather not talk about it, if you don't mind.'

'Okay,' he said, 'of course.'

Henderson had a very high regard for Sarah, and even though it was pretty easy for him to guess what the problem was from her response, he wasn't one to pry. She knew she could always talk to him if she wanted to.

* * *

'Good morning, how are the happy squad this morning?' asked Bill Reed, affably, as they passed through his domain on their way into the building.

'Morning, Bill,' said Henderson, but all Sarah could manage was a grunt.

'Oh dear,' teased Reed. 'Has someone been kept awake all night?'

'Sod off, Bill,' she mumbled. 'I'm not in the mood.'

'Well, I'm sorry if you're in a crappy mood, but you need to snap out of it, because you're going to need to put on a full-scale charm offensive when the DCI gets here.'

'Why? What the hell's happened now?' asked Henderson, realising this would almost certainly mean trouble for him.

'I suggest you look at the local newspaper as soon as you get upstairs.'

'But it doesn't come out until Friday, does it?' asked Henderson.

'Check out the online version,' advised Reed.

'Why? What about it?'

'I won't spoil it for you,' said Reed with a cheery smile. 'You can see for yourself when you get upstairs. It'll give you a good idea what the front page story's going to be on Friday, and if I was a betting man, I'd have at least a tenner on Whaffham wanting to know who leaked the story!'

* * *

Henderson went straight to his office after the morning briefing and read the article on his PC.

'Bloody hell!' he said to Sarah when she joined him five minutes later. 'It says here we've charged someone for the burglaries and the murders. The old man's going to think this is your doing, you know that, don't you?'

Sarah groaned. As if she didn't have enough problems! At the same time, she understood only too well why the DCI would think such a thing. After all, the writer was Sarah's sister, Mandy.

'I promise you I haven't spoken to her. I haven't even seen her since we brought in Gillian Bowden, and anyway, you know I never share anything with her.'

'Yes, but we've obviously got a leak somewhere, and Whaffham's not going to believe it's not you, is he?' said Henderson.

'I'm sorry, but I'm really not sure I can deal with this today, Don,' said Sarah, close to tears.

'Hey, you really are in a bad way, aren't you?' he asked, genuinely concerned. 'Are you sure you don't want to talk about it?'

'I'm not sure I can right now,' she said. 'Maybe later, if that's okay?'

'Of course,' he said.

Just then his phone buzzed. He snatched it up and listened for a moment.

'Ah, yes, of course, sir. I'll be up right away.'

He glanced at Sarah as he listened some more.

'DS Southall? Err, no, I'm afraid she's out at the moment,' he replied. 'How long? I'm not sure, it could be a while, but there's no need to wait. Why don't I come up now?'

As he put the phone down, he spoke. 'As you probably guessed, that was DCI Whaffham, and he wants to speak to me. He's not in a very good mood so my guess is he's already seen the article. As I've just told him you're not here, it's probably a good idea if you disappear for a while.'

'You don't have to do this—'

'DS Boulting should have been back at work yesterday, but he didn't turn up,' continued Henderson, ignoring her protests. 'He's still not here this morning and we've heard nothing. As I'm concerned for the welfare of one of my officers, I've asked you to go and check him out. Understand?'

'Yes, thank you,' she said.

'I'll call you when I think it's safe to come back.'

'While I'm out, I'll go round my sister's and see what she's playing at.'

'Following up on a lead, you say? Good idea,' he said, getting to his feet. He gave her a reassuring smile. 'Wish me luck!'

'Good luck,' she said, 'and thanks.'

'Never mind thanks,' he said, 'just make yourself scarce. I wouldn't want my lie compounded by him coming down here and finding you at your desk.'

* * *

Two hours later Sarah sneaked back into the building and made her way up to Henderson's office.

'How did it go?' she asked.

'Oh, you know, the usual. Hellfire and damnation, fire and brimstone. I've still got a job, so I suppose that's something.'

'Pretty bad, then?'

'Probably the worst one to date,' he agreed, 'but the good news is he's gone away to another conference for a couple of days.'

'So we can all relax, then. That's a relief.'

'Not exactly. He's decided it's down to us to sort this mess out with the press, and the way we have to do it is to make sure the story is right.'

Sarah looked confused. 'Eh? How are we supposed to do that?'

'We are supposed to do that by making sure we do what the story says, and make the necessary arrests.'

'Oh, right. So no pressure then,' said Sarah. 'You can't just make arrests because he says so. He must be mad.'

'Mad? He's absolutely livid,' joked Henderson. 'But enough about my troubles, how did you get on? Did you manage to find your sister?'

'Sorry, I'm afraid not,' she said.

'What about Grinder? Perhaps if he comes back to work he can make the bloody arrests we so desperately need. I'd be happy to eat an enormous slice of humble pie.'

'I don't think you'll be eating that humble pie any time soon. I've hammered on his front door, and I've hammered on his back door. I've stood outside and rung his landline. I can hear the phone ringing inside, but it just goes to the answering machine. I've tried his mobile, and that just goes to voicemail. I've peered through all the windows, but there's no sign of life, and his car's not in the garage. It was the same on Saturday. I think he must have gone away.'

'But where would he have gone?'

'I have no idea,' she said, 'but I'll tell you one thing: looking at the state of the house, I'd say he's struggling to cope a lot more than we thought. If you want my opinion, I think he's falling apart.'

'You're really worried about him, aren't you?'

'Yes, I am.'

Henderson considered this for a while. He couldn't pretend he liked Grinder, but even though he was an argumentative so and so, he was still one of their team. As such, they all had a duty to look out for him.

'I tell you what we'll do,' he said, finally. 'If there's still no sign of him tomorrow morning, we'll both go round there. Maybe we need to think about breaking in, even if it's just to try and find out where he's gone. Does that sound okay?'

'Yes, I think that's a good idea.'

Henderson smiled. 'Right, that's a plan. Now, believe it or not, there is actually some good news.' He handed her two forensic reports. 'Read these. I think you'll find one or two things start to make sense . . .'

Sarah took the reports and sat back to read them. As she did, Henderson's phone squawked, and she listened in as she read.

'Ah, Sergeant Reed,' Henderson said, sarcastically. 'What a pleasure it is to hear your dulcet tones. I hope you've got better news now than you had first thing this morning.'

He listened for a few seconds. 'And who might this someone be?'

Although she wasn't giving Henderson her full attention, Sarah was tuned in enough to pick up the sudden surprise in his voice when he next spoke.

'Really? Well now, that is a surprise. Put him in interview room one, and give him a cup of tea, please Bill, we'll be down in a few minutes.'

'Well, well,' he said, as he put the phone down, a big smile on his face. 'Jason Blackwell's just walked into reception asking to talk to us.'

'That's handy,' she said, brandishing the two reports, 'because we certainly want to talk to him. It'll save us going to pick him up.'

'Yes, he couldn't have timed it better really, could he?'

'How do you want to play it?' she asked.

* * *

'Good morning, Mr Blackwell,' said Henderson, genially, as they entered the interview room. 'Sergeant Reed tells me you wish to speak to us?'

'Yes,' said Blackwell, looking nowhere near as sure of himself as he had the last time they met. 'I read the story about the arrest, and that you're going to charge someone with murder as well as the burglaries. It's Gillian, isn't it?'

'If you mean Gillian Bowden, I can admit we've been questioning her—' began Henderson.

'I knew it!' said Blackwell. 'I knew it must be her. But you're wrong if you think she's murdered anyone. We never had anything to do with those murders. We didn't know the first woman who died, and we weren't even here last weekend.'

'We?' prompted Henderson. 'According to Gillian, it was all her own work.'

'I can't let her take the blame for all of it, and you'll probably find out eventually anyway.'

'Well, now you're here, why don't you save us all some time and tell us about it?'

'That's what I've come here for, but we didn't murder anyone. You have to believe that. You won't charge us with murder, will you?'

'I'm not going to promise anything,' said Henderson. 'Why don't you tell us what you know, and then we'll decide what we're going to charge you with.'

'I find the victims for the robberies,' he said.

'Yes, we've worked that much out already,' said Henderson. 'Single, mid-thirties, with a few small valuables at home, are we right?'

'That's right,' he admitted.

'And then you take them out twice, is that correct?'

Blackwell nodded his head. 'The first date is when I decide if it's worth the risk. If I think it is, I take an imprint of their door key and get a copy made.'

'How do you manage to get the key imprint?' asked Sarah.

'If you make them happy and get a few drinks inside them, they relax. Then it's remarkably easy to slip your hand inside their handbag. Sometimes they even leave their bag unattended when they go to the loo. Anyway, once I know I can get the key made, I make a second date. When I've got them out on that second date, Gillian goes in and nicks the stuff. That way there's no risk to Gillian, or the victim, and no-one ever gets hurt. We nick stuff, we don't kill people. You've got to believe me.'

'Actually, Jason, we haven't charged anyone with anything yet,' said Henderson, with a smile. 'And we know you and Gillian haven't murdered anyone.'

'But that online newspaper report said—'

'I don't know where they got their information, but it wasn't from us,' said Henderson. 'I suppose it just goes to show you can't believe everything you read.'

Blackwell looked as though he'd just dug a big hole and fallen in, which, of course, he had.

'So tell me about Gillian,' said Sarah.

'Tell you what about her?'

'Well, you could start by telling me why she uses a stolen identity.'

Blackwell laughed, nervously. 'What d'you mean? I don't know anything about anything like that.'

'Really?' said Sarah. 'That's a pity. I was sure you'd know all about it.'

Blackwell licked his lips and fidgeted nervously but he said nothing.

'So who had the bright idea to start doing these burglaries?' she asked.

'I dunno, I can't remember.'

'All a bit hazy, is it? I expect that's because you've done so many now you've lost track, is that it?'

'I dunno what you m—'

'We've done our research, Jason. Over the last three years you've done dozens all over the south coast, haven't you?'

Blackwell didn't need to say anything; it was quite clear Sarah had scored a bullseye.

'The thing is, your speciality is conning money out of lonely women, isn't it? That's what you went to prison for.'

'Yeah, well, I can't help it if women like me, can I?'

'Life is certainly full of surprises,' said Sarah, looking suitably unimpressed. 'But you didn't have to break into their houses to do that, did you? That's not your thing, is it? The sort of con trick you specialise in takes a bit of time and patience, doesn't it? I bet it can take months sometimes. But now you've changed the way you operate. Now you're part of a double act. You do the short con and get the key, Gillian gets into the house and gets the goodies. So who had the idea to team up?'

'I dunno. I can't remem—'

'Yes, you said,' interrupted Sarah. 'The thing is, we think we've worked out whose idea it was.' She waited for Blackwell to say something, but he seemed to have lost his voice. 'Do you want to know who we think it was?'

'It looks like you're going to tell me whether I want to know or not,' he said sulkily.

Sarah smiled at his discomfort. 'Yes I am,' she said. 'We have reason to believe it was your brother, Jolyon.'

Blackwell laughed. 'Jolyon?' he scoffed. 'What possible reason could you have for thinking that?'

'Because breaking in was his thing, wasn't it? He went to prison fo—'

'Yeah, alright, so he went to prison for it, but I haven't seen him in years.'

'Is that right?' asked Sarah, thoughtfully. 'How many years, exactly?'

'I dun—'

'You dunno, you can't remember; is that what you were going to say? Well, let me tell you how long I think it's been, and perhaps it will help you remember. Is that alright?'

'Yeah, you carry on if it makes you happy.'

'I think it's been about three years since you last saw Jolyon.'

Blackwell's eyes flitted from Sarah to Henderson and back. Then he licked his lips again. 'How d'you work that one out?' he asked.

'Because that's when Jolyon Blackwell became Gillian Bowden, isn't it?'

Blackwell's mouth dropped open and the shock showed clearly on his face before he managed to get some semblance of control.

'You don't know what you're talking about,' he spluttered. 'That's bollocks, that is.'

'Is it?' said Sarah, sliding a sheet of paper in front of Blackwell. 'Then how come Gillian's fingerprints are an exact match for Jolyon's?'

Blackwell stared at the report, trying desperately to think of an answer. 'That can't be right. There must be some mistake!'

'Oh, come on, Jason, don't play games. There's no mistake, and you know it.'

'It's a coincidence, that's what it is.'

'No chance,' said Sarah. 'Do you know what the odds are against that? It's one in sixty-four million.'

* * *

Sarah and Henderson were sipping coffee in the canteen.

'Well, that's the easy one sorted,' said Henderson, with a mirthless smile. 'All we need now is for the murderer to come in and confess, and we'll be sorted.'

'We must have missed something, somewhere,' said Sarah. 'I can't believe someone could carry out two murders and not leave a single clue.'

'It does seem unlikely, doesn't it?' agreed Henderson, gloomily. 'You'd have to know a lot about procedure and evidence gathering, and even then it would take a lot of luck. This guy's done it twice now and apart from a small piece of material from a blue shirt he's not left a shred of evidence. We still don't even know how he got into the houses.'

'Maybe this is going to be one of those cases that drags on and on,' suggested Sarah.

'We can't let that happen,' said Henderson. 'The longer it goes on, the more likely we are to have a third victim.'

The doors to the canteen burst open suddenly and Parrott rushed in. He took a quick look around and then headed for their table.

'I hope you've come to tell us there's a murderer downstairs waiting to confess,' said Henderson, as the young DC stopped before them.

'I'm sorry?' said Parrott, looking confused. Then the penny dropped, and he smiled brightly. 'Oh, right, I see. Sorry, it's not the murderer, but there's a lady downstairs who might be a survivor.'

Henderson had just taken a mouthful of coffee, and he almost sprayed it everywhere. 'What did you say?'

'She saw the story online this morning. She says she was attacked a few months ago, but she was too scared to report it before.'

'Bloody hell, well done, Parrott,' said Henderson. 'Come on, Sarah, maybe this is the break we've been waiting for.'

* * *

The woman waiting in the interview room twiddled the handle of her handbag nervously as Sarah made the introductions.

'Good afternoon, Mrs Morrisey, my name's Detective Sergeant Sarah Southall, and this is Detective Inspector Henderson. I understand you want to speak to us about an attack?'

'Yes, that's right,' she said. Sarah studied the haunted face before her. She guessed she was probably about the same age as Sonia Morrisey and, like the two murder victims, she was about the same height and weight, too. Sarah thought this was unlikely to be a coincidence.

Over the next half an hour Sarah encouraged Sonia Morrisey to share her story.

'I was at home on my own when someone knocked on my door,' she told them. 'It was a man. He told me he was a police officer and that there had been a break-in a few doors down. He said he was checking all the neighbouring houses to make sure everyone was safe and secure.'

'And you let him in?' asked Sarah.

Sonia looked embarrassed, and stared at her hands. 'He showed me his warrant card, so I thought he was the real deal,' she explained. 'He offered to come in and check all my windows were locked, so I let him. I was feeling a bit scared after he'd told me one of my neighbours' houses had been broken into . . .' She looked up at Sarah. 'I suppose that's exactly what I was supposed to feel, wasn't it?'

Sarah nodded. 'He was playing on your fears. First scare you, and then offer to protect you. I'm sorry.'

'Yeah, well, I fell for it alright,' said Sonia. 'He certainly played me for a fool.'

'It's not your fault,' said Sarah.

'I've been telling myself that for the last six months,' said Sonia, 'but it hasn't done much good. Maybe if I hadn't felt such a fool I would have come forward earlier and those other two girls would still be alive.'

'We can't know that,' said Sarah. 'We can't even say if it was the same man.'

'Did you read the warrant card?' asked Henderson. 'There would have been a name.'

'No, I'm sorry. Like I said, I was a fool, and I was scared. I just assumed it must be genuine . . .'

'Can you describe the man?' asked Henderson. 'Was he tall, short?'

'He wasn't much taller than me,' she said.

'What's that? About five feet six, or seven?'

'I'm five six,' she said. 'He couldn't have been more than five eight.'

'What about his face?'

'He was at the door, with the light behind him. I couldn't really see.'

'Hair colour?'

'He had a hat, a trilby.'

'What about when he came into the flat? You must have seen his face then.'

She shook her head miserably. 'I'm sorry. I didn't take much notice. He walked straight through and started checking windows. He had his back to me. He suggested a cup of tea would be nice, so I went into the kitchen to make one.'

'You said he attacked you,' said Sarah, gently. 'What happened?'

'I was in the kitchen making a cup of tea. I had my back to the door. Suddenly the light went out and he grabbed me from behind and spun me round. But I had a mug in my hand and I smacked him across the head with it.'

'Did you hurt him?'

'It must have hurt. It made him stop and grab his head, like this.' She clutched at the top of her head with both hands.

'Then what happened?' asked Sarah.

'I was spitting feathers by then,' she said. 'How dare he come into my flat and make a fool out of me? So I rammed my knee into his balls, and then I got the claws out and tried to scratch his face?'

'The claws?' asked Henderson.

She flexed her fingers and revealed ten long, immaculately manicured nails. 'I would have poked his eyes out if I could, but he'd slipped on some sort of protective goggles so I couldn't, but I got my claws into his neck. Now that really must have hurt because I actually drew blood! Then he decided he'd had enough, and he pushed me to the floor and made his getaway.'

Henderson knew this must have been a seriously frightening experience for her, and he realised she would have been in shock afterwards, but inwardly he was cursing. When she scratched him she probably had his skin under her nails!

'Can you remember the date when this happened?' asked Sarah.

'Yes, it was Thursday 28th September.'

It was as if Sarah had suddenly been jolted from a deep sleep. 'Are you sure?' she asked.

'I'm not likely to forget it, am I? It's not every day something like that happens to you.'

'Err, no, sorry, of course not. I didn't mean to suggest you didn't know. I just wanted to make sure I got it right.'

They carried on talking for a while, but while they had no doubt Sonia Morrisey was telling the truth, they were equally sure she had told them all she could.

* * *

'It's a pity she didn't report this at the time,' said Sarah, later that afternoon, as they were getting ready to go home. 'We'd have his DNA on file.'

'Yes, but that's been typical of our luck with this case, hasn't it?' said Henderson. 'Assuming it's the same guy, of course.'

'If he's using a warrant card to get in to these places, it would explain why we've never found any sign of a break-in.'

'That's true enough, but somehow I don't see our murderer getting kneed in the balls and scratched. I get the impression he's much too clever for that.'

'Maybe it was his first attempt,' suggested Sarah. 'Perhaps he realised he had to up his game after that one. That could explain why it was a few months between this attack and the first murder.'

'Oh well, at least we know one thing for sure now,' said Henderson. 'If this is our murderer and he's only five feet eight, it can't possibly be Blackwell or his brother, and your Kenny must be over six feet tall.'

Sarah didn't respond to his comment, and he studied her face, looking for some clue as to her thoughts. 'You don't still think he could do something like this, do you?'

'It's that date,' she said.

'You mean the one that made you look as if you'd been poked with a cattle prod?'

'I had my baby that night. Kenny didn't get there until late. He missed the birth, said he'd got held up at work, but I know he wasn't even at work that night.'

This time Henderson didn't respond. He was thinking of the most obvious reason why Kenny might have missed the birth of his only child. Whatever Sarah might think, he was sure it wasn't because he was attacking Sonia Morrisey. Besides, there was no way a big six-footer like Kenny could possibly pass himself off for someone five feet eight.

'Look, Sarah, I know your personal life is none of my business, but if you insist on suggesting Kenny's somehow involved in these murders, we're going to have to start investigating him, and I'll have to take you off the case. Do you really want that?'

'If you mean do I want everyone else finding out what a complete mess I've made of my life, no, I don't. But he's been acting so suspiciously over the last few months.'

Henderson was concerned about Sarah. He regarded her as a friend as well as a colleague, and he could see whatever was going on in her personal life was tearing her apart. It could only be a matter of time before it began to affect her work.

It seemed obvious to him why Kenny had been acting so suspiciously, so why hadn't Sarah considered the possibility? He had been struggling with how, or even if, he should broach the subject, but now he felt he had no choice. It was time to help her open her eyes.

'Look,' he said, with the distinct feeling he was walking on eggshells. 'Has it occurred to you there might be some other reason for his behaviour?'

'Like what?' she asked, warily.

'Well, I can think of at least one reason that makes loads of husbands act suspiciously, and it's not murder. In fact, it's not even illegal.'

She looked at him defiantly and shook her head. 'No chance. He wouldn't do that to me.'

'You don't think you're in denial, do you?' he suggested, cautiously.

'No, I don't,' she snapped. 'And if you knew Kenny as well as I do, you'd know better than to even suggest it.'

She began to collect her belongings to leave.

'I'm sorry if I've upset you, and I certainly don't want to fall out with you,' said Henderson, 'but I am concerned for you. I know you want me to shut up now, but I'm going to say one more thing you might want to consider on the way home. I might not know Kenny as well as you do, but I know him well enough to know he's not capable of murder. I'm sure, deep down, you know it too.'

'I'm going home now, if that's okay?' she said, trying hard not to listen to him.

'Of course,' he said.

CHAPTER TWENTY-NINE

Sarah arrived early next morning, and was waiting when Henderson arrived shortly before 7 a.m. She followed him to his office.

'Could I have a word?' she asked, through the open doorway.

'Sure. Come on in and close the door.'

She did as he asked and stepped inside.

'Err, I think I owe you an apology for last night,' she said, awkwardly.

'Last night? I don't know what you mean,' he said, innocently.

'Yes you do,' she said. 'I was acting like a stupid kid, and you know it.'

'Don't worry, I'm not going to hold it against you,' he said, with a warm smile. 'You're going through a tough time. We all do, from time to time.'

'I had no right to behave that way, and I'm sorry.'

'Look, I probably shouldn't have said what I said about Kenny—'

'No, actually, I think you're right,' she confessed, miserably. 'I had a long chat with my sister last night and she agrees with your assessment that I'm in denial. As Mandy put it, "I've been wearing blinkers for the last year".'

'I'm really sorry, Sarah,' said Henderson, sadly. 'And I understand about the blinkers. I don't think anyone ever wants to admit something like that could happen to them.'

He tore open an envelope that had been left on his desk. It was a forensic report. He read through it and then passed it to Sarah.

'I know this probably won't be much consolation,' he said, 'but . . .'

The report confirmed Kenny's shirt was not a match for the button and fabric recovered from the murder victim.

Sarah looked at Henderson and offered a sad little smile. 'I suppose I'd prefer to admit he was a shagger than a murderer,' she said.

'If you need some time away—'

'No, thank you. I'd rather be here working than sitting at home wondering what if. It won't change anything, will it?'

'No. I suppose not,' agreed Henderson.

'But if you feel I'm not helping by being here . . .'

'Don't worry, I'll soon let you know if I think that's the case,' he said, 'but how about we just try and carry on as normal? If we find there are any problems, we can deal with them if we need to. And don't forget I'm your friend as well as your boss. If you want to talk . . .'

'Thanks, Don, I appreciate that, I really do.'

'Right. Let's get on then, shall we? I'll take the briefing . . .'

* * *

It was just after 8 a.m. The briefing was long finished and everyone had dispersed. Sarah and Henderson were the only ones left in the incident room. Once again Grinder hadn't shown up, and still there was no message to let them know where he was. Sarah had tried both his phone numbers but they were still going to voicemail.

'I know he's not my best mate,' said Henderson, 'but I have to admit I'm beginning to get a bit concerned. This just isn't like him, is it? I think we'd better send someone round there to take a look.'

As he finished speaking, a PC came into the room carrying a small parcel.

'Is there a DS Southall here?' he asked.

'That's me,' said Sarah.

'This parcel just came through the post,' he said. He handed her the package and made his way out of the room.

Sarah weighed the parcel in her hands, and felt it. It was a medium-sized padded envelope. It weighed hardly anything, and was soft and pliable to the touch. She could feel no hard edges inside. She studied the address label, but it was smudged enough to make it almost unreadable, so it didn't tell her much. Carefully she peeled back the flap, peered inside, and then tipped the contents onto her desk. A folded sheet of A4 paper landed on the desk and she unfolded it to reveal two pairs of panties!

'What the hell?' she exclaimed, jumping up from her seat.

'What's up?' asked Henderson, rushing over to her. He looked down at the contents of the package. 'Wow! What's that all about?'

She had stepped back from her desk as if something poisonous had spilled from the envelope, but now she stepped forward again to take a closer look.

'Someone is taking the piss,' she said, angrily. 'If I find out who it is . . .'

She picked up a biro and separated the two items, careful to keep her fingers well away.

'There's something written on the paper,' said Henderson.

'Hang on, I've got some gloves in my drawer.' Sarah opened the top drawer of her desk and produced two pairs of latex gloves.

Henderson slipped on a pair of gloves and picked up the sheet of paper.

'For Sarah,' he read, 'I hope you're happy now.' He studied her face. 'This seems to be aimed at you. It's a bit personal. Any idea what it means?'

She had a sudden sinking feeling. What if Grinder had decided to make things public. But why send panties? What if he had told someone he was the father of her baby? Maybe this was that someone's idea of a joke!

'I'd love to be able to say I have no idea,' she said, guiltily, 'but there is one possibility I can think of. I should have told you about it before, but, well, what with one thing and another . . .'

'I think you'd better tell me now, don't you?' he suggested.

She sat down and heaved a sigh. 'You remember that time, the Christmas before last, when we combined celebrating solving a big case with our Christmas do?'

'Where we all got so pissed we ended up booking hotel rooms?' asked Henderson. 'Yeah, I remember. No-one wanted to share with Grinder, because he was such a miserable git, but in the end you volunteered.'

'Actually, I seem to recall I didn't have any choice,' she said. 'You all volunteered me.'

'Yes, that sounds about right. We probably did,' said Henderson. He was trying to remember that night, but it was all a bit hazy. He doubted if any of them could really recall much about it.

'The thing is,' she continued, 'Grinder's got it into his head that because of that night, he's the father of my baby.'

'What?'

'He seems to think we had a night of unbridled passion.'

Even though it sounded absurd, Henderson was so surprised by her story he just couldn't stop himself speaking. 'You didn't, did you?'

'No, we bloody didn't!' she snapped indignantly. Then, less convincingly, 'At least, I don't think we did.'

'Oh, come on, don't you remember? You'd know, wouldn't you?' asked Henderson, in disbelief.

‘Can you remember everything that happened that night?’ she asked. His face told her the answer. ‘No, you can’t,’ she answered for him. ‘And neither can I.’

‘You’re not suggesting he ra—’

‘No, I’m not suggesting he raped me, if that’s what you were going to say. I think I’d remember that!’

‘But he was legless, wasn’t he? Didn’t we have to help you carry him upstairs? He wouldn’t have been capable, would he?’

‘According to him, I told him Kenny was away and I was gagging for it.’

Henderson wasn’t sure what to say to that. In fact he wasn’t quite sure what to say to any of it.

‘And was Kenny away?’

‘Yes, he was. He’d gone over to the US. They had a problem with an aircraft, and he was one of the few people who knew it well enough to fix it.’

‘Yes, but . . . father of the baby?’

‘Work it out,’ she said. ‘I had her in September.’

‘Yes, but I expect you and Ken made up for lost time when he got back, didn’t you?’

‘Yeah, we did,’ Sarah agreed, sheepishly, ‘but there’s something you don’t know about Kenny.’

‘What? What don’t I know?’

‘We had a big argument the other night. It turns out he had a vasectomy when he turned forty.’

‘Oh, Jesus,’ said Henderson. ‘So he can’t be . . .’ He left the sentence unfinished.

‘No, he can’t be, can he?’ she admitted, sadly.

‘He wasn’t just saying that in the heat of the moment?’

‘I don’t know,’ she said, wearily, ‘but he says he knew right from day one it couldn’t be his. That’s why he’s been staying away so much. That’s why he’s moved out.’

‘Oh, Sarah,’ said Henderson. ‘I’d guessed you were having problems, but I didn’t realise it had got that bad!’

There was an uneasy silence as Sarah tried to come to terms with having revealed her problems to her boss. She wondered how it would affect their relationship. For his part, Henderson was wondering the same thing, and trying to understand what he'd just heard. He wanted to believe they would be able to get past it and carry on regardless, but right at this moment he was shocked.

'What's happened here?' called a cheery voice. 'You two look as if you've just found out Santa Claus isn't real!'

Unnoticed, Parrott had come into the room and was heading over to join them. He'd caught them unawares and for a moment neither could think what to say.

'Is this to do with the case?' he asked, pointing to the items on the desk. 'Can I have a look?'

'Err, yes,' said Sarah, absently. 'Don't touch, though. I was just going to send it all off to forensics.'

'Is it a clue?'

'Sorry?'

'A clue? Is someone trying to tell us something?'

'How do you mean?' asked Henderson, his mind still reeling from what Sarah had just told him.

'Didn't you find a card at the first murder scene that said: *For Sarah*?'

'Yes, but we couldn't find anyone called Sarah who was connected to Miriam,' said Henderson.

'But wasn't there also a note at the second one — "I hope you're happy now", or something like that?' insisted Parrott. 'It's a bit of a coincidence, isn't it? And what about the panties? We had no way of knowing if any had been stolen from the two murder scenes, did we? Maybe this is the answer.'

Henderson looked at Sarah, who would have been quite happy if the ground had opened up and swallowed her right there and then. She had been so consumed with self-pity this morning that she hadn't even considered the package might have nothing to do with her personal situation.

'Parrott, you're a bloody genius,' said Henderson, kicking himself inside for allowing Sarah's insistence that it was about her to have distracted him from the obvious.

'I am?'

'Of course you are. We've both been sitting here wondering what it could mean, and you come along and solve it straight away.'

'But it's just a guess. I'm probably miles away from what it really is.'

'But perhaps it's a guess we need,' said Henderson. 'We're all agreed that whoever is behind this has been leading us a merry dance, aren't we? And, frankly, I think we can also agree we've got almost nowhere by following procedure.'

'But why would someone who had got away with murder send us a clue?' asked Parrott. 'It makes no sense to me.'

'That's because you're assuming a murderer would think in the same way as you or I,' explained Henderson. 'But if they thought like us, they wouldn't have murdered anyone in the first place, would they? What if this person is beyond clever and wants to prove it? What if this is some sort of bizarre game designed to prove to the world just how clever he is?'

'I still don't understand why he would send us a clue,' said Parrott.

'Perhaps he's got bored because we're so far behind him. Maybe it's no fun if there's no risk of getting caught.'

'You mean he wants to get caught?'

'How will anyone know we've been led a merry dance if he never gets caught?' suggested Sarah.

'No offence, but I thought that sort of thing only happened in books or on TV,' said Parrott.

'But we've got nothing else, have we?' said Sarah.

Henderson pointed at the panties. 'Is there any way we could compare these with the ones at the murder victims' homes, Sarah? Would it tell us anything?'

'I don't think it would give us any definitive proof, but it might be worth a try,' she agreed.

'Right, let's go and take a look then,' said Henderson. 'A change of scenery might help us to think, and figure out what's going on.'

‘What would you like me to do, sir?’ asked Parrott.

Henderson thought for a few seconds. ‘As your brain seems to be the only one working this morning, I think you’d better come with us.’

* * *

Henderson felt rather guilty about bringing Parrott along, but thought he’d probably made the right decision. The normal rapport between Sarah and himself had been replaced by an awkwardness that was almost palpable. It was understandable, given the revelation she had made, but even so, it would make for an uncomfortable working relationship if it persisted. Parrott would act as a temporary buffer between them, at least for today.

‘I was going to send a couple of uniforms over to Grinder’s, but he is one of ours, and it’s not that far out of our way,’ said Henderson. ‘We might as well look in while we’re passing.’

Sarah pulled a face but didn’t pass comment.

‘It was your idea we should check up on him,’ Henderson reminded her.

‘Yes, I suppose it was,’ she admitted, unhappily.

Henderson had never been to Grinder’s house before, and as he turned into the drive he was shocked to see the state of both the house and the garden.

‘Bloody hell, it looks derelict,’ he said, slowing down to take it all in. ‘Are you sure this is the right house?’

‘It used to be beautiful,’ said Sarah, sadly. ‘His wife made sure of that. She was the gardener. Three years she’s been gone, and now it’s all gone to pot.’

‘She meant a lot to him, didn’t she?’ said Henderson, guiltily, realising he had probably been much too quick to criticise Grinder when he had obviously needed help and support.

‘Evie didn’t just mean a lot,’ said Sarah. ‘She was his life.’

As she stepped from the car, Sarah spoke. ‘Look, someone’s been here.’ She pointed to tyre tracks that led up to the garage doors. 'These weren't here yesterday.' She marched over to the garage and stood on tiptoe to peer through a gap between the doors. 'His car's in here.'

'Parrott, you come with me,' said Henderson, heading for the front door. He stopped and pressed the doorbell but there was no ringing sound from within. 'Not really a surprise, looking at the rest of the house,' he muttered. Then he began hammering on the door, but there was no sign of life from inside.

'I'll try calling,' said Sarah. Then she realised she'd left her bag in the car. 'I just need to get my phone,' she said, heading back to the car.

'Let's try round the back,' Henderson said to Parrott.

Sarah swung the car door open, leaned inside and rummaged in her handbag for her mobile phone. As she pushed the car door closed and turned to walk back to the house, she started to scroll through her contacts looking for Grinder's number, stopping as she found it and thumbed 'call'. As she waited for the call to connect, she looked up at the house. She thought she could see something through one of the windows, but at first she couldn't make out what it was. Then her blood ran cold, and her mouth dropped open in a silent scream as she realised what she could see.

* * *

Henderson led the way down the side of the house, stopping to peer through a filthy window, allowing Parrott to pass him and continue round to the back of the house.

'Sir!'

'What is it?' he called, as he ran the last few steps to catch up with the young detective who had ducked back from the kitchen window.

'The kitchen light's on.'

'Anyone in there?'

'I don't see anyone.'

Henderson stepped past Parrott and peered round the edge of the window and into the kitchen. There was no-one there. Somewhere beyond the kitchen he thought he heard a telephone ring.

'Come on,' he said, leading the way past the window to the back door. Parrott followed closely behind, scarcely daring to breathe. When Henderson got to the door, he tried the handle. It turned rather noisily, and the door opened an inch or two. Now the sound of the ringing telephone was louder. He turned to Parrott, raised his eyebrows, and then nodded towards the door.

'Be careful, and try not to make too much noise,' he whispered. 'It's probably nothing, but something doesn't feel right.'

He pushed the door and it slowly swung open, making a barely audible creaking as it did. When the door had opened as far as it could, Henderson stepped inside, Parrott following closely in his footsteps. Suddenly Henderson froze as he heard a woman's voice, then he realised the telephone had stopped ringing and he was listening to the recorded voice on the answering machine asking the caller to please leave a message.

'D'you think that's his wife's voice?' asked Parrott, quietly.

Henderson nodded, ruefully. 'Yes, I think it probably is.'

They quickly looked in each of the downstairs rooms, but, although there were plenty of signs of a man in decline, there was no sign of the man himself. Henderson, now fairly confident the house was empty, nodded towards the stairs and then led the way up. There were five doors leading off the landing at the top.

The first one was open, and they could see it was a bathroom. Henderson pointed to indicate Parrott should look inside, then turned his attention to the next door, carefully easing it open to look inside. It was a bedroom that had obviously once been used by Grinder's wife as a dressing room. It was obvious because it was still filled with her things.

Henderson pointed to the next room on the left, and Parrott stepped across to the door while Henderson took the room to the right.

Parrott eased his door open and stepped inside.

'Bloody hell!' he gasped, stopping to take it all in. 'Sir?' he called. 'You'd better come and see this.'

But Henderson had already entered the bedroom opposite, at the front of the house. Now his shout was louder. 'Quick, in here! I need help!'

Parrott bolted into the front bedroom, hardly able to take in what he was seeing. Grinder was suspended from the ceiling by a noose around his neck, and Henderson was struggling to lift him high enough to keep his weight from the rope.

A fallen chair bore testimony to how Grinder had hanged himself. As quickly as he could, Parrott stood the chair up and climbed on it, helping Henderson to support Grinder's weight while he eased the rope from his neck.

'Christ, you stupid sod, Grinder,' muttered Henderson, as he gently laid him on the bed. 'Why didn't you come and see me if you were that depressed?'

'I'll call an ambulance,' said Parrott.

Feverishly Henderson felt for a pulse, but he already knew it was futile. Grinder was cold, he must have been hanging there for hours.

'I'm afraid it's a bit too late for that,' he said, sadly. 'He's long gone. I didn't realise he was so depressed. I should have known.'

'I think you should take a look in that other room before you start blaming yourself, sir,' said Parrott.

'What?'

'The other room. I—'

He was interrupted by the sound of footsteps rushing up the stairs. 'Is he alright? Did you find him in time?' called Sarah. 'I saw him from outside. I'm sorry, I froze.'

As she burst into the room, Henderson reached to stop her. 'I'm sorry,' he said, 'we're too late. He's gone.'

'Are you sure? Maybe he just needs—'

'Sarah, he's cold, luv. I'm afraid he's been dead for hours. We weren't even close to stopping him.'

'Can I sit with him?' she said. 'Until everyone else gets here? He's spent so much time on his own, it doesn't seem right to leave him now.'

'Of course,' said Henderson, gently. 'You sit with him while we make some calls.'

He nodded reassuringly to Parrott and then followed him from the room, closing the door behind him. He placed a call and then spoke while he was waiting for it to connect. 'You said something about the other room.'

'Yes, sir. I think you need to see it before you do anything else.' He pushed the door open and ushered Henderson through.

'Jesus!' said Henderson. 'What the hell's this?' He walked into the centre of the room and looked around. There wasn't a single item of furniture, but every wall was covered in photographs, mostly of Sarah, some taken while she was pregnant.

'He's been stalking her, hasn't he?' asked Parrott, in disbelief.

'For well over a year,' agreed Henderson.

On the wall behind the door, there were three enlarged head shots. Sarah's was in the centre with a murder victim either side of her. The two victim photos had a large 'X' scored through them. Above Sarah's photo, the words 'Happy Now?' had been written.

'Aren't they the two murder victims?' asked Parrott.

'Yes,' agreed Henderson, grimly. 'It's easy to see just how much they look alike now, isn't it?'

'Do you think she was next?' asked Parrott.

'I don't think so,' said Henderson. 'He was besotted with her, but I don't think he wanted her dead.'

Unheard by them, Sarah had crept into the room. 'Oh my God,' she said as she saw the photos. 'I think this is my fault.'

Henderson spun round, surprised by her voice. 'Don't be absurd. How could it be your fault?'

'I told him I'd like a nice juicy murder to investigate.'

'Yes, but we all say things like that when it's quiet,' said Henderson.

'He did this to please me.'

Henderson was confused. 'I'm not sure I understand.'

'You'd better read this.' She had a note in her hand and now she held it towards him.

'What is it? A suicide note?' He took it and read it out loud. 'For Sarah, you said you wanted a nice juicy murder. I gave you two. I hope you're happy now.'

CHAPTER THIRTY

Two Days Later.

'Are you sure it was him?' asked Whaffham. He had initially been pleased when Henderson had notified him that they had successfully concluded both cases, but the news that one of his officers had been responsible had rather spoiled the celebration.

'I've no doubts,' said Henderson. 'We've got the suicide note confession, of course, but to add to that, Dr Morgan believes the scars on his neck were almost certainly caused by scratches from long fingernails.'

'That ties in with your theory that his first attempt ended in failure when the victim fought back?'

'That's right, sir. And one of those scratches had never properly healed, which explains why Boulting always seemed to be scratching at his neck.

'There's also the footprint found at the first murder scene. It's a match for a pair of boots found at his house, and imprints on the notepad found at his house suggest he wrote the "*I hope you're happy now*" note found at the second murder scene. Handwriting analysis suggests he also wrote the "*For Sarah*" note found at the first scene.'

'It's a pity he hanged himself,' said Whaffham. 'It's almost like he's got away with it.'

Henderson wasn't quite sure he agreed with his boss on this point. He didn't feel Grinder had 'got away' with anything, and was still feeling guilty that one of his team had obviously been in such a bad way and he had chosen to ignore the problem. Deep inside, he held himself responsible for the two murders and Grinder's suicide.

'And what's this about an obsession with DS Southall?' asked Whaffham.

'When Boulting's wife died, three years ago, he became quite depressed. DS Southall made the effort to look out for him. She was the one who was prepared to listen when he needed someone to talk to. I think maybe her kindness made him see her as a replacement for his wife.'

'She didn't do anything to encourage these feelings?'

Henderson shook his head. He thought there were probably some things his boss didn't need to know. 'I believe it was the fact she didn't reciprocate his feelings that pushed him over the edge.'

'And he thought he could impress her by murdering two innocent women?'

'She made the mistake of saying she would like a nice juicy murder to investigate. It was a throwaway comment made when she was bored, but it seems Boulting took it literally. In his head, he thought it would make her happy . . .'

'My God,' said Whaffham, in disbelief. 'How is she coping?'

'I think it would be fair to say she's not coping at all,' said Henderson. 'I spoke to her father yesterday evening. Nervous breakdown, he called it. According to him, she won't be back at work for some time.'

THE END

THE JOFFE BOOKS STORY

We began in 2014 when Jasper agreed to publish his mum's much-rejected romance novel and it became a bestseller.

Since then we've grown into the largest independent publisher in the UK. We're extremely proud to publish some of the very best writers in the world, including Joy Ellis, Faith Martin, Caro Ramsay, Helen Forrester, Simon Brett and Robert Goddard. Everyone at Joffe Books loves reading and we never forget that it all begins with the magic of an author telling a story.

We are proud to publish talented first-time authors, as well as established writers whose books we love introducing to a new generation of readers.

We have been shortlisted for Independent Publisher of the Year at the British Book Awards three times, in 2020, 2021 and 2022, and for the Diversity and Inclusivity Award at the Independent Publishing Awards in 2022.

We built this company with your help, and we love to hear from you, so please email us about absolutely anything bookish at feedback@joffebooks.com

If you want to receive free books every Friday and hear about all our new releases, join our mailing list: www.joffebooks.com/contact

And when you tell your friends about us, just remember: it's pronounced Joffe as in coffee or toffee!

ALSO BY P.F. FORD

THE WEST WALES MURDER MYSTERIES

Prequel: A DATE WITH DEATH
Book 1: A BODY ON THE BEACH
Book 2: A BODY OUT AT SEA
Book 3: A BODY DOWN THE LANE
Book 4: A BODY AT THE FARMHOUSE

Printed in Dunstable, United Kingdom

71203359R00143